T0289058

# NORTHERN LIGHTS

*Writings from an Unbound Europe*

■ □ ■ □ ■

# DRAGO JANČAR

# NORTHERN LIGHTS

Translated from the Slovene by Michael Biggins

NORTHWESTERN UNIVERSITY PRESS

EVANSTON, ILLINOIS

Northwestern University Press
Evanston, Illinois 60208-4210

Grateful acknowledgment is made to the Ministry of Culture of the
Republic of Slovenia for its support of this translation.

Printed in the United States of America

10 9 8 7 6 5 4 3 2 1

ISBN 0-8101-1838-6 (cloth)
ISBN 0-8101-1839-4 (paper)

**Library of Congress Cataloging-in-Publication Data**

Jančar, Drago
    [Severni sij. English]
    Northern lights / Jančar, Drago ; translated from the Slovene by
Michael Biggins.
    p. cm. — (Writings from an unbound Europe)
    ISBN 0-8101-1838-6 (cloth : alk. paper) — ISBN 0-8101-1839-4 (pbk. :
alk. paper)
    I. Biggins, Michael. II. Title. III. Series.
PG1919.2.A54 S4813 2001
891.8'435 — dc21                                        00-012337

■ ☐ ■ ☐ ■

# NORTHERN LIGHTS

■ □ ■ □ ■

# 1

OUTSIDE THE RAILWAY STATION ERDMAN CAUGHT SIGHT OF THE gloomy facade of some building. High up above, two windows were lit. For an instant it seemed as if the huddled city's eyes were watching him. He walked down the empty street through wet, snowy slush. When he turned the corner past the house with the shining eyes, there was a human shape wavering in the darkness. The street had been deserted, making the appearance of this phantom before him unexpected. It had to have come out of an entryway, or from behind some pillar, if it hadn't just sprouted up from the ground. Behind it were the dark facades of old buildings and in the early morning darkness it was scarcely even possible at first to make out the figure.

"*Khristos voskrese,*" the man shouted. "*Voistinu voskrese.*"

He swayed and bent at the waist, and his whirling arms jabbed strange shapes in the air. For an instant Erdman may have been frightened of this bearded man in ragged clothes; he may not have been quite sure what the words meant, what the point was of this bending and arm waving. To be sure, at first he couldn't decide whether the man in front of him was drunk or dangerous or just slightly stupid. He tried to sidestep him, but with a sudden leap that no one would have thought his twisted shape capable of, the other blocked his way. Erdman had the rumble of the train in his ears, the glare of deserted stations in his eyes, and here he was accosted by the empty silence of this street, a dark morning with the dilapidated facades of unknown buildings and then, suddenly, this contorted face and wobbly human form that refused to let him pass.

He set his suitcase down on the dirty, slushy mess of snow and human footprints. He heard only silence and waited for a human voice to speak to him again out of the red cavity of a mouth before him. Erdman was tired and for a second he felt as though the street were sliding out from under his legs. He ascribed the strange sensation to the long train trip, yet he still propped himself up with a hand against the wall. The other bent at the waist again and stretched his neck out, turning his face upward. Then he straightened and stepped up to him. Erdman could feel the other's warm breath on his face, and he really felt like going. He would turn around and go. He didn't turn around. He didn't pick up his suitcase, and he didn't push the phantom out of the way. Because at that moment, he noticed the other's tiny pupils, which were completely at peace. Completely at peace in that bearded, distorted face, in that body nervously jerking back and forth. Erdman couldn't stop staring at the other's eyes, which were hollow and deep, as though they were the precipice leading into a chasm, as if they concealed a bottomless darkness. He stood there and stared at those eyes and at that face that was furrowed by something inside it, and he could see that these were in fact very quiet, very still eyes. These weren't the eyes of a drunk or an idiot. These were eyes that were afraid of something. Not just anything, but something that was simply, surely going to happen and that could not be avoided. These were Fedyatin's eyes. This was exactly how it had to be. Fedyatin's face and his quiet eyes, his tiny black pupils, and the deep, dark abyss behind them were what he had to see on this morning, with dilapidated buildings in the background, the slushy street, a morning that was quiet from earth to heaven. And Erdman had to start when he saw the dark red stains on the other's coat, when he concluded that those spots were from some blood or other. The street slid slightly from under his feet again, and he held tighter onto the wall.

He may have thought then that he should just turn around and go back where he came from. He didn't turn around and he didn't go back. Who in this world has left a city where he wanted to find out something, based on some vague intuition? Who has ever held back on account of any intuition at all? Intuition exists to propel you even more decisively toward the inevitable. And so that early-morning phantom with the black pupils and dark red stains on its coat was nothing but a drunken, rumpled man with a slightly idiotic face. And so Erdman stayed and he remained standing there in the street even after Fedyatin, still bending ceaselessly, disappeared amid the dark facades of the buildings, after he vanished into the facades, the morning herald and agitator of the resurrection. Erdman stood alone beside a wall on Alexander Street, overwhelmed by the powerful, throbbing silence of that morning, a shuddering silence that hovered over Central Europe, echoed off the walls of streets in Prague, and soundlessly beat and gnawed the shores of Duino. He looked over toward the Franciscan church and waited for a bell up above to ring.

That was early on the morning of the first of January 1938.

■ □ ■ □ ■

## 2

NOW IT'S EVENING AND THE MUSIC HAS STARTED DOWNSTAIRS.
The sounds strain upward, as if they were coming from underground. I can sense the contours of a melody, although I can't
quite put it all together. I'm anxious in this room, in this city,
which has been empty and quiet all day. The first signs of life
appeared in the streets just a few hours ago, and individual
voices started to dart through the hotel's stairways and halls,
colliding with the door of my room. It's evening and people
are waking up. The kind of day when everything gets stood on
its head. At the station the conductor had been bleary eyed in
the morning darkness, if not also a little drunk. He'd rattled off
his litany and ducked back into the train. Some lady was running toward the exit. When I'd gotten off the train, she was
gone and there was no one else there. Outside the entrance
there were nearly squared rows of porters' handcarts. I'd set my
suitcase down on one of them and stepped back onto the platform. I could hear the train puffing away in the distance. I
knocked on a door. Nothing. No cabdrivers, no cabs, no
bus—deserted. Piles of dirty snow on the empty street, dilapidated facades of old buildings, the flickering light of street-
lamps. So this is the bright, airy city that my folks wanted to
see one more time. This dusk, these lamps, these piles of snow,
these tiles peeking out from under the crumbling stucco?
Memory is a comforting ally of old folks, it colors things for
them so nicely and lies. And singing from some window back

there, music from a record player or a radio, and shrill female laughter. Then silence. And that strange man. Slush underfoot. A brief, fitful sleep in this room that will be my home. Around ten o'clock I'd tried to have breakfast. A mess: stained tablecloths, overturned chairs, leftover food, and other remains of a wild night on the tables and floor—ribbons, confetti, part of a jawbone (the remains of a pig's head), horrible stench. Now it's evening, the familiar anxiety of a strange hotel room, and downstairs the music is getting louder and louder. Went down to the river at noon. Black water. The riverbanks were dark, with branches jutting from some lonely trees. The snow had shaken off of them, or some sudden south wind had melted it. Some birds or other, ducks floating on the river. One shore steep, the other low. City on both sides of the river, with buildings getting sparser and smaller, and gardens and fields as you went farther out. Suddenly I seemed to remember those fields, the way they cut in between the houses, and the crude wooden fences. No, it won't do, I don't believe in memories from early childhood. Somewhere along the way I must have picked up that image, some words uttered by Father over an evening's soup. There wasn't that freshness down by the river that there's supposed to be. Not even the slightest gust of wind to disturb the heavy masses of slightly tepid winter air. Strata of air warmed in the streets wafted down from the city, from both shores and settled among the patches of mist that hovered on the water—there was nothing good or innocent about this day. One of the birds that I thought were ducks took flight and circled over the water. It was a gull, a river gull, a wild duck. It took flight, serenely moving against the backdrop of the dark riverbank opposite. I'd gone down to the river to drive the clatter of the New Year's Eve train out of my ears, to drive the glare of passing streetlights and desolate stations out of my eyes, in hopes that running water would clear the confusion out of my head. But it wasn't any better there either. The sky weighed down on the earth, and beneath the sky— the gull in its slow circling. It could barely make it, it could barely overcome the endless cycles of its flight. Only some senseless physical law kept it up in the air, but even it was drawn down into this black water, which, when the bird got there, was obviously going to suck it right in. And in my memory this bird keeps circling and circling in the waltz time that unrestrainably seeps through the walls from downstairs, up through the hallways and right through the closed door into my room. And still, it was peaceful, unusually peaceful down by the river, in the midst of this winter day, overwhelmingly peaceful from east to west. I thought again of Prague, where this fall I had crept out of some tavern into the empty morning streets. I thought this same peace was there, and that somebody was hurrying down a narrow, winding street. And to the north and south, whichever way you turned your gaze or your mind, everywhere there was this overwhelmingly peaceful Central European landscape captured at midday, with its rivers and shores, its hilly, rolling countryside, mountains and lakes, with its medium-size cities. The same identical day everywhere on the first day of the new year.

Somebody had shouted something after me as I'd made my way toward my room. How long did I plan to stay, or something like that. If only I knew, if only I knew. The tousled bedsheets, the suitcase in its place. These hotel rooms, these patterns on the walls, these same hotel smells, redolent of yesterday's stale cleaning. White sheets and the washbasin in the corner, the dark brown wardrobe, and the window with its broken handle. The music from downstairs, another waltz, the hum of the customers. I'm drawn to them, whoever they are.

■ □ ■ □ ■

**3**

THE REDHEADED RECEPTIONIST HAS STOPPED ASKING HOW LONG I plan to stay. Nor does he try to engage me in conversation anymore. I've given him the critical details, so that he can pass those on, the way all the receptionists in the world do. Now he and I are reconciled. He even says hello nicely. Yesterday morning the commotion outside woke me, but today I slept fine. How quickly we adjust, like some animal to its stall. Missed breakfast both days. Walked up and down the main street. Typical January street: grim faces, work, end of the holidays, gray faces, and still the dirty, slushy snow. Read in the afternoon, then just lay down on the bed and stared at the ceiling and watched the images form on it. A throng of unfamiliar faces from outside, eyes, noses, mouths, swarming arms and legs, all of it running across the ceiling, and chaotic voices through the window. I think I fell asleep for a while. When I woke up or came to, I tried to open the window. The handle's broken. I can't even air the place out. The whole place is motionless and stuffy and I'm losing interest in waiting any longer.

For sure: a misunderstanding. I can't imagine that anything would hold Jaroslav up. He's always been punctual. And he was even in such a terrific hurry that I had to drop everything and spend my New Year's Eve on a train. And now I've wasted two days here, going on three.

The postal clerk has red cheeks and unbelievably white teeth. But when she got up to send the telegram, I could see she had a serious limp. I wired Jaroslav that I'd wait until the seventh and then go back, no matter what. Assuming the telegram even reaches him—he could already be on the road. The worst of it is that in a sense it's all my fault. Can get there in three days, I'd said: Marburg on the Drau. Fine, Jaroslav said, we'll get started on the first, I'll arrive there from Trieste. Then Zagreb and the push to the southeast. We'll have a network of representatives established by the end of the month. All right, it's a long way to the end of the month, and Jaroslav will get here this week. The problem is that I got myself into this provincial mousetrap. I could have said Trieste—that train went all the way to Trieste—and could now be taking walks along the waterfront or eating spaghetti in some cozy, humming little trattoria. But I said Marburg on the Drau, which they call Maribor here, and I said it only because back up there in that cozy kitchen of ours my folks kept talking about some ball in a church and about how I waddled through some garden and trampled some flowers and how we ate some big, fat beans. Now that garden and that house are nowhere—only mud and piles of filthy snow and gray faces and a hotel room—and Jaroslav is nowhere to be seen. But I do remember the ball in the church— it has to be somewhere. I went to the movies to try to distract myself. *Der Streit um den Knaben Jo,* a film with a wonderful story, as the poster said. Inside the movie theater the floor was black, and the fellow sitting next to me tapped and tapped on it with his hiking boots the whole time. I kept giving him looks but couldn't quiet him down. Lil Dagover, a fabulously beautiful actress, kept distracting him and making his feet dance on the black floor. I noticed several young girls and thought of Lenka. She's probably thinking that Jaroslav and I are somewhere far to the south, buried to the neck in work. If only she knew I was sitting in a movie theater and someone in hiking boots was tapping on the floor because Lil Dagover wouldn't give him any peace. Bought a newspaper that reports that something's up in Moscow again, something to do with

Trotsky again, some group or other of his has been discovered. Went walking through the suburbs again, looking for that house. It should be set back from the street, with a large front yard and grapevines growing on trellises by the door. I didn't find it. Everything looked hopelessly the same and monotonous, and everywhere there were dogs snarling at you. And anyway, what do I care about those big, fat beans, what do they have to do with me? The fact that I came back with muddy shoes and trousers, that's what. And the fact that I have only myself to blame for thinking up a rendezvous in this city. At lunch some big, heavyset guy sat next to me. A fat watch fob was hanging over his vest. Presumption and ostentation. Still, I talked to him—what was I supposed to do, I can't just keep meandering through the suburban slush or lying in bed in my room. The big guy was very curious. All my answers were dry and uninformative. Before long I got up and left. I can't live with people, I can't live without them. There's got to be something wrong with me. Maybe I've worked too hard the last few years, maybe I've lost the knack of spending free time. That's what this is—free time, aimless time, this is why they invented Sundays. Not for resting, but so that people know how absolutely pointless their existence is if they're not chasing after work, or money, or bread, or some damned fat beans that put me at a dinner table with that Pešić, or whatever the show-off's name is with the fat watch fob. And now finally something that interests me. Way down at the bottom of the page in the paper: the wonder of Parisian anthropologists. A young woman covered with animal fur. This is the third monkey woman this scientist has discovered. I've forgotten his name. Her face is covered with freckles, and there's a tuft of hair sticking out of the skin on the right cheek. Intellectual circles in Paris are all abuzz. Anthropology of a vulgar sort—the sort this newspaper goes in for—but they probably didn't make up the basic fact. It could really be an interesting case, if only these simpleton reporters would furnish a few more details: where they found her, what her mental and physical faculties are, her level of culture, and things like that. But all they care about is the fact that there's a tuft of hair sticking out of the right side of her face. This afternoon I dozed off again. This evening I sat in the restaurant, drank some wine, and listened to the music. Back in my room another one of those evenings when you just don't know what you want. Due to my afternoon nap I kept waking up all night.

Around two in the morning I looked at my watch and for a while had no idea where I was. Then Jaroslav suddenly entered the room. His face was shaggy, he had long hair growing on his face, even on his forehead, like that case from Borneo, and in the midst of it the red hollow of his mouth and his dark eyes kept opening and closing. He paced back and forth and, his face distorted, he bent down over me where I lay on the bed. They're investigating me now, he said, they don't know what it's going to lead to. I tried to answer him, I wanted to ask him if it was in Trieste, if they were investigating him in Trieste, but I couldn't get a single word out of my throat. By the end of the month, he said; we'll take care of everything by the end of the month. Then I noticed that the wall behind him was full of some kind of glass laboratory tubes, equipment that was familiar to me. He opened that red hollow of his mouth, groaned something, and then said, Now you see, now you see they really are investigating me. I looked at my watch again, it really was two o'clock, I really was in the hotel room, and there on the floor in the corner Jaroslav really was groaning. I thought to myself, I'm dreaming this and these dreams mean nothing other than that something bad has happened to Jaroslav, and that something was going to happen to his sister, too, that all of us are somehow doomed and that I'm trapped, too, and that there's no escaping at this point. But my mind kept working. How could I be dreaming when I could see my wristwatch over there on the nightstand with perfect clarity—it shows 2:00 A.M.—and what is Jaroslav doing here with a hirsute face? Intellectual circles, Jaroslav said, are all abuzz about our case. Our case? I thought. You, too, he said, they're all abuzz about you, too. Don't get up, I wanted to say, don't lean back, but Jaroslav had gotten up and had leaned back against the wall, causing the test tubes and the elaborately bent glass tubing to rattle and start breaking and shattering, and Jaroslav was suddenly a bloody mess.

When I turned on the light, I saw that I was holding the watch in my hands and that it was three in the morning. So I had the dream at two. But how the hell could I have been dreaming if I was looking at the watch? I was soaked with sweat, unable to understand a thing that was happening to me.

I've delivered my second telegram to the cute, limping postal clerk. Now it was clear that something's up. At lunch I sat with that sales representative. Pešić, from Zagreb, he sells motorcycles and his business is booming; of course he wears a big fat chain; it's because of his booming business; how could you not see that? He uses the local Germans to import the machines and has them expedited on farther south. "Expedited," that was the word he used. He wanted to have some fun, but I couldn't help him with that. In the lobby I ran into some Czech who was also talkative, so I talked with him, too. Now I've begun talking with anyone who wants to. I've become the hotel's regular chatterbox. And I know why. I felt a need to distract myself. This uncertainty was starting to gnaw at me. I really didn't know what to do. If I left and then Jaroslav showed up, then he'd have to wait, and then when would we ever get started? If I stayed . . . So I talked with the Czech. He brightened when I told him that I work for J. Stastny and Company. The *J* stands for Jaroslav, I explained. In Germany? Yes, in Germany. But from Vienna, J. Stastny is from Vienna, he's a Viennese Czech. We drank coffee, he talked about politics and I talked about anthropology. The Czech wasn't interested in anthropology and I wasn't interested in his political speculations. He had her on display, this anthropologist—an ape woman, a young girl, full of life—but what was he going to do with her once the show was over? Lock her up in a cage? Give her Voltaire to read? The Czech wasn't interested. Some drunk started bawling me out so viciously that I lost my bearings. He was staggering around me and shouting something and I had no idea what he wanted. Was he mistaking me for someone else or had something in his drunken head just totally snapped? For a second I thought he was going to hit me. The blow would have been just as unprovoked and logical as his shouting was weird and pointless. The Czech got him out of the hotel with the waiter's help. Maybe there's something wrong with me. Maybe there's something I'm doing that's so provocative, I myself don't know what it is, and it causes everyone to attack me, day and night.

In spite of everything, the Czech calmed me down. He was a good listener, even if he wasn't interested in my stories, and his voice was even and gentle. This evening I looked him up and we shared a good bottle of wine. His name is Ondra and he's an engineer, an expert in textile machinery. He's come here to inspect the local textile magnate's installation, I forget what his name is. Ondra comes from some village in Moravia, but he lives in Brno now. Brno is a black and dirty town with stucco crumbling off the buildings, just like here. In his memory it really is black, but at least it's full of pretty girls—at least that. Like this place in my mother's memory, where I trampled the flowers, and in my father's memory, where he ate big, fat beans. In spring Ondra's village is so beautiful, everything is green and in flower, and in summer the fields are fragrant. He'll never get used to living in these Central European K. & K. cities, all of them alike. Even though he'll live his whole life in them. His Moravian village is completely different. But what to do? There were no textile mills there. Funny, I've always lived in cities, not counting this one here. I can't imagine a village where the flowers bloom better and the fields smell better than in any other. It's not a matter of "better," Ondra said, it's a matter of "nicer." I can't imagine that either. Just the opposite. I suspect it smells a lot like manure, and that people have to slog through mud in autumn, and that it's always just a little musty in those tiny rooms.

■ □ ■ □ ■

**4**

AT FIRST I WALKED ALONG THE RIVERBANK, STRAYING EVENTU-
ally among the gloomy taverns through the damp, narrow
streets that lead uphill toward the town center. Suddenly I
caught sight of a face that seemed familiar. An old man wearing a rumpled coat, with a wild beard, red nose, veined face,
and dark, feverish eyes. He was waving his arms and muttering to himself. As he came closer I could tell he was speaking
Russian, hurriedly, gulpingly, so that it was impossible to
make out individual words. Then I remembered—this was
the old man I'd met several days ago, the one who'd spoken to
me about Christ's resurrection that first day on Alexander
Street, who'd given me some kind of Easter greeting at that
late, lonely hour. In his battered shoes and thin jacket he
stopped for a moment at the door to a tavern, muttered something else, and then vanished inside. Some unthinking, idle
curiosity drew me after him. I entered the taproom, which
was so dark that at first I couldn't make anything out. The
heavy scent of brandy, of male sweat, of a slovenly and airless
bar assaulted my nostrils. Four men wrapped in clouds of
tobacco smoke sat at one of the tables, noisily playing cards.
The old man sat on the other side, in the corner, alone with
his muttering, fussing with his hands over the table. The bar-
keep gaped at the newcomer with an unconcealed curiosity—
betrayed by his wide-open mouth—that verged on simple-
mindedness. The newcomer thought to himself that he'd

never seen quite such a miserable tavern in his life. I've known taverns in Prague and in Germany, and I've wandered into a few suburban holes in the wall, but none of them were this dark in the middle of the day, and none smelled so horribly of liquor, bad liquor, distilled from lord knows what. Still, I ordered a brandy, and while I sipped it and struggled with nausea and stomach cramps and a whole organism that was rejecting the vile liquid, I found out from the bartender that the old man really is a Russian, that he lives in the city asylum, that he's always wandering around the vicinity, and that Russian émigrés look after him. His name is Fedyatin and the local Russians see something very special in him. But the bartender thinks the old Russian is nothing more than an ordinary, drooling, schnapps-drinking fool. Now the bartender wanted to ask the questions, but I wordlessly paid, stood up, and left.

## 5

I TOLD ONDRA, THE CZECH ENGINEER FROM THE MORAVIAN village where everything smells "nicer," not "better," about what I'd seen down there. Ondra anxiously nodded. His local colleagues had warned him on his first day here that he'd better stay away from that area down there, unless he wanted to lose his wallet, watch, or hat. Lose something at best, and possibly also come away with something, like a scar from a knife wound for the rest of your life.

"As for that Russian of yours," Ondra said, "what's his name again?"

"Fedyatin."

"Right, Fedyatin. As for the Russian, it's very simple. He's a holy man. Before the Bolshevik takeover, there were thousands of them in Russia, tens of thousands. Every village had at least one. They wander near and far, these holy men, endlessly talking about Christ's resurrection. Nobody touches them, because they're holy, and when they're in a trance—they're usually epileptics—they have apocalyptic visions and whatnot. They're peasants, but in the years before the revolution the upper classes were also infected by this Russian craziness. You do know about Rasputin?"

"Sure."

"Well, there you are. Rasputin was one of them. So they had a holy man when everything went crazy and bloody in that dark Russia of theirs." Ondra also had an explanation for what's happening now. It's all religion, he said. Even Stalin came out of a seminary. It's a movement of ancient religious sects that joined up with some Western, German, and Jewish concepts of equality. But I was interested in Fedyatin. A shiver went down my spine whenever I remembered how he appeared before me on the street that morning.

"There've been times when holy men have caused outright mass hysteria," Ondra said. "Self-flagellation and orgiastic experiences and barefooted pilgrimages over rocks and thistle and the devil knows what else. And they call that Christianity, for God's sake. No"—Ondra shook his head despairingly— "you and I as Central Europeans can't even imagine it all. Even their Christ is completely different. A grim Christ. The mistake is in taking things so literally—that's how I see it."

I expressed surprise that a Moravian mechanical engineer, inspecting the textile machines here and thinking the whole time of his native village, would have these kinds of thoughts.

"Why not?" he said. "We have lots of them, too."

"Holy men?"

"Russians, I mean," he said, "and probably a few holy men among them, too. Can you imagine the enormous multitudes that flooded Europe from out of those wide-rivered steppes after the Bolshevik revolution? Ships in Constantinople were bursting with noblemen, priests, peasants, White soldiers. All of Europe smells of their Orthodoxy and incense."

Ondra spoke in vivid and interesting terms, but it was all too theoretical and it just went past me. Fine, you can explain these things that way, but I want to know what it's like for a holy man like that, what the visions are like. There are so many scientists wrestling with telepathy, psychosuggestion, and similar things, they're obsessed with finding someone with psychic capabilities. But no one has thought of putting a Fedyatin—primal man—under the microscope and doing a serious scientific analysis. There's no way they can extract lord knows what out of that famous Eva C. Even if she is the best medium that's ever been, she's lived her whole life in salons and with those women. Her visions do go beyond the potential of her own self-projections, but they have no trajectory, at most they only extend to erotic visions, male organs. But Fedyatin is a whole different world. I have no doubt, because that night something touched me, I still don't know what, I still can't figure it out rationally, it was something dim. And now as he walks around this city, which is something completely different from his Volga River plain, or wherever he's from—does he realize now that everything has changed? Still, he keeps doing those things with his hands and his body and his eyes, as if there's nothing that can change or replace something inside of him. You can also look at the whole thing in its bizarre aspect, like the bartender did: an unusual idiot, perhaps, but ultimately just another drunk, drooling idiot. However much I try in my imagination to subject that ghost to common sense, like the tavernkeeper's, I still can't stop wondering why he was waiting for me in the first hours of the new year, why he wandered the streets on New Year's shouting his "*Khristos voskrese*" to the people. And besides, they've got these scheduled differently somehow. Something must have disturbed him—the merrymaking, the lighted windows, the drunk people on the streets. Why I had to meet him I'll never understand.

■ ☐ ■ ☐ ■

## 6

ALL THE SIGNS ARE THAT THE SOLITUDE OF MY ROOM IS DISSI-
pating. Before, I thought I wouldn't be able to stand another
hour in this cell waiting for Jaroslav, but now suddenly
there's almost too much conviviality. When you come to a
new city, you don't get to know the locals—it's the other
strangers you meet. We see each other in the hallways, at dinner or supper, and eventually we start greeting each other out
in the city. Finally, in the evening, we even drink together. At
Emeršič's, a restaurant on Alexander Street. Pešić with his
watch fob, Ondra, and I. Ondra talked about his Moravian
village and the wine grown there. Pešić became loud and arrogant. He started attacking a Serbian officer who was quietly
eating at the next table and stroking his mustache with the
back of his hand.

"Look at him," Pešić said quite loudly, certainly loud enough
for the officer to hear, "behaving as though he were at home
everywhere, as though he owned everything, as if the whole
country were his cavalry barracks." Truth be told, however,
the officer was not behaving like that, not this evening. Pešić,
however, was.

"His stinking cavalry barracks," Pešić added. At the next
table the officer's jaw started working faster and faster and his
mustache began to twitch. All at once it wasn't clear anymore
what I was doing there. The officer had his soldierly honor,
Pešić had his fat watch fob. I stood up and walked away

wordlessly. Ondra called out after me. I didn't feel a bit treacherous or cowardly about it. All of it simply didn't have anything to do with me. That was a world I was not ever going to enter.

That's what I thought. But that very night I did enter it. I entered it just as irrevocably as I'd decided not to.

At the post office my toothsome girlfriend told me there was no reply. But that I shouldn't worry, because as soon as the telegram came she would deliver it to the hotel. Nothing, then. One more night, then, in this town that doesn't like me and that I keep turning away from with greater and greater discomfort.

When I returned to the hotel I was met at the desk with a message that someone was waiting for me in the restaurant. My heart beat faster. Jaroslav? Impossible.

Of course it was impossible. It was Ondra. He introduced me to a red-haired gentleman, his colleague in the textile machinery business, engineer Franjo Samsa, senior textile supervisor at the Hütter factory, all in one breath.

THE CITY IS NOT A PRISON OR AN INSANE ASYLUM. FOR MOST travelers the city is a way station on their journey. But no one knows the final destination. The city has been situated in its own space, halfway between Vienna and Trieste, and with its streets and buildings, salons and taverns, inns and sanctuaries, jails and hospitals, asylums and morgues, it waits for its own and for strangers, for newcomers and travelers. Everyone can get off the train whenever he wants. In 1860 the poet Ivan Sergeyevich Aksakov got off the train. He left his luggage at the station and went with a handbag to the Hotel City of Vienna. The surrounding city, he wrote in his diary, was almost totally unpaved, misshapen, uneven, surrounded by mountains, rich with cabbages, poplars, gardens, and derelict property. A total mess, with silence and boredom reigning supreme. For Aksakov the city and the entire countryside on down to Trieste were a kind of terra incognita which became an object of fascination to his explorer's eye. This terra incognita lay at the edge of the world and was populated with Slavic patriots. In his room, by the light of a guttering candle, Aksakov wrote to distant Moscow—the center of the world—about this extraordinary land where he'd had to drink bottle after bottle of wine with some Slovene scholars in the middle of the day. All of the scholars were Catholic priests, yet in spite of that, Aksakov wrote, they shared our Slavic soul.

In 1938 Franc Gregurič, a native of Zagreb, and Edita Lieber, daughter of a wealthy Moravian industrialist, come here from Brno. They choose the city as their trysting ground. But several days later Mr. Lieber also arrives. A nasty dispute follows at the police station, because Edita and Franc want to marry, while her father insists that Franc convert to Judaism if he wants to win her heart. Both lovers proclaim that they can't live without each other, but they'll have to live without each other, they'll just have to, because Mr. Lieber takes Edita back with him and the police detain Franc a bit longer for routine questioning. Thus the city for some is the sorrowful end of a sensational love affair, as the local newspaper reports in its sensational roundup of events. It's a different story for Austrian citizen Peter Galowitz, forty seven, a mechanic who, for no apparent reason, suddenly collapsed in the Castle Café and never got up again. Because he's dead, and no one knows why he had to drop dead precisely here. It's a different story for the Viennese symphony conductor Stolz, who can't forget his arrival. When he got off the train he saw such hideous facades that his aesthetic sensibilities went into shock, and after a brief engagement, he fled. It's a different story for Princess Elisabeth Obolensky: she got off the train straight into a trap that she wouldn't be able to leave for twenty years. She had fled the Bolsheviks, and she worked in this city at the edge of the Slavic world (pace her compatriot Aksakov) as a librarian for twenty years, and she would flee again with the Germans in 1945.

In January 1938, 1,417 guests were staying in the city: 239 Austrians, 31 Czechs, 113 Germans, 4 Romanians, 6 Poles. On January 1, 1938, in the first dark hours of the new year, a solitary man, an Austrian citizen, got off the train and headed down Alexander Street to the hotel.

The city of January '38 lies here in wait. Most of the 1,417 will move on or go back. The few who fall in and get trapped will be claimed by the jails, hospitals, police stations, or missions. A simple business, it would seem, but the mystery lies in the fact that none of the fallen or trapped knows beforehand that the thing that is to happen to him will happen to him right here and nowhere else. There's also the asylum waiting for those who get off the train for no good reason they can explain. These last will wander through the unknown land simply because they carry terra incognita in themselves.

■  □  ■  □  ■

# 8

ENGINEER FRANJO SAMSA WANTED TO TREAT ONDRA TO SOME
Czech beer, but Ondra wanted wine. At this point I already
knew that it was going to end in a headache. Because soon
Samsa was all irritated. In fact, it was his exterior that appeared
irritated—his head went completely red, even though his gestures remained measured and his words boring. Because Ondra
kept rattling on about how good the wine was, Engineer Franjo
got a little angry—within the boundaries of collegiality, of
course—contending that this wine was wretched and that the
two of us didn't even know what good wine was. Good wine
was the wine he produced himself. The wine that grew from
vine to bud to grapes and must under his caring hands. From
there it was only a small stretch to the decision that we had to
try that wine. And that we had to try it on the land where it's
produced. But this is winter, I hazarded to remind him. Doesn't
matter, Engineer Samsa said with authority, wine tastes best on
the land where it's produced. Ondra was enthusiastic about this
proposal. So we drove off somewhere into the evening gloom in
Engineer Samsa's car. He told us it was near Trojica and that it
wouldn't be all that damned far, if only the road was decent.
But the road wasn't decent; it was horrible. If we can just make
it to the crucifix, Samsa said, from there we can walk the rest of
the way. I wasn't one bit excited about walking through the
snow at night, but Ondra was as enthusiastic as ever. What I
feared would happen, happened. The car got stuck in the snow.

We trudged on on foot but got no farther than some ramshackle cabin. Samsa's winegrowers lived there, his people, as Samsa kept repeating incessantly. He banged on the windows, which were small and seemed to be at ground level. A little man came out, an old man with a furrowed face. Samsa asked him how the road was. The old man discouraged us from trying to climb any farther. "The road crosses through a hollow, and the snow is deep. Even though it isn't far, it's better not to go." Samsa was enraged. His plan had been ruined. I suspected that he just wanted to show off his country house to his Czech colleague. Then we all squeezed into a tiny, dark room where some old lady stared at us in surprise. There were no children. Everything happened abruptly, emptily, pointlessly. I didn't care where it was all heading anymore. The old man set some wine out on the table. I don't think he said a word all evening after that. Ondra praised it, and Samsa was making faces over his winegrower's product. Ondra taught us a Czech song: Wherever the folks drink beer, there's good living you hear, or something like that. We all had to sing with him. Wine, I corrected him. Beer, Ondra insisted. You can't change a song, you can't change the world, you can't change anything. He started to doze off. Samsa was talking about his concern for his winegrowers, while the old man and woman nodded and professed affirmation from the bottom of their hearts. Samsa had a remarkable social conscience, sensibility, heart. Suddenly Ondra demanded a song. He wanted to hear a real Slovene song in its fitting environment. The old man and woman had to sing the way children sing for a drunken father. For a long time they wavered, then even Samsa coaxed them, and finally they wetted their lips with some wine and timidly started to sing. She sang in a grating falsetto and the old man grumbled an accompaniment, not one word of which I could understand. Ondra said how gentle, how Slavic, what a gentle soul, what a special soul. He explained to us about the Slavic soul. At his emotion and tears, even I could sense some drunken Slavic soul of my own.

Then we pulled the car out of the snow. Then we rang the bell on a door that bore the nameplate ENG. FRANJO SAMSA, SENIOR TEXTILE SUPERVISOR. Then a very interesting, possibly even beautiful, but slightly hostile and disheveled young woman opened the door.

"My friend," Samsa said, "my friend Josef Erdman, he's come back to us, see, to his childhood."

She stared at me vacantly. She had a tired gaze.

"Firm of J. Stastny and Company, special laboratory equipment," Ondra added.

"The *J* is for Jaroslav," I said.

"We'd be very glad to have you visit sometime," she said, and Samsa sobered up in an instant. All the red drained from his face.

"Marjeta," he said, "how can you? My friend Josef and my friend Ondra."

I groped my way back down the steps. Somebody tugged at my jacket, trying to explain something. I wandered through empty streets into the nth night of my pointless sojourn in this city. Back in my room, I turned the key twice in its lock. The ceiling was spinning, and the bed and city spun, and everything spun and that gull continued its endlessly revolving, upturned flight over the water's black surface, and something drew it toward the water as though it were going to get sucked in, and I clearly remember that in the midst of this incoherent rambling I was seized by the clear and razor-sharp realization that I was locked up in this room and in this city, that Jaroslav was not going to appear, and that I would never get out of here again.

## 9

HER NAME IS MARGERITA, OR MAYBE MARJETA AS HER HUSBAND calls her, but she doesn't appear to like that. Nor does she like the three drunken men who try to come into the apartment in the morning, even if one of them is Franjo Samsa and the other two are his friends. She doesn't like standing at the half-opened door in the morning, disheveled and in her robe. She does like oriental rugs, fringed lampshades, and discussions of hypnosis and the women's movement.

I'm not really sure why I went there, and what's more on the evening after our failed early-morning excursion among the vineyards and winegrowers of Engineer Franjo Samsa, senior textile supervisor at the Hütter textile works. Some-times I think I don't know how to say no when I need to most. On top of everything, I'd wanted to spend that evening alone. Suddenly there were too many acquaintances and social events. But I suspect that for a moment I was afraid of the loneliness and anxiety that would pervade my hotel room—the voices from outside, the clattering of cups in the hallways, the staring at the ceiling, killing time. But as I stood once again in front of the door where that morning I had tried to explain that the *J* stands for Jaroslav, I may have been even more afraid. I was afraid, even more than of the lonely room, of the strangers I would have to meet, the empty con-versations, and especially their horrible curiosity, which, out of sheer, provincial boredom, they would be unable to stem. I was afraid of the probing and the genteel interrogations that would inevitably follow, just as inevitably as I find myself standing here at the door with a stupid bouquet of flowers, ringing a doorbell that produces a stupid sound, as though somebody on the other side were striking gongs of different intensity and pitches on the tonic scale.

Of course it was just as I had expected: deadly dull. If, that is, I disregard her and one of her actions that I don't really know how to explain, although there are several explanations, several explanations as plain as day. Of course, with her you can tell right away what she likes and what she doesn't, and she makes it clear in a way that doesn't brook any opposition. What she probably likes most of all is that she can move easily through as large a crowd as possible and that, in an unobtrusive way—or rather in that particular unobtrusive way that doesn't brook any opposition—she can be the center of attention. I sat next to the fringed lamp, obviously in some seat of honor, and I listened to the engineer's endless, endless paeans of praise to his enlightened industrialist for the way he supposedly looks after his equipment and his workers and his managers, consequently also after him, Samsa, and soon something astonishing became clear: This person simply didn't have any other topic of conversation. I remembered that he did have one other topic—his vineyards—but even the night before, he'd mostly spoken on his main topic of social welfare, apartments, textiles, and his great master's employees. Several comparably great minds were present with their ladies that second evening, and they were all terribly self-confident, quite comfortable in each other's presence, but maintaining an appropriately reserved distance.

I was struck by a doctor with a perfectly smooth bald head who smiled enigmatically the whole evening, as though he had this whole group figured out, including my position in it. I'm even tempted to say his smile contained a dab of derision. The doctor's name was Bukovski. I was struck by a handsome young gentleman with a handsome young mustache, the owner of a small business that produces flytraps under the trademark of Bussolin. Two women twittered, drank tea mixed with wine, and laughed out loud—what else were they to do? And finally, I was struck by an incident that had to do with this gentleman and Margerita, and apparently also me, to some extent. Someone was speaking about the occult, most likely the doctor with the smooth bald head. Without really being prepared, I entered into the conversation and briefly mentioned Eva C. Marjeta, that is to say Margerita, or rather Mrs. Samsa, was fascinated by Eva's ability to channel. She sat down next to me and proposed that I speak about Eva C. to the Feminist Culture Section of the Women's Society. But that isn't the point; the point is that she sat right next to me and suddenly touched my arm with the back of her hand. It was the kind of touch that creates a magnetic field that shakes you, I have to admit. I was truly surprised. Especially because she hadn't done it accidentally on purpose, while she was talking, or even unintentionally. Clearly and in full view she had touched my arm while I was speaking. I could tell that almost everyone who was present at that moment had noticed the incident, and I could tell that especially Bussolin—or whatever the flytrap manufacturer's name was—had noticed. It was instantly clear to me that these people had something going on between them and that this obvious, demonstrative touch meant something. Most of all for Bussolin, who was obviously disturbed by it. A bit later I could hear him at the other end of the room letting out tasteless witticisms about flytraps that were better than his, or something like that.

Whatever's going on between them, I refuse to be involved in their party games. I'll even stop going there. Anyway, in spite of everything it was deadly dull. I'll wait a day or two more for Jaroslav, or at least for some communication from him. I even imagine that postal clerk with the white teeth smiling at me enigmatically, and before I fall asleep I see her white teeth and her smile weirdly pasted onto the bald doctor's face. Then, in my dream, Ondra appeared after having left for his

Brno the day before. By now he's probably in that Moravian village, contentedly smiling at the flowers that smell better. In bed I completely forgot that it was winter outside and that there weren't any flowers anywhere and that likewise Jaroslav was nowhere to be found. When I awoke, even I had to smile at that swapping out of enigmatic smiles.

# 10

THE POSTAL CLERK WHO ACCEPTS AND DISTRIBUTES TELEGRAMS walks with a heavy limp. She limps the way people do whose hips were seriously damaged from birth. This means there's nothing—no amount of practice or agility—that will disguise the limp, because the entire body rises and moves forward unevenly. Every day she has to endure her Calvary from the suburb of Magdalene, where she lives with her elderly mother, over Government Bridge, and through Main Square down narrow Cathedral Street to the post office. She has slightly red cheeks and white teeth. Supposedly some people learn to live with their handicaps, but the postal clerk in charge of telegrams was one of those who never manage to reconcile themselves with the fact all their lives. Consequently, every day for her is spent in the tension between torment and joy. Every morning and every afternoon, gritting her teeth, she avoids the eyes that glance from her face down her body to her hips and legs, then return back upward, disturbed by her misfortune, with a mixture of pity and pleasure at their own physical soundness. She knows every kind of glance, as well as the involuntary thoughts that are triggered behind the eyes and forehead. All of the tension is released when she sits down at her window, although she knows she will have to get up and type telegrams. But this is the place she controls, and the few paces there and back are not a long, endless walk among a multitude of evenly striding legs and upright torsos. This is the place where people come with their sad and happy faces, with problems or joy, with their dead and their newborn. In her solitude, which is interrupted every two weeks or even less often by nocturnal visits from the married electrician who works in the telephone department on the second floor of the post office, she has developed an extraordinarily strong sense of the moods of the people she deals with. A week in advance of an actual illness, she can tell for certain that the seeds of the illness have begun to collect in her old mother, even though there are no apparent signs—no pain, no malaise, nothing. She prepares in advance whatever a customer entering the post office might need: condolences or best wishes. Sometimes this really isn't hard to guess. But there are plenty of people who are good at concealing their pain or their happiness. Yet not from her. Here, the masks fall even before the customer has written or said a single word. The electrician who comes to take her body during night shifts or after a carousal, when the taverns have all closed, has long since stopped lying to her, the way men lie to women they visit only for sex. With extraordinary acuity, yet at the same time with a strange kind of tact, she has deprived him of any inclination to babble the way an adulterer normally would. She is aware of this advantage of hers, and he quietly admires her for it. This woman harbors no spite for healthy people, no intolerance. This is why she herself doesn't understand why it's so difficult for her to make the trip each day from Magdalene to the post office.

The postal clerk who distributes and accepts telegrams was the first to determine with all certainty that this person was in some kind of trap. She knew this the first time he stood in front of her, and she wasn't in the least surprised when his telegram was returned stamped RETOUR INCONNU. She knew he would come back, and she sensed he had no way out. This city was his trap and he had stepped into it.

■ □ ■ □ ■

# 11

I WAS QUIET FOR A LONG TIME BEFORE I SPOKE. I LISTENED TO them patiently. The topic of the evening was the occult. With tea, wine, fruit pastries. Bussolin is a newspaper reader. In his flytrap workshop (trademark Bussolin), amid the stale, thick, sticky smell of his flytraps, day after day Bussolin reads the newspapers. Day after day the newspapers contain perfectly serious reports of the extraordinary phenomena and experiments that scientists the world over are performing on mediums. Today's issue: Can crimes be perpetrated under hypnosis? Crime is an ideal topic for them. But not crime as it takes place in some Maribor suburb or in the highlands northeast of the city, where it's more likely to smell of rotgut than blood. Crime in Corsica, vendettas, blood feuds. Or in Chicago, among gangsters. Or crime in an unhappy love affair. Far-off, alien crime. Hypnosis is more familiar, especially among these thick oriental carpets and shaded lamps with fringe that sends shafts of light falling onto her pale cheek. Bussolin claims: Hatred can be realized under the influence of hypnosis. The criminality already lurking in man can suddenly burst forth with all possible violence in a state of hypnosis. Then follows a long string of anecdotes about how somewhere there was a rapping on somebody's window and then somewhere somebody died; about how somebody dreamed about an event that then really happened; about how somebody thought of someone he hadn't seen for years, and then that person showed up at the front door or sent a letter.

I noticed Margerita listening wordlessly. I watched her face, oddly illuminated through the fringe, and it struck me that she was being drained by an unspoken anxiety. It wasn't to add to the pleasant agitation that the company was subjecting itself to in this room, but on account of her anxiousness, her compressed lips, that I spoke up. I couldn't bear to see Bussolin's tales from the daily papers, from his flytrap factory, cause the pallor and the anxiousness on her face. I asked to speak. I spoke about Eva C. About her emanations and her torments in the process of channeling, about her spasms and the slow and tortured dying away after an event like that. I described several experiments. Most of them had been performed on her when she was still very young. Day after day and night after night they worked with her. If she's still alive, she would be very old. She would be very tired and would have to suffer horribly whenever she remembered what all they did to her. The world has never again known a guinea pig the likes of Eva C. No animal has been injected with as many experimental drugs as there were torments inflicted on her. It was having an effect. Margerita leaned back, into the darkness, and I could see her hands trembling slightly. It had shaken her. The others were listening attentively, too. I stopped for a moment and enjoyed the startled and curious looks on their faces.

Then I went on and ruined everything. Aside from the famous Eva C. and her performances in Paris and Munich, which are probably best understood by taking her hysterical predisposition into account—supposedly it's true that she didn't distinguish well between reality and fantasy—aside from her and the spirits she channeled, there's only one other thing of interest in occult biology and physiology, and that's telesthesia. A. Beau de Rochas observed that the body's boundaries expanded in the process of channeling, as though a sphere of sensitivity formed around the body, within which there was a kind of feeling without touch. This sphere extended from two to three meters around the body, but it was divided into layers, the closest and most sensitive of which extended from three to four centimeters outward. But so what, if Margerita remained far outside of that range, way over on the other side of the room, not even in the sphere's outermost layer.

Her lips weren't compressed anymore, and the pallor was gone from her face. She was smiling. Only Eva C. had interested her, only the things they had done to her. Bussolin was reaching for his wineglass more and more often, and some female hands were crumbling fruit pastries. Engineer Samsa was overtly bored. What he cared about was social measures on behalf of the workforce, and when it came to mysteries, then at most the mystery of the creation of fabrics. Only bald Dr. Bukovski was still looking at me with any interest. I went on, but not for the doctor's sake, or for the sake of his theoretical expectations. I went on because I couldn't just stop in the face of the smiling and the fruit pastries. I gave definitions of magical occultism, of the bases of occult medicine, and of the difference between white and black magic. I talked about suggestibility and the subconscious, about channeling and about emanations again. When I stopped, I was astonished to find that nobody was listening to me anymore, that these people were all talking about something among themselves, and that only the bald doctor was still nodding encouragement my way: Just rattle away, pal, you're doing fine.

The whole thing was quite a defeat. I was left sitting alone, sipping tea with wine and shoving that fruit pastry back and forth inside my mouth. The others were excitedly discussing an evening of Russian dance with jazz which, apparently, was inevitably and swiftly approaching. So why had they been telling those horrible stories? Was it because we all still have a trace of those dim peasant huts inside us, where at night the talk is of strange, improbable happenings and pleasant, fearsome ghosts, so that sleep comes easier? Was that why? Or was it because they could sense that someday something really awful was going to happen in this town, or maybe even to them?

Or maybe none of it amounted to anything at all. These people wanted some excitement and a little less light. From the kitchen I could hear the doctor's wife explaining with her mouth full (of fruit pastry?) to some woman: "We have to keep an eye on her. Whenever she drinks too much, she gets strange. She always does something unusual. Did you know that she once disappeared for two days?"

"Impossible."

"Oh, but it is possible."

"And for two nights, too?"

"Just one, but she was away from home for two full days. Her husband says alcohol has some rare effect on her nervous system."

"Really? On her nervous system? Hmm. That can't be good."

"It's not, it's not." They were talking about Margerita.

I didn't mean to eavesdrop. It just happened that I involuntarily overheard it all. Each one of us bears a germ of insanity inside himself. We loners know this best of all. When we look at ourselves in the mirror and don't know where we're going or where we've come from. However: If the doctor's wife talks that way about Marjetica, it doesn't mean anything, not at all. Even if her bald Bukovski says it does.

Next time I'll tell them about how Swedenborg, pale and shaken, saw his house in Stockholm go up in flames. He saw this from Göteborg, fifty miles away. Kant writes about that. A bit more powerful than some rapping at the window. I won't tell them about Eva C. anymore, no. That jackass is going to talk to me about nervous systems? What am I supposed to say, while I'm waiting for Jaroslav?

■ □ ■ □ ■

# 12

MOST PEOPLE WHO DEAL SERIOUSLY WITH SPIRITUALISM ADMIT that the biggest problem is seeing into the future. Even the best mediums in the most favorable circumstances have yielded poor results in that respect. In '38 there are all kinds of prognostications about the future of mankind, all of which at this moment are highly unlikely. The postal clerk doesn't care about the future of mankind, and even at the séances of the occult circle, she got no tangible results concerning the electrician's and her future. The most she attained was a torturous state of despairing uncertainty and fear in the form of her own image, fleeing at a limp down an empty street, with healthy, athletically healthy, types in pursuit, and it's clear to her that she can't escape them. But she'd seen this kind of thing before in her dreams; she didn't need a red light and a séance to see it. If she could see ahead to where she can't see, then in May of '45 she would glimpse her electrician sitting at Beranič's tavern on Vodnik Square. She would see him waving his hands around, drunk, picking up a glass with those hands and flinging the contents in a liberator's face. Then several more liberators wearing uniforms of the Bulgarian People's Army run in and drag her sweetheart by his jacket, by his undershirt, by the hair, out from behind the table. They drag him through Beranič's tavern like a sack of potatoes, tables collapsing and people flying in both directions, toward the walls. They drag him outside into the sunny May afternoon, set this human sack down in the middle of the dusty street and then back off several paces. They unshoulder their rifles and release the safeties. When her drunken sweetheart sees the rifle barrels in front of him, his knees wobble and in mute, drunken terror he drops onto them in front of the Bulgarian, whose eyes flash as he wipes the wine off his face with his sleeve. She would see herself limping out of the tavern, trying to run. As they raise their rifles she is almost there, and she sees that she's drawn the flashing eyes toward herself. She shields her sweetheart with her body, then throws herself onto the road, onto her knees. The Bulgarian shouts, walks up to her, and tries to drag her away, but she grabs on to him with both hands. Hands raised in the air, the Bulgarian sways back and forth, trying to break loose from the disheveled, crazy, limping lame woman, then he shoves her away with his rifle butt. He pants, standing over her, and catches his breath. She can feel the horror receding down the street, which channels it downhill, toward the Drava. The Bulgarian sets the butt of his rifle on the ground. The others begin shifting around. The Bulgarian sets the safety on his gun and slings it back onto his shoulder. Her sweetheart lies in the dusty road, vomiting. Then he tries to stand up, but can't make it onto his feet. His whole body shakes. His whole body is drenched and all around at that moment there is the stench of totally evacuated bowels. One of the Bulgarians says something. The rest laugh and head back into Beranič's tavern. She would then see herself dragging him like a human sack down Carinthia Street, like the Bulgarians did just beforehand, over National Bridge and onto Magdalene Square; she would see a cripple dragging a horribly stinking man through packed streets, along the route of her Calvary. And she would see her sick mother, frightened and sobbing while she washes that man in their apartment and brings him back to life.

And finally, she would see him sneaking down the steps that night, as always, but with the difference that this time he would never come back.

■ □ ■ □ ■

# 13

THE TIME IS APPROACHING WHEN A DECISION WILL HAVE TO
be made. Either I'll leave, or something will happen to me.
I've gotten really comfortable with these people here and it's
interesting that they don't even ask me anymore when Stastny
and Company will be starting its southbound journey. As
though I were at home in this city that had been waiting for
me on my journey and into which I've crawled like some
embryo into its mother's belly. Today this memory struck me
again. At first as I was walking past a church. That blue ball
that I once wanted to have, that some saint was holding—it
had to be in one of these churches. I reached my hands out
toward it, wanted to have it. I haven't found the house in the
suburbs with flowers and fat beans growing in the garden, and
I never will. But the statue seemed so close that something
familiar that had happened flashed past me, though I can't
make sense of it. I wanted to take hold of the ball, wanted to
hold it in my hands, and I seemed to hear a childish voice
demanding the ball for itself in the middle of the church and
the shushing of women trying to quiet it. Did I dream it, or
had I really sat in a church in this city in some woman's lap,
sensing the cool, smooth surface of that ball from up close
and wanting to take hold of it with both hands? Amazing,
how the mind can't grasp something that almost certainly
happened to me in some church here, in my dreams, or perhaps someplace else entirely. Later, when Margerita and I were

walking down Carinthia Street . . . there was a wall in the space between two buildings, and in the wall there was a wooden door. The door was slightly ajar and I knew that behind it was not a house, and not a courtyard, but a whole grassy world that sloped gently down toward the river. I stood in front of the door and slowly pushed it open. At first I was actually a bit surprised when I saw an open space covered with snow and not a blade of grass anywhere. But the open space sloped downhill somewhere and there was sure to be grass under the snow.

I explained to her what was happening to me. She listened attentively, but then shrugged even so.

"Human beings don't remember any of what happens up to their third or even fifth year," she said. "I don't remember a thing. And you're probably just imagining that you remember something. What could there be to remember, anyway?"

A ball in a church and a grassy lawn sloping toward a river, I told her.

"You're a stranger here," she said, "and you don't remember anything. You'd like to remember something, since you're here now and waiting for this Jaroslav. But you could just as easily be in some other town remembering something, maybe something in that town."

Or maybe something that simply exists, exists someplace in the world and exists in some life and has suddenly intruded into my consciousness, which is now trying to turn it into a memory. But there is no memory, no place, and no past, there's only me waiting here for Jaroslav, less and less certain how I got here on some January morning, and here I am walking down some Carinthia Street on a warm winter's day, slogging in wet shoes through the wet snow on the black pavement, and the street is narrow with black houses and tightly shuttered windows on the right-hand side and the black interstices of alleyways that lead down to the river on the left-hand side. That's what I wanted to tell her. And that the ball in the church existed.

And so I've become so comfortable around these people, but especially around this woman, that I can tell them about balls in churches and grassy slopes that lead toward rivers, and it wouldn't make one bit of difference if I told them about balls on grassy slopes or little grassy slopes amid crèches in a church—it would be a matter of complete indifference. The one true thing is that something has happened to my memory, or whatever that is; that something has come over me in all this and that none of it changes a single thing.

I went with Margerita down Carinthia Street to one of the apartment houses that are the property of the Samsa family, their real estate, their very real real estate, bringing them a certain revenue every month. Her job is to collect the rent. Her job is to maintain both houses. Aside from the preparation of tea mixed with wine, fruit pastries, and participating in the Adriatic Night, her job is to collect the rent in a vacant apartment. The apartment has two rooms. In the kitchen there are two chairs and a table, behind which she collects the rent. In the main room are a wardrobe and some kind of couch or bed with a silk cover spread over it, and several more chairs jutting their legs in the air. The apartment serves as an office where people come to pay. And I have to admit that her job isn't easy. People either don't have any money, or they use it for other things. People don't want to pay. And so her job is also to bicker with her tenants and threaten to sue them. Not a pleasant job, after which she is in a foul mood and after which, as she says, she feels more than a little dirty. People gather in the courtyard and outside the door to the vacant apartment whenever Mrs. Samsa collects the rent. They grumble, but then ultimately they pay. Two of her tenants are a pair of sweet young things pushing middle age. Their names are Gretica and Katica. I was hanging out on the covered walkway that juts out over the courtyard, leading to the front door of the "office," which is how I met Gretica and Katica. They said there were leaks and that the plaster was coming off. They said that during the long April rains the water sought out every possible crack and leaks started. Margerita was not happy that I'd talked to Gretica and Katica. She said they were queer birds. But she said it in a way that made me think she envied them their birdlike freedom or something. She was in a really bad mood as we walked down the street. She'd probably had to listen to her renters citing funerals and illnesses as reasons for not paying. She walked down the street with her head bowed and her lips pressed tight. Her extortionate chore is ugly, but she's beautiful. The uglier her chore, the more beautiful she is.

■ □ ■ □ ■

# 14

TOWARD EVENING I WAS DRAWN TO THE POST OFFICE. I WANTED to ask about a response. But when I remembered the clerk would look at me with those white teeth, and that she'd limp over to a table and shuffle through stacks of papers—when I remembered her, I headed downhill. I could hear raucous singing coming from those ramshackle taverns down there in the narrow streets that lead to the river. Behind their windows was a muffled light, behind them were crowds of male bodies, behind them the air was thick with deep voices and tobacco smoke. And when I opened some door, I saw him. He was sitting at his table, and through all the thick barroom air I saw his dark face and feverish eyes over in the corner. He wasn't alone now. Some man with a bull neck and smooth-shaven face was sitting next to him. He turned his head toward the door, this man, and stared at me. I didn't go in. I walked away. But I'd memorized his face. Not just because he was sitting with Fedyatin, the Rasputinesque peasant, not just because of that. I'd memorized it because his face was dark, and not Fedyatin's, as Ondra the Czech engineer might say. His face was dark. The look on Fedyatin's face was feverish, but the other one's gaze was calm and fixed, and his cheeks were clean shaven. Yes, and even his bull neck which was turned toward me was smooth shaven. Later, as I walked through the well-lit streets, I couldn't look at all the young and boisterous people walking around and back and forth endlessly: I had Fedyatin's image before me, and that man sitting next to him. I'm going to expunge them from my memory this very night, because I know that people you think about too much, especially late at night, wind up being drawn into your orbit. And what business did I have with a couple of shady types out of some dank tavern? True, I had met Fedyatin the morning of my arrival. That was why he'd made such an impression. Otherwise, the answer was none. None whatsoever.

# 15

ON THE WEST SIDE OF MAIN SQUARE, BEHIND A HUGE IRON door and set toward the back of a paved courtyard, is the Church of St. Aloysius. On the east side of the square is the inconspicuous Jewish Street with its abandoned synagogue. Midway between the two is a monument to the plague. The Silesian architect Johann Fuchs built St. Aloysius, completed in 1769, in a rather unusual way. From the street you could easily miss its facade, since it stands squeezed between the neighboring buildings of a former monastery and a secondary school, and consequently the whole nave, together with its mighty altar and lofty windows, stands removed far above the humble houses and taverns and squalor of the Lent district at its feet, tending toward the river, as if having sailed upstream at the end of a voyage over some vast and distant sea, then suddenly landing here.

In this harbor the luminous and silent Church of St. Aloysius stands at anchor, with Gabriel and Raphael, with Ignatius Loyola and Aloysius, with soaring vaults and walls of stone, with a gigantic wooden cross against the wall and the Savior on it. For many years the patron saint of studious youth gazed down at the soldiery that had chosen this ship at anchor for its barracks; he listened to their oaths and orders, their quarrels and fights, the nighttime sighing and dreams of distant lands and battles, of wives and children from other places that visited the sleeping army.

On the far side of the altar the river flows on its steadfast and unchanging course. That's behind the altar, which reaches from floor to ceiling, with statues of Peter and Paul in the foreground, and with Tunne's enormous figure of Saint Aloysius. And at the very top there are sculpted clouds and sunbeams. All the intricate carving of the late Baroque intertwines up there over the tall, smooth pillars, and peeking out through it are little human heads, little children's heads, as though they'd been chopped off from somewhere with their sweet features and placed up there among the clouds that the Holy Spirit dispatches to every corner of the earth and heavens. To the right is the Son of God with a great cross, and at his left his slightly hunched old man with gray hair, two putti, and a sphere. Clustered around the blue sphere are those chopped-off little heads that don't know what the gray-haired old man knows: that man's heart must become the heart of a little child. The old man knows this because it's he, after all, who is this world's creator, and it's he who invented all of this, including the sphere he's holding in his hands. There are some who contend the sphere that God the Father holds in his hands is the sphere of the earth. Others think it stands for the cosmos. But the child who once had a little head just like the ones chopped off up there in heaven, and who also had little arms that reached out for this blue ball back then, sitting in his mother's lap, also had the heart of a little child. Which is why he didn't know that the sphere on the altar wasn't a ball that he could reach for, grab, roll, or kick, but that it was the sphere of the earth.

And he can clearly remember that all through Mass he demanded the ball for himself. It was way up there and he wanted to have it. He wouldn't be placated. They had to carry him out of the church, crying loudly. Later they bought him a blue ball, but he kept talking about the one the old man held and refused to let go.

## ■ □ ■ □ ■

## 1 6

SHE FOUND ME AT THE CAFÉ CENTRAL. I WAS BROWSING THROUGH the German newspapers and listening to the rustle of paper, the muffled exchanges, footsteps on the sidewalk, the clinking of coffee cups. A gloomy, aimless, winter-morning-provincial-coffeehouse atmosphere. When time stands still, even though the newspapers are full of commotion—portentous speeches, mass meetings, trials, torchlight parades, marches, and crowds shouting. Suddenly she was standing in front of me in that quiet, dimly lit café, and she stood there without a word of greeting or a smile. I offered her a seat and blurted out a few inane sentences, the way you do in chance encounters like that. For a long time she stared out the window at the dim January morning's frail light. I could tell she wasn't hearing my point-less, incoherent phrases, although she nodded several times. Her mind was clearly elsewhere as she distractedly fumbled through her purse and stared vacantly at the morning gloom outside. For some time we were silent, and that appeared to be the best thing. I thought that last night, as she'd sat pale faced under that lamp in the corner, something upsetting must have happened to her, that the occult discussions must have been especially quiet and sinister and disturbing. I thought that some-thing probably really was wrong with her, that her thoughts ran their own course and that her heartbeat was always a little irreg-ular. I thought about that calculated and faintly impudent touch, about the conversation I overheard in the kitchen, "She always does something unusual," and I could sense a kind of trembling in the air between us, a shuddering that came from this motionless silence, and I thought that here she was doing something strange even now. I wanted to say or ask something, but she stopped every possible word of mine with her absent stare. And she was staring at me the way she had been staring out the window.

Then, in a perfectly calm and straightforward voice, she asked if I was going with her. She had some business down on Carinthia Street involving roof repairs. Although she had come unannounced and though her question was unexpected, from that moment on it was evident that she had come to the café on her own and that she had come to the café for me and no one else. We rose, and I couldn't help noticing from the corner of my eye that a number of customers were watching us from behind their newspapers and over their coffee cups as we walked through the café. I helped her on with her coat and could feel that, despite the calm voice and all the matter-of-factness, her shoulders were trembling.

■ □ ■ □ ■

# 17

SOME OF THAT TREMOR PASSED INTO MY HANDS, AND I COULD feel this as we walked down the gloomy street. People were turning their collars up, but Margerita was carrying her velvet cap with the shiny clasp in her hands. She was silent the whole time. Even on the narrow staircase she walked slowly ahead of me, as though she were in a meadow looking at the flowers underfoot, not climbing a stone stairway licked smooth by countless footsteps. Between walls on which the dampness had etched huge, black spots. An older man coughed his way past us and gave a raspy greeting.

At that moment a presentiment began to rise somewhere inside me. It pressed against the top of my stomach, and I could feel it pass through my wildly beating heart up toward my neck. She took a long time unlocking the door on the wooden walkway. Someone slammed a toilet door behind him, and I could hear newspaper being torn to bits from inside. Before we went in, she first looked at me. A little despairingly, I thought, as though she were just then doing something that was against her will, but that had to happen.

We stepped into that empty apartment, as clean and white-washed as a hospital room. The door to the bedroom was open, and I could see curtains fluttering way in the back. She set her cap down on the entryway table where last time she had sorted through the papers in such haste. She walked through the open door and crossed the room straight to the window.

She stopped in front of the curtains. I followed behind her. At the bedroom door I stopped, too. I assumed she wanted to look out the window, but she stood there motionless, gazing into the white curtains. Strangely, the room wasn't cold. In as big a room as that, with just an old wardrobe pushed up against the wall, and on top of the bed opposite the legs of overturned chairs jutting into the air, it should have been cold, clouds of warm breath should have formed in front of our mouths. I figured that her renters on both sides must be burning their last sticks of firewood for the winter, warming the walls of our room. I went up to her and lifted my hands. She shrugged her shoulders, as if escaping my importuning hands that didn't even touch her. I wanted to help her, but she did that with such decisiveness, my hands were left awkwardly hanging and I didn't know what to do with them. On the bed there was only a thin silk cover, with long fringe falling at the edges.

She took her coat off and threw it over the headboard. She looked at me now for the first time. Or rather, she caressed me with her eyes. I could feel without any hesitation that it was a caress. Then, in an unusual gesture, she ran the back side of her hand over my cheek, as though she were checking whether I had shaved. She unfastened the buttons on her dress one after the other, and I lifted my greedy hands to reach for her. Again she escaped them in midair. She dropped the top of her dress down over her shoulders. The fabric fell as far as her hips and caught there. I was loosening my necktie. I knew I would have to take the tie off, and that undoing the tie was always the clumsiest and most ridiculous part of this whole business. My fingers refused to obey me. I was too nervous. A half hour ago I had been sitting in the Café Central reading a newspaper, and now here I was with this beautiful woman who'd dropped her dress down to her hips, who had white shoulders and beneath her white slip the outlines of small, round breasts. All of it was too sudden. I just wasn't prepared for the direction things had taken. I took off my jacket and threw it over a chair. She did absolutely nothing to ease my embarrassment. She stood there watching my jerky motions.

This was a scenario she'd planned in advance. Who knows how many times she'd played it out in her mind? And up to this point it had been flawlessly performed, too. She had carried her hat down the street in her hands. While everyone else was bundled up to the ears, she'd carried it as though it were the warmest day of spring. She'd walked through the sludgy snow in the courtyard as though it were wildflowers. She'd gazed thoughtfully toward the windows, in order to seem beautiful and alone, despite the fact that she was in the room with a man who, in accordance with her plan, fervently desired her beautiful body. She'd taken her coat off and she'd let her dress fall from her shoulders. She'd refused to let any sweaty male hands grope her until she wanted it to happen. But above all—and this part seems to me the most important—everything, and that means absolutely everything, had to be completely different from the way it was with her Franjo. I don't want to get into speculating about how it was with her Franjo, whose face turned beet red whenever he drank a couple of glasses of his excellent muscatel, but I do want to say that I wasn't the least bit comfortable with this game she was playing.

It's cold, I said, even though it wasn't cold at all and that isn't what I was thinking either. Everything in me resisted assuming a role for which I didn't know the words, the steps, or the moves. Everything I said misfired. When I said it was cold, it came out as a thinly veiled hint that we ought to warm ourselves, and that again didn't conform with her illusion. So I let the necktie go, elaborately and tightly knotted as it was. I walked over to where my jacket lay on the chair, felt through it for my cigarettes, and lit one. Some wordless rage was building up inside me, because I was sure I was about to spoil and waste everything. But it turned out that her scenario wasn't so strict and that there was still room for improvisation. Because she pushed her dress down over her hips and let it drop to the floor around her feet, then she stepped over it and took the cigarette out of my hand. She drew on it, then threw the cigarette onto the floor and stepped on it. Maybe this is how she'd planned everything. She took hold of my hands and drew them around her waist. We sat down and kicked the shoes off our feet. Then I could feel and hear her rapid, warm breath on my neck. Jerkily, I lifted her slip. Suddenly we were undressed. I ran the palms of my hands over her thighs, which were cold above the stockings, but warm and pliant closer to the hem of the panties. I caressed her belly and with a convulsive, clawlike motion shoved my hand into her underwear. She stopped my violent hand with force and withdrew. She wanted it differently. When I overcame her and reached my fingers between her barely parted legs, where it was amazingly warm and moist, she whispered: Not like that, not the fingers. That was all she said that morning.

Later, as I was moving on top of her, I could see she had sunk her teeth into her lower lip. She had probably imagined this part differently, too, but now she had forgotten. Now she wasn't thinking of anything. Then, at the end, all I could think was how ridiculous, here I am spread-eagled and practically naked, but with my necktie still on.

# 1 8

THE CITY IS OLD, AND THE BUILDINGS IN IT ARE OLD, TOO. THE oldest quarter has at its core the rectangular Main Square, out of which radiate the main streets of the old town, intersecting at right angles: Carinthia, Vetrinja, and Noble Streets. From there the center of city life stretches down along Alexander Street to the main train station and south over the river. To the north lies the business district, with its newer office buildings, schools, and apartment buildings in grassy settings, with broad tree-lined avenues and parks that culminate in affluent neighborhoods nestled in the foothills. To the south and east, especially in the Magdalene district, there are red-collar neighborhoods, as well as industrial and military installations. There are also a lot of shantytowns that have been thrown up, due to the sudden population influx. One of those areas has been named by its residents "Abyssinia."

If we exclude the parkside villas in the north and some of the new apartment buildings in the center of town, then most of the population lives in old, poorly maintained buildings. The owners behave like slumlords, investing practically nothing in their property. Most of the old houses have those wooden walkways in the courtyards, assembled from weathered planks that have been worn smooth by innumerable footsteps. One of these wooden walkways juts out from the building like a rib or a shelf, and this is how you get into the apartments. The street side just has windows, while the courtyard side reveals the doors. Every time you walk through the main courtyard door, you survey your whole world, which is a nice and clever arrangement. The entry into the courtyard is secured by two doors, the outermost of which is wooden and locked at night. The inner door is wooden only halfway up, with the top part made out of glass panes set in wooden frames. Behind one of the doors on Carinthia Street a little early-morning adultery takes place. Behind one of the others a tuberculosis victim coughs. He does this in a year when tuberculosis has almost been completely eradicated in this country. In the previous year only eighty-eight individuals had died of the disease. And since this year has barely just begun, it's possible he'll be the eighty-ninth, since his cough is so violent and incessant that he can be heard through the thick walls and out into the courtyard. But outside the wooden water closet at the end of the walkway there is a third door. Behind the third door are Gretica and Katica, drinking some of Pristovšek's liqueur. The walls and ceiling have dark water stains on them, because the roof on Samsa's house leaks, and it's winter, and the southerly wind has melted the snow, which also goes dribbling over the edge of the gutters. The bigger the water stains on the walls, the more violent the coughing and the faster the rain comes streaming off the roof. But if we forget about the stains on the walls and the ceiling, their apartment is neatly appointed. There are doilies, coverlets, and flasks everywhere. The doilies are Katica's handiwork, because Katica stays at home and sews. The flasks are Gretica's, because Gretica occasionally works at an eau de cologne bottling factory, and now and then she'll bring a sample home. Gretica has a picture of some girls in German folk costume on the wall. The girls are shown next to their bicycles, because Gretica is a member of the Edelweiss cycling club. She also likes the song of that title and often twitters it to herself, especially when Pristovšek brings some of his liqueur by. When Gretica starts singing "Edelweiss" very loudly, then old lady Gruden on the ground floor shouts back

and calls her a Bundist. Then Gretica runs out onto the walkway, bends over the railing, and tells her off. Then Gretica feels
better, goes back to Katica, and starts singing out loud again.
It's that nice. It's that nice to sit in a warm kitchen on a winter
morning, even if there are water stains on the ceiling and walls.
And it's that nice when Gretica and Katica chat:

"I knew he'd come," Gretica says, "and now he's here."

"Well, so what of it?" Katica says.

"He's a nifty fellow, that's what," says Gretica.

"Not many of them around," Katica says.

"Did you see how his trousers were pressed?" Gretica says
and thinks for a moment. "A man has to have pressed trousers,
otherwise what's the point," she adds.

"You've got trousers on the brain," Katica says as she
threads a needle.

"He doesn't have trousers on . . . at all now," Gretica says
with satisfaction. Katica giggles into her sewing. Then she
sips some liqueur and then practically spews it all out in
another fit of laughter. Gretica has fallen to thinking again.

"All Germans have pressed trousers," she says after a pause.

"Oh, those riding breeches," Katica says.

"Sure, they wear riding breeches," Gretica says. "A sight
handsomer than our men in uniform, with the butts of their
trousers hanging down to their knees."

Katica stops contradicting her. She puts her sewing down
on a table and walks to the door. Out of habit she pushes the
curtain aside and looks out onto the courtyard. She always
does this when she walks to the door, if only to see if old lady
Gruden is peering out from behind a curtain across the way.

"Hey," Katica says with a start. "There's one at the door."

Gretica gets up and fixes her hair and adjusts her dress.

"Not our door," Katica says, "her door. There's one in an
overcoat standing at her door." Gretica shoves Katica away
from the door and takes her turn pushing the curtain aside.
She bites her lower lip nervously, then suddenly opens the
door and goes out onto the walkway.

"Who are you looking for?" she calls out loudly, causing him to flinch in confusion. Angrily he drills her with his eyes, then he turns around and suddenly vanishes down the stairs. Agitated, Gretica walks back into the kitchen. She catches her breath so that she can say something serious.

"Hey, Katica," she says. "That wasn't just some man. That was one of them."

"One of whom?" Katica asks.

"One of the snoops from the police," Gretica says.

"How do you know?" Katica asks.

"I know what they look like. And the regular ones don't wear overcoats like that. This one was the secret service, I can tell, I can tell from a mile away, from the overcoat and the trousers."

"Oh, come on," Katica says.

"Come on nothing," Gretica says. "I know, because I was a political on account of belonging to Edelweiss."

"Gretica," Katica says, "come on, now, Gretica, you know you weren't a political, you know it was on account of that repossessor, because his wife reported you."

"It wasn't because of my repossessor," Gretica says, hurt and angry. "I was a political."

"Sure, fine," Katica says.

"Sure nothing," Gretica says and is absorbed in thought. She thinks for a long time, then says, "Something's going to be wrong here. There's going to be a problem with that fellow who's with her. When a person's being tailed by a trench-coat type like that who snoops around after politicals, then something's wrong. That much I know."

■ □ ■ □ ■

# 19

I DREAMED I WAS WALKING DOWN SOME STREET IN VIENNA, BUT the buildings were so small that it seemed like Linz. I heard my father's voice. He was saying something that I repeated after him, but I didn't understand any of it—neither his words nor my own. I remember that. And when I woke up, everything around me suddenly seemed wholly unreal, too. Even what had happened. I had to walk down to Carinthia Street to convince myself. I walked beneath the windows of the vacant apartment and through the dank entryway, then stood in the courtyard for a long time. It was all there, and even though she wasn't there, everything else was so very much there, that it was real. Then, not thinking, but filled with her silent image and absent gaze, I walked alongside the river. I walked over a little bridge, and high on the bank up above me caught sight of the bell tower of a church. My heart beat faster. I practically ran along the wide path that led up the wooded hillside and stopped, completely out of breath, in front of the door to the church. For a second I stood there, and then I shoved it open, revealing the hollow and empty nave gaping before me. I went in and heard the sound of my breathing inside the huge space. At the same instant, I realized this wasn't it. It wasn't that church. Even so, I went up to the altar. Other saints and other gods were standing up there, and other scenes of the Way of the Cross hung everywhere on the walls. Back outside, I cooled my burning forehead and temples with a fistful of snow.

I took a different way back into the city. I bought a news-paper at the tobacco stand near the main bridge, with a picture up above of a Turk with crossed legs. I meant to return to the hotel and to my room, but they were filled with that obscure speech of my father's and my own obscure words. I kept going and ended up in the park, stopping alongside the skating rink.

I watched that couple: him in his plus fours and her in a wide black skirt, spinning relentlessly, as though they had been wound up, spinning around some invisible axis. The axis was invisible and the music inaudible. Amid all the relentless spin-ning, the dancers had to be humming some tune or keeping time: one-two-three, two-two-three, in incessant waltz time. They had to have some tune in their ears—they were so wound up that all they had to do was keep the beat and hum, while a mighty Viennese orchestra boomed in her ears and before their eyes billowed the waves of the blue Danube— which isn't blue at all, but filthy and brownish. The two of them perceived this world differently from me, who saw them as downright ludicrous in their endless, taut spinning and grinding of ice beneath their skates. Just as the man who sud-denly approached me must have known of some utterly differ-ent world. It's a world I don't know, though he's profoundly convinced that I exist in it, that I'm a part of it. I have to admit I gaped at him in total surprise when he approached me and suddenly asked, "Have you come from lunch at the hotel?"

He just asked outright have you come from lunch at the hotel. Actually, it was even less ceremonious than that, more like Didja have lunch at the hotel, and I had no idea if he was mistaking me for someone else or if he was just some insane person who hung around the park and skating rink in the mornings, approaching strangers. He was hatless, with closely cropped hair and a silk tie visible under a dark overcoat. I don't know why I remembered that tie, of all things, but it was a white silk necktie covered with some kind of pattern—the kind of tie you'd probably prefer not to remember. In the con-fusion of the moment I probably answered in the affirmative, because after lunch there actually was a knock on my door. When I opened it, the first thing I saw was that bright necktie. That morning's stranger from the skating rink was standing in the doorway. May I? he asked and came in. For a moment he paused in the middle of the room and looked around him, then he just sat down on my bed with his overcoat still on. He sat down on the bed, as if he were at home, though he could as easily have sat on a chair. He looked me straight in the eye and I sensed that somehow my face didn't suit him. Indeed, he paused before he began speaking, mysteriously.

"Are you in touch with Kasper?"

"Kasper who?"

"And what about Ondra?"

"You mean the Czech engineer?"

"That's right."

"He's gone. . . ." I didn't understand a thing, myself included, or why I was answering these extremely opaque and pointless questions. Again, I sensed that something was getting confused and that some misunderstanding was going to sprout from this, too.

"Listen," I said in something of a daze, "you and your Ondra Kasper—"

"Kasper is one thing, Ondra is another."

I noticed that his hand was impatiently fumbling through a pocket, as though he were about to pull something out of it. He fumbled as though he were playing with marbles, fidgeted a bit, then fixed his eyes on me again. I just stood in the middle of the room in my undershirt and slippers, watching him as he sat on my bed in a winter overcoat and spoke of contacts that to me had no apparent beginning or end, or even sense.

"You're right, of course," he said. "The conspiracy comes first. But you don't need to worry. . . ." I wanted to say that I wasn't worried, or rather that I was worried, but about totally different things. And that as far as he was concerned, my only worry was that he was making himself at home on my bed, playing with those marbles in his pocket and asking me ridiculous questions.

"Excuse me, stranger," I said, but didn't get any further than that, because the words caught in my throat. I wanted to say that I had no business with any Kasper, that I had only casually met some Ondra here, if he was thinking of the same Czech who was infatuated with the mud of his Moravian village. Finally, I wanted to say that I had no business with him either, forcing his way into my room, where he had absolutely no right to be, and sitting on my bed in his overcoat. The words got caught, because he abruptly asked another question.

"How are things in the nest?" What nest, for God's sake? This person was beginning to annoy me.

"How are things in the hawk's nest?"

I gave no answer and thought I could see him begin to waver. He was becoming impatient and a little testy. I was also becoming impatient and a little testy. His hand fumbled around in his pocket, and I could see his knuckles moving through the material of his trousers as his hand massaged some marbles or maybe a rosary. He gave a deep sigh and then began speaking patiently and slowly, as though talking to an idiot who would eventually understand, if you just kept trying till it dawned on him.

"How are things in Prague? Are all our people safe?"

Connections began colliding and meeting in my head. Ondra is a Czech. The hawk's nest is Prague, the center of the Sokol, or hawks', movement. They have something going on there, somebody who's in touch with Ondra, and now they think I'm also—no, all of it was just too ridiculous. I had to be decisive. I went to the door and opened it. "Sir, you've made a mistake," I said. But he leaned back on the bed, as though he were planning to sit here all day, playing with his marbles and asking me questions. I closed the door. I was somehow helpless in the face of this presumption. For a second I thought of going downstairs and calling the concierge. But to do that I'd have to put on my shoes. I couldn't run down to the concierge in my slippers and call for help, when all outward signs were that this person meant me no harm and just wanted a few answers. And what if I put on my shoes—should I have to flee my own room, for God's sake? And what if I grabbed him by the jacket so that his buttons popped off and that white silk necktie cinched up around his neck? What on earth for? He isn't showing the slightest sign of violence, if you don't count as aggression the fact of his sitting here on my bed, in his overcoat. All the options were so pointless that I capitulated and closed the door. I sat down on a chair and, beaten, said, "Listen, sir, I simply don't understand any of this."

I could see he was beginning to realize that this really was some kind of misunderstanding. That in all likelihood—in all likelihood, don't you see—I simply was not the person he thought I was for who knows what reason. Slowly he stood up, went over to the mirror, and adjusted first his white silk necktie, then his scarf, and then finally straightened out the collar of his overcoat and began to button it. He left the marbles in his pocket.

"I don't know what has happened here," he said slowly, looking into the mirror, "but I'm going to brief you as I've been instructed to do. It's not my place to judge; I'm just an intermediary. Do you understand? Just an intermediary and nothing else, don't you see?" I don't see shit, I thought, but he went on to brief me as he'd been instructed.

"Philip wants you to know," he said, "that they've decided on lots of dancing at the wedding. But first, in the next two weeks there will be a big sale of printed, and I stress printed, material, at heavily reduced prices. The date will be set just before the sale. The sellers are ready, but the buyers don't suspect a thing. Is that clear?" I nodded. He nodded back. There was a mixture of anger, surprise, and nodding in his gesture and in his eyes. He reached back into his pocket and fumbled with his marbles and rosaries and keys and whatever else was in there, then he went slowly over to the door. He turned around one more time and looked at me distrustfully. He shook his head. With resonant footsteps, he left with his surprise and with the objects in his pocket.

Afterward I thought how similar this had been to the couple spinning on the ice this morning, he in his plus fours, she in her wide skirt. The grand melody of a Viennese waltz and all the sounds of a symphony orchestra echoed in their ears, while all I could hear was the ice crunching beneath their skates, and at most their humming. I watched their taut, mildly ridiculous spinning, while they—who knows where they were soaring, maybe in the stratosphere. Of course I exaggerate a little; but what marches were blaring in the head of this man in the white necktie with marbles in his pocket? I could only see that white necktie and hear his garbled speech. But he has his job: He knows exactly what he's doing, and he sees all the threads and connections. Although he obviously got some wires crossed, still he's part of some gigantic, tirelessly functioning machine. Its engine is there, in far-off Moscow. And what do I know about those people? About those Communists and Bolsheviks and anarchists and Trotskyites? What do I know about this machine, about this organism with its heart beating in the center of darkest Russia? Today the papers are full of news from that country. There's some trial under way in Moscow. A Soviet diplomat vanished mysteriously in Bucharest. The Soviet ambassador to Oslo, condemned to death, is on his way back to Russia. He's been recalled immediately on counts of espionage and anti-Bolshevik propaganda linked to Trotsky. His two sons are being held in Moscow as hostages. And what else do I know? I know that they organize strikes, that they get arrested, that in practically every corner of the globe there's some intrigue they're involved in. Even in the city where I'd like some peace and quiet, even in my hotel room. And what else? That the medication we gave him had its effect. This is what seventy-year-old Dr. Pletnev said to some other doctor, a Dr. Byelostok. Byelostok gave a written deposition about it, and at the same time Yagoda, the former head of the secret police, confessed that he'd given orders for the elimination of people, including an order to poison this man. He vigorously denied having anything to do with the death of Menshikov, the previous head of the secret police, or of Peshkov. The medication that had its effect had been given to Maxim Gorky. Man—how noble that sounds.

■ □ ■ □ ■

# 2 0

EVERYTHING SEEMS AWFULLY CRAZY AND AWFULLY MIXED UP: what the newspapers write about, and what strangers here tell me. And this thing with Margerita that's happening to me. I haven't gone near, I've needed some time to think through what's happened. I've thought about the Hütter works engineer, the owner of the vineyards and the souls that live there, the owner of apartment houses. I've thought about their apartment, covered in oriental rugs, and I couldn't go near it. But at the desk there was a note in a pink envelope waiting for me: *Why don't you come visit us? Have we offended you somehow? Margerita Samsa.* So that's how it is, I thought. Social life goes on. I'll have to drop by there and hear about some new incident of a tapping on shutters and some new crime committed under hypnosis. Which means that what happened, in fact, didn't.

My heart was racing when I rang the bell that evening, and when she opened the door I knew again that I wasn't dreaming that black January morning in the Café Central, that it wasn't some story I'd read in a cheap German novel. We had fruit pastries. As hostess, Margerita was cordial and said just the right thing to each of her guests. Not a single sign, nothing. Boris Valentan—Bussolin—was telling a story about a woman who had all of Corsica at her feet. Her husband, an outlaw and bandit, was murdered in a vendetta, or blood feud, by a rival. She then married her husband's killer and together they killed innocent travelers. Next followed a story by

Dr. Bukovski about an unhappy schoolteacher named Milena L. and her even unhappier lover. As this story was being told, some of the absent gaze and charming pallor under the fringed lamp returned to Margerita Samsa's face. The story was reputedly a true one, but there was some question as to how much of its shock value would survive the taste of fruit pastry. It had happened not far from here. A mother had convinced her son, who worked as a porter in sleeper cars, to quit his job due to the rising number of assassination attempts on international routes. The son was persuaded and returned home. Their life was happy, but only for a short time. The son fell in love with Milena L., a young teacher. He became so infatuated that he began to rave in unrequited love. One day he went from house to house, totally deranged. Then he pulled out a knife and murdered Milena L. He went home and there he plunged the knife into his own heart. In horrible agony he begged his neighbor, who had run over, to shoot him. The neighbor couldn't oblige and the young man slowly expired amid mad shrieks.

A Hungarian named Iris Farczardi had taken sick and fallen unconscious. It appeared she was going to die. Then she came out of her coma and recovered. Now she began claiming she was a Spanish peasant named Lucia Alvarez. She spoke some Spanish dialect and they had experts determine it was for real. She also claimed she had fourteen children in Spain.

There were lots of other little stories, even more frightening and bizarre than these. With the exception of the Hungarian named Iris Farczardi, or rather the Spanish peasant Lucia Alvarez, this time none of them was about the occult. This evening amid the carpets and fruit pastries was for bloodletting.

A TRIP INTO WINEGROWING COUNTRY. A SUDDEN SOUTHERLY wind had drenched the whole countryside in warmth. Sunlight flooded the city streets, too, and all at once the morning gloom that just yesterday had been grinding people down evaporated. At the home of the engineer and owner of apartment houses it was decided this was a unique opportunity for a trip out of town. Off to winegrowing country in the middle of winter. Off to spring in the middle of winter, to see the snow gleaming in the sun and dancing in its brilliance. They were concerned the car might get stuck in the mud, but then, after exhaustive consultation, they determined to drive only as far as that roadside cross, because the road was paved to that point. From there it would all be on foot.

On Sunday morning we drove off along Alexander Street and through the neighborhood of Kosak toward Lenart. The engineer's Ford was all polished and bright, and so were the people in it.

I sat in the back seat with Margerita. She was in high spirits, constantly looking back and waving through the rear window at Bussolin, who sat proudly at the wheel of the second car. They could feel their status as ladies and gentlemen. Playing tennis and going for a drive are the only ways they can really feel their genteel status. In the apartment, full of oriental rugs, you didn't have that atmosphere. The world was small there, the air was heavy and full of unspoken nastiness.

Their thoughts there kept drifting back to the filthy apartments of their tenants, who refused to make good on their obligations and who constantly had to be forced to pay up. There they thought of the hateful stares of the factory workers and the thick, sickening smell of the flytrap workshop. Marjetica squealed in delight when Franjo stepped on the gas, causing the car to lurch. Bussolin didn't give up. His was the more powerful motor, and soon he was right behind us. After a while, even I thought it splendid to be racing through the sunny countryside and having people on all sides turn and stare at those two damned cars.

We left the cars at some intersection, near the roadside cross where I'd already been once, one dark night, at the beginning of this story with them. This time we sat the whole day in that big room, looking out the window. I forget what we talked about. Mostly about wine and grape harvests, I suppose. We ate a lot, and the engineer kept bringing wine to the table. I went outside just one little time, when it was already afternoon. I walked down the path that ran behind the house and sensed somebody walking behind me. It was Marjetica. We leaned against a tree in the orchard and kissed for a long time. As we walked back, people waved to us from a neighboring house. They conferred for an instant, then apparently they decided that the two of us were going to stop by and pay a visit. They had come from town, too. They introduced themselves: first of all, property owner and landlord Millonig (more or less the equivalent of Herr Engineer, only on a larger scale), next businessman Janesch, and finally real estate magnate Markoni.

I whispered to Margerita that in that case I was just a meal-plate magnet, as some great man once said in a similar situation, and it tickled her. She couldn't forget it, and one after the other she called the people in her entourage aside to tell them the excellent, if unoriginal, joke. You could see that the two groups spoke each other's language, although it was obvious that these gentlemen associated with each other only in the country. Back in the city they would avoid each other, and presumably more and more as time went on. After we graciously parted ways Bussolin yelped, "Those Kraut pigs, they'll get theirs." And no one argued with him. On the ride back, Marjetica stroked my calves too brazenly with her patent leather shoes, intended only for driving.

We came back exhausted. The car was covered with mud, and we were all deflated and a little drunk.

And so I definitively became an inseparable member of this group. A friend of the family, if not the pet.

What was I still doing here? Was I just going to hang around?

I forgot: There was a fourth German, whom we'll call Maestro. And all of them had delightful wives and beautiful children, fearsome Teutons.

■ ☐ ■ ☐ ■

## 2 2

A CLOSED, TRIANGULAR PLATFORM THAT NARROWS AND BENDS
gently toward the Drava. It feeds directly out onto the bridge
and in the morning it offers a nice view of the red roofs of
the old quarter of Lent, drenched in sunlight. In the midst of
the platform is a green island demarcated by a painstakingly
pruned living border, a fence made of hedges. Across from the
public toilet on the east side of the bridge is a small building
so tiny that it resembles the alchemists' shops in Prague's Zlatá
ulička, or Golden Street. Over the door there's a large picture
of a Turk with his legs crossed, holding a water pipe in his
hands. The tobacconist who opens this shop early every morning is some sixty years old. When he was still young and help-
ing his mother run the shop, he knew the triangular square
on the right side, the south side of the river, well—a square
out of which life streamed in all directions, to the east and
west alongside the river, to the south toward the mountains,
and toward the big factories in the southwest. When he was
still young and they sold different cigarettes and different magazines and when everything was different, the square had a
peaceful and even slightly beatific name: Magdalena Platz. In
1915, when the tobacconist had grown ripe for the muddy
trenches of Galicia, Kaiser Wilhelm stepped onto the square
with his drums, his crown-princely trinkets, and the distant
rumble of his cannon. The tobacconist returned with some
long-delayed transport from Italy just in time to see the KAISER

WILHELM PLATZ street sign being taken down. That was in 1919, and the Kaiser was replaced by a stocky Serbian hero, King Peter I, at the mention of whose name patriots had visions of rugged Albanian mountains, heard the squeak and rattle of carts, saw the blue Adriatic around Corfu, and smelled the gunpowder of the battles for Thessalonika. As he observes the life of King Peter Square from morning to night through the glass panes of his shop, the tobacconist—getting on in years now—thinks of it as the heart of the new city that's beginning to grow to the south, and the streets running in all directions are the veins and arteries. In spring of 1941 the street signs will crash to the pavement, as will many other signs, as bundles of old newspapers will go flying into the river, and just as everything else will fall. From then on, the square will carry the athletic name of Friedrich Jahn Platz. From under his Turk with the crossed legs the tobacconist will watch life rush on, and he'll watch as the wall of his building under the sign with the name of the inventor of the horizontal and parallel bars is covered with posters, one after the other, listing hostages recently shot. One winter, as he locks up his shop in the dark of evening, he will suddenly notice blood slowly seeping out from under a poster to all sides. After that, he will anticipate with trepidation every new proclamation pasted onto the side of his Turkish house, and he will try not to look at it in the evening. In May 1945 he will watch from behind his counter as the units retreat, and in the evening he will run outdoors. He will pry the poster off of the stucco with his penknife. But amid his own loud, panicked heartbeats he won't be able to hear the shouts coming closer and closer. There will be a hollow explosion in his head, caused by a rifle butt striking him in the skull. He'll be bedridden for several months, fighting for his life, and when he recovers, street signs bearing the glorious name of Thessalonika, King Peter, will adorn the square once again. As an old man in the years to follow, he will more than once hear workers setting up their ladders, tin dropping to the pavement, hammers banging. At first, the place where he'd spent most of his life, sold every kind of magazine and brand of cigarette, and seen all sorts of uniforms will be called May Ninth Square. Shortly after that, the facades of the buildings will sport the name of the victorious Red Army, and just when the street activists will have gotten people used to the new name, the Red Army will drop to the pavement, too, and from then on, this will be Revolution Square. And so the tobacconist and the reposing Turk above him have watched, instead of blessed Mary Magdalene, hordes of heroes, drums, rifle shots, artillery, armies, liberations, and revolutions, all accompanied by the banging of hammers. A short while later, as hammers drive nails into the tobacconist's coffin, his place in the shop will be taken by a comrade who would never even think of comparing this piece of the world, which she stares at in boredom for most of the day, to a heart, and the streets to arteries.

There were fewer artillery barrages, echoes of distant battles, fewer kings and armies on other squares of the city, and as a result the *Kulturkampf* that took place on the facades of those buildings was a bit less frenetic, but just as fanatical. In 1919, Goethestrasse had been replaced by Prešeren Street. In 1941 it would go back to Goethe, and in 1945 back to Prešeren. Levstik would drive Lessing out, as Bismarck did Maister. The Medved Street of 1934 would become Grillparzerstrasse. Trubar and Luther, Dvořák and Wagner, Smetana and Mozart would all take their turns. The Slovenes would replace the Austrian Emperor and Hungarian King Franz Joseph with Frankopan; the Germans would replace Frankopan with Hindenburg; and then the Slovenes would replace Hindenburg with Gorky. Hegel would get Prečna Street, Hunters' Lane would become Hubertusgasse, Factory Lane would become Kruppgasse, and then all of them revert back again. A street with the strange name of Deadend would change in '41 first to Sackgasse, then a year later to Mondgasse, and then in '45 it would become Deadend again. The only names that more or less avoided controversy were Minoritengasse, which would become Minoritska, and Workers' Lane, which remained Arbeitergasse. And yet, under the

German occupation—or liberation, depending on how you looked at the name changes—there were some streets that got decidedly Slovene names: Bračič, Gornik, Hočevar, Petek, Bubak. These were the Germans who fell on Main Square in 1919 under the Frankfurt flag, shot down by troops of the Slovene general Maister.

■ □ ■ □ ■

## 23

HER ENGINEER WAS AT HIS FACTORY, HER CHIVALROUS FRIEND Bussolin was making flytraps, and Dr. Bukovski was dismembering corpses at the morgue, while the two of us spent the day lying on the bed, listening to the wind press against the wooden walkway, and watching the new snow fall against the windowpanes and slide wet down them.

We smoked. Gently, she lifted my arm and examined it for a long time, as though she were trying to imprint it on her memory. Her expression was gentle, too, and she spoke in a soft voice. She told me about some village that was her home, supposedly on the south side of the Pohorje range. She talked about the rustling of the Pohorje pines, where you didn't have a driving wind like the wind that pounded now against the wooden walkway jutting out into the courtyard, but where it rustled through the tree limbs and sang its songs, at times sorrowful and at others dark with its own roaring. Once, when she was little, she had been afraid of those languishing songs as they passed over their house in the mountains, and at night she would hide under the blankets and even her pillow. Now she enjoys listening to the wailing, and whenever they go skiing, she goes out into the snow until she's nearly buried in it, and just as the others start to worry about her, she comes back all white and soaked. Why don't I go skiing with them, it suddenly struck her to say, since that Jaroslav what's-his-name—Stastny, I said—since that Stastny isn't going to be here anytime soon. Involuntarily I nodded, horrified at the thought of going with them to ski and then furtively making love with her in a dark hallway of some mountain cabin. But she was confident it could be pulled off. She couldn't get by without me. They would go skiing for a week, she said, how was she supposed to get by without me for a week? I told her she'd have to, because one day, sooner rather than later, I would leave for real, and for a lot longer than a week. She pressed her hand to my mouth and then wanted to hear my story about the sphere or the ball I was looking for again. She couldn't understand, she said, how that could mean so much to me. Those spheres were such an ordinary part of Baroque altars. I couldn't explain it. I said that I had to find it, that in this one and only life there were certain things you had to figure out. She said she hated that turn of phrase, one and only life. She wasn't with me because she was afraid of that truth, I'd better not think for a minute that she was with me because of this one and only life. And much less because I was some stranger about whom people were already saying all kinds of things. What kinds of things? I wanted to know. She didn't answer. Why was she with me? I wanted to know. She didn't answer. Then we were both silent and listened to the driving winter wind, to the groans of the wooden planks in the walkway, and to the jolts that shook the door.

Amid the wailing of the wind you could hear through the walls the spasmodic coughing of the consumptive who refused to become number 89.

I tried to imagine the wind as it sang and roared in the Pohorje with its endless forests, and the drawn-out song of the Pohorje pines. I tried to imagine her afraid of those songs, and how she might look then.

She rested her head on my chest. I stroked her hair and then she said she could hear my heart beating.

# 2 4

SOMETHING IS HAPPENING. SOME PEOPLE ARE LOOKING FOR ME again. For three days in a row the concierge has told me that some man has been looking for me. He said this in a voice that suggested something was seriously wrong.

For a long time I tried to think where I saw her for the first time. I was certain I saw her before my first visit to their place. I think it was in front of the Ford dealership on Alexander Street, shortly after I arrived. I was standing there, looking at the display floor, while two female voices talked about cars behind my back. This surprised me so much that I turned around and saw her: a young lady who was talking about cars and probably also traveled in them—in Fords, of course. How could I not have recalled that when I went to visit them? On the other hand, of course, it's possible I'm wrong. That it's just my imagination. I keep getting the strong impression that I've seen her before somewhere, in some other city. Of course I've seen her. She was exactly the one I was looking for.

This man is starting to worry me. He keeps looking for me when I'm not in. Today at lunch I thought of him. I thought, Why the hell doesn't he come now, during lunch? Surely he can figure out I would be in the hotel for lunch. Then I had a sudden, strange, chilling doubt: He always comes to look for me when I'm with Marjeta.

I walked around with that thought for a long time. Outside an employment office there was a long line of people.

What could they be looking for there in the afternoon? An officer was standing outside an army depot—I think he was a lieutenant—and I watched as he struck a soldier. This had a powerful effect on me. I could see the soldier's startled eyes. I could hear the blow explode across his face. This sudden violence in the street seemed senseless to me. The nape of the officer's neck was clean shaven, just like that of the man who had sat with Fedyatin in the tavern. Suddenly I was at the train station. Travelers were milling around, waiting for some other train. Locomotives puffing, train cars shifting. I could feel the ground shudder under their wheels, beneath their heavy freight. I sat down on a bench and waited. No trains arrived. I would have boarded the first train that stopped. I would have left and then, at some big station where there were lots of people and cabs waiting, I would have transferred to some other train. I sat motionless with that warming thought and most likely would have stayed seated until a train arrived. But then, behind me, I heard a familiar voice—so familiar that I flinched. Cautiously, I turned to look over my shoulder, and saw standing several yards behind me Engineer Franjo Samsa together with two men unknown to me. All of them were wearing dark overcoats. Most likely colleagues of his, experts in textiles, or maybe machines. I tried to decide whether I should stay seated and wait for that train that had to arrive from somewhere. But it was too risky. Samsa could notice me at any moment. He could walk over to me and ask what I was doing here. I wouldn't have an answer. He could ask if I was waiting for someone. Again, I wouldn't have any answer. He could ask if Jaroslav Stastny was due to arrive on the next train. I could tell him that he wasn't, but that I was going to leave this instant, without any delay. But where's your luggage? he could ask. Luggage? I would ask. I don't have any. I don't have any, and I can't leave until I get it and until I find that blue sphere. When I return to Linz, I'm going to have to tell them whether I found that blue sphere or not. The men standing behind me laughed loudly. I carefully got up and tried not to turn my head. As soon as I turned my head, he'd see me and ask if I was waiting for someone. I walked several paces, taking care the whole time to walk behind his back, not to enter his field of vision, because he could have also noticed me out of the corner of his eye. I would look familiar, he would call out to me and then ask what I was doing here. I wouldn't be able to explain. I stepped behind a pillar and listened to their loud conversation. I didn't mean to eavesdrop, and I couldn't make the words out anyway. But they were very loud and self-confident, probably making some good business deal. People who came walking past gave me strange, puzzled looks, since I was standing behind the pillar stock-still. I really didn't mean to attract attention. I really didn't want to explain what I was doing here. But the looks of the people walking past could have given me away. So I turned around and leaned a shoulder against the pillar and lit a cigarette. That improved things, though now there was cigarette smoke coming out from behind the pillar. I was petrified at the thought that the wife of this gentleman, Mrs. Margerita Samsa, who was afraid of the wind howling through the Pohorje pines, could also happen by. It's not that I would have been afraid of the encounter, even if all three of us then had to look each other in the eye, one after the other. It's that she would also ask me what I was doing here, and I wouldn't have any answer for her either. It was just that I'd prefer not to meet anybody today. That senseless violence on the street, that blow—the officer could just as easily have killed him. I feel all slack today, as though some not very stable, not very firm axis were wobbling inside me, and I can feel the ground swaying underfoot. That's from the trains shifting back and forth to the shouts of the railwaymen, and from the noise as the trains go rumbling past. Sometimes so much that it seems as though the earth were giving way. That's why I regretted not being able to sit. Then a train came in and released its steam, engulfing us all for an instant in fog. I watched from behind the pillar as the three men in black parted. Two of them got on the train, while Samsa stayed on the platform for a bit and kept talking with them as they leaned out a window. Then they shook hands, though their hands barely touched, since two of them were high up above. The train pulled out, but even then Samsa remained standing for some time, watching the puffing serpent as it receded into the distance. He lit a cigarette, adjusted his muffler, and then walked almost straight past me through the door to the street. I could feel I was shaking. For a long time I caught my breath. Then I followed him out and watched his fast-moving car, as water and slush flew up on both sides of it.

I stood on the street outside the station and looked with curiosity at the facades of the same buildings that had watched me with their high-set pairs of eyes on my arrival. It was only now that I realized the earth wasn't shifting from the weight of the train cars bending the rails. Here, too, the street was giving way slightly beneath my feet. I leaned up against the doorway to the station, as the face of some fellow in a railway uniform approached. I pulled myself together and with all my might shoved off from the wall and headed down the street. With determined steps I went straight to the hotel, closed the door of my room behind me, lay down on the bed, and pulled the covers over my head. I thought of Marjetica and the way she sometimes buried her head when the wind roared. But I bury my head when that axis shifts, either inside me or deep within the earth, I don't know which.

■ □ ■ □ ■

**2 5**

OVER AND OVER I KEEP SEEING SOME PAINTING OF HIERONYMUS
Bosch. I can't actually recall the entire picture. Those little details
in the background are what come so intrusively and persistently
to mind. In the foreground, right in front of me, some twisted
human business is going on, but I get real clarity and sense
only in the background. What's in the foreground—misshapen faces and blasphemous scenes—leaps out at me so
suddenly and forcefully that it passes in practically the same
instant and fades out of memory. But in the background there
are eerie flames that persist. They radiate out of the bowels of
the earth, and among them far, far in the distance there are gallows. Tiny people move among them, setting up ladders.
That's where the premonition comes from. From that terres-
trial glow, from those openings into which the people walking
among the gallows can surely see. What depths are those and
what do they hold? Can they see to the bottom of the abyss?

This is how I know that I also have to look to the bottom
of my memory. It's in this city and I'm going to find it. Is it
the lawn that slopes down toward the river? Is it that sphere
in the saint's hands? The chill and quiet of some church? The
light in its windows? The sphere must be big and blue, and I
must be small, sitting in a woman's lap. My arms reach for
the sphere but never grasp it, because that powerful man on
the altar holds it tight in his hands. Whenever I try to grasp
that memory with reason, I realize all at once that I under-

stand nothing. I understand so little that certain associations break apart, leaving everything close up and far away, yesterday and today at the same time. Reason is so utterly helpless that I'm immersed in a feeling of such uncertainty and obscurity, it verges on real, physical illness, and I have to grab on to something, to think of something that's in my immediate vicinity. So I don't get sucked into a dizzying vortex that I can't escape. So I don't fall into that limitless abyss that's at the bottom of memory. If man's heart does not become the heart of a little child, he cannot enter the kingdom of God, Christ said.

Will I hear a little child's heart beating in that church? Hear the scarcely audible palpitations of a child's excited heart, and see its eyes looking at the world?

And maybe then, in that church, for an instant, I'll be able to escape the chaos, the confusion consuming and corroding its walls on all sides.

■ □ ■ □ ■

## 2 6

MORNING. THE ROOM IS IN TOTAL DISARRAY. MARGERITA LEFT about two hours ago. She left such an empty space behind. The room seems as big as an auditorium, and out of the broken faucet drops of water relentlessly strike against the porcelain basin, echoing against these walls like hammer blows. She knocked on the door at two in the morning. I didn't wake up right away. She knocked on the door impatiently. She had come from a Russian party. In the doorway she latched on to me so tight that I was frightened for her. My dearest, my dearest, she kept saying. Then she sat down on the bed, shaking. I thought something bad must have happened to her. Awkwardly, I stroked her, trying to comfort her. Turn the light off, she said. She undressed. Under the covers she pressed up against me. I feel good here, she said, it's warm here. Did anybody see you? I asked, but she pressed her hand against my mouth. Don't say anything, she whispered, don't say anything.

In the morning she clung to my neck again. As though she would never, ever leave.

Something has happened between us that simply can't be fixed. There's no going back anymore.

Everything is wrong with me, too. This room is so huge and empty, now that she's gone.

I have to get out of here. I think I have to leave town.

She left a message for me. We met in Magdalene Park. Then we went to the orphanage of the Benedictine nuns. Being in the company of those women helps her. I waited for her at Government Bridge. Then we went walking alongside the river again. She said one of the cooks in the orphanage kitchen had been telling her how fresh the brains were. Just this morning they'd still been thinking. At this comparison, and at the sight of a huge heap of raw brains, she got sick. If she knew how they get at the brains, she'd have been even sicker. They smash the calf's head with a hammer. They take the brain out and then remove the little slivers of skull. That officer could do it. I treated her to that story. The last time, when I told her about Eva C. and how they examined her throat and then thoroughly searched her vagina because they suspected she was hiding something there during the channeling experiments, how they examined her mercilessly and by force, I thought then that I could see the color drain from her face.

■　□　■　□　■

## 2 7

I WOKE UP IN THE MIDDLE OF THE NIGHT. I HAD SEEN Margerita's face. She was laughing, too, only in a completely different way. She was saying something and I couldn't understand what she wanted. But it was something so totally bold, something against all the rules of her life, of her engineer and householder, of her tennis and her Bussolin. It was something that she would have liked to be. Then it came to me in a flash. Suddenly everything was as clear as day. Why those stories about unusual women make her so very uneasy, why all that business happened to us in that empty room, on a horsehair mattress with no sheets, in that damp space, why we made love next to a tree where anyone could have caught us in flagrante at any moment and given us away, why these visits and long silences, why the shameless explosions at poor, stalwart Bussolin, why her mysterious two-day disappearance. She is all of those things. She's strangely predisposed toward those mysterious feminine destinies. She'd like to be the girl with the phenomenal mind, an Amazon among the savages. She'd like to be Eva C. with her incredible gifts for channeling. She'd like to be the woman with a tuft of hair sticking out of her face, being examined by Parisian anthropologists. She'd like to experience a sensational love affair like the one in Brno, and the strange obsession of young Rosette. She'd give anything in the world if she could be Iris Farczardi, the Hungarian who woke up as the Spanish peasant Lucia Alvarez. My dear, sweet Margerita would like to be anything, she just doesn't want to be what she is. She doesn't want to be Marjeta, collecting the rent from those poor couples and suing them ruthlessly. She doesn't want to be the wife of Engineer Franjo Samsa, and she doesn't want to listen to endless tales of Hütter's social consciousness and technological achievements. She doesn't like the oriental rugs that she's used to carpet her flat, she doesn't like Bussolin the flycatcher, or vineyards, wine, or winegrowers. She doesn't like Real Estate Magnate or Maestro. She doesn't like operettas or plays, coffee shops, or Russian parties with jazz. To experience the thrill and the piteous fate of poor Milena L. she'd even let herself be murdered, if she could come out of it alive.

■ □ ■ □ ■

## 2 8

I BOUGHT SOME MAGAZINES AT THE TOBACCONIST'S BY THE
bridge, which is located in an interesting little building that
has a Turk with crossed legs painted over the door. I strolled on
with the freshly printed paper rolled up under my arm, and
again I found myself in a suburb where the houses and yards
were scattered around so strangely that for a while I didn't
know where I was. I asked some man standing beside a fence
how to get back. He gave me a kind of imbecilic look and said
nothing. A woman wearing an apron appeared in the doorway
of the one-story house. Not until I turned around to walk away
did he start shouting and waving after me, pointing me in the
other direction, but I kept going and eventually wended my
way out of the labyrinth. This place must be totally green in
the spring, with kids hollering on the streets, lettuce and beans
growing in the gardens, and possibly even a flower bed or two.
But for now it's a wretched and wet winter, with wet, ragged
snow suddenly falling from the sky, soaking my magazines in
an instant.

I sat in my hotel room and tried to unstick the wet roll of
magazines, which kept tearing wherever I touched it. Something within me was resisting, some resistance to these printed
pages. As though there wasn't a live human being I could talk
to. As though I didn't have Marjetica and didn't know a
whole bunch of people who surround her, including her husband, after all. As though I didn't know the postal clerk, the

tobacconist, those two women Gretica and Katica. As though I didn't know Real Estate Magnate and Maestro, the wine-growers, the concierge, even that insane Russian, after all—Fedyatin. And it was true, I suddenly thought: I know all these people, and yet I'm so damned alone. If I could just be with her more often—she's the only person I can relate to, who's close to me, very close, in fact, so close that I miss her more and more. I wadded that wet roll of paper up and went out into the hallway to the WC and threw it all into the toilet bowl. I lay down on my bed and lit a cigarette. Suddenly I realized that even in the course of unraveling the wet roll of paper, on the wet pieces of paper that clung raglike to my fingers, on those shredded strips I had just read a whole bunch of things. Damned involuntary reading that impresses itself on your memory like some song you hear in the morning and can't get out of your head for the rest of the day. How many times have I told myself I'm not going to read that stuff anymore? Not just because I don't want to have anything to do with politics anymore, but also because it never changes. Every day things happen, and taken all together none of it means anything. Now the Communists have hatched some plot against the Greek government. So? How many of these plots have there been already, and the sky in Greece is still blue. Sensational changes in the leadership of the Reich: A. Hitler has become commander-in-chief of all German armed forces. H. Göring is promoted to field marshal. It could only interest Real Estate Magnate, and Maestro not at all. Still, what Real Estate Magnate really cares about more than anything in the world is viticulture. More Communist riots in Prague. The rightists are preparing to march on Budapest, anti-Jewish measures are being taken in Romania and Poland, and something really awful is happening in Paris—they're having a plague of rats. Several years ago they were furiously fighting fleas. Now a legion of rats has infested the city, reportedly attacking children and house pets in city parks in broad daylight.

Who's going to put an end to all these legions and riots and underground machinations? Even here they supposedly have their share of problems with the Communists. Recently some local judge joined our group. He had some interesting stories to tell. Every week, his circuit court convicts some revolutionary or other, mostly for distributing forbidden pamphlets. Several days ago he had one he says behaved pretty brazenly in court. The judge suspects the fellow was counting on appellate court to save him. But he was wrong, because appellate doesn't have any patience for that kind of crime. The judge said he couldn't understand why they assign these characters to him, why they don't just remand them to the court of national salvation. As it is, he can't slap more than a month in jail on him for distributing seditious material. He said these people have an incredible faith in Russian socialism, which they think will rescue them. But they forget, he said, that there they'd get several years in Siberia for distributing seditious pamphlets, the same as under German socialism. Siberia? someone asked and everybody laughed.

But what difference does all this make to me? Why does it keep going through my head? It's the loneliness. Every phrase a lonely person reads, every word he hears, burrows into his brain so deep that he can't root it back out. For all I care, the earth can shake. For all I care, it can swell up and churn under humanity's feet, it can even explode. Just as long as it doesn't explode in my head.

# 2 9

COMMUNISTS, SPIES, ROBBERS, BURGLARS, THIEVES, SWINDLERS the local newspaper reports in a big banner headline. Characteristic of the times is the use of statistics. The greater the crisis, they clearly demonstrate to us, the more deeply we sink into perdition. Last year a total of 3,684 individuals were incarcerated at the "Graf." Police arrest accounted for 778 detainees who spent a combined total of 1,401 days in jail. Of all detainees who spent at least one night in jail, 739 were delivered to municipal police headquarters, 40 to the district attorney's office, 13 to the commissioner of the border patrol, 145 were deported, 54 taken to the city hospital, 1 to a reform school, 2 to orphanages, and 1,557 were driven out of the city into other locales. The violations that brought about arrests and punishment were extremely varied. There were some instances of insulting the King, or distributing leaflets and antigovernment information. Many more of the detainees were Communists and spies who had covertly tried to subvert the government, but whose activity was caught by the watchful eye of the law—or, more precisely, whose own incompetence had given them away, because they weren't suited to that kind of activity. Several were arrested for robbery, and two for attempted suicide. Moreover, the police had to deal with women who tried to dispose of the fruits of sinful love. Among those arrested were 1 arsonist, 2 extortionists, 5 miscreants who had damaged their own property, 17 burglars, and 128 thieves. Twenty-two smugglers and 105 persons who had crossed the border illegally all went to jail. Fifty-nine Austrian political refugees also found shelter at the "Graf." Seventeen were arrested for fraud, 2 for concealment, 5 for embezzlement, and 2 for failing to pay for their drinks. Infliction of serious bodily harm got 24 arrested. Also, last year covert prostitution became very widespread, and 17 of these cases were punished. The police were lucky and caught all of them. There were also 4 individuals in the city who were unable to identify themselves and who showed clear signs of being mentally disturbed. Upon interrogation, they were turned over to the mental hospital for psychiatric observation.

■ □ ■ □ ■

# 3 0

A NARROW RAY OF SUNLIGHT, OF FRAIL WINTER LIGHT, FELL from the upper window behind police chief Benedičič's head onto the floor, a little piece of sun catching on the desk, while the rest cascaded onto the floor. The same sunlight came between us, with the little particles of dust that rose off the carpet shimmering in that comforting band. There would be such peaceful morning calm in this room, if only I didn't hear those heartbeats throbbing in my rib cage, for what reason I don't know. If only I hadn't been thinking that this was a police station where they investigate, interrogate, and occasionally rough people up and knock them around. So we sat there for a while and all that was audible was the shuffling of papers as he moved them from one pile to the other. Pink fingers wearing a fat gold ring, all the blackness of those records, all those flickering letters that somewhere spelled my name, alongside worthless or invented details.

"Listen, Mr. Erdman," he said, "if that really is your name . . ."

"It really is," I said.

"Born here, if you really were born here, employed by the Stastny Company, if they really are your employers, waiting for the arrival of Mr. Stastny, Jaroslav. Come on, Mr. Erdman, why don't you tell us what you're doing in our city?"

"I've told you," I said. "I've explained everything to you." This person, this policeman, has a spongily amiable face and a soft, gentle, patient voice.

"And you say your parents left here before the war. You say your father was an employee of the postal service, and you say you're a specialist in laboratory equipment, and you say you're waiting here, and how much longer do you intend to wait here? Try to understand," he said, "that all kinds of people are drawn to this city, that all kinds of people were here even before, that we have to check on things. You can imagine," he said, "what all goes through this office. People scheme, don't you see—"

"Yes, they scheme."

He stood up and I could see the ray of sunlight turning the hair on his head red, making things up there even thinner and brighter than before.

"They spy."

Beneath that light his face was dark, very dark, and beneath that light it was almost invisible.

"They kill, they steal, they swindle, they break and enter, they assault, they drink, they smuggle, they undermine the public order and disturb the peace."

And I thought about how all of that went through this office, or at least a lot of it, if not all. Through those pink fingers of his wearing the gold ring. And what did I have to do with all that? I must be involved somehow if I was sitting in this office where it had become so silent that you could hear with utter clarity the rustle of a crumpled pack of cigarettes and the explosion of my lighter as I lit one.

"Actually, I can't do anything to you, and I don't want to," he said after a long silence. It struck me that the blaze of sunlight had stretched across the entire room. I could feel the veins throbbing in my hand holding the cigarette. Slowly, surely that throbbing, which was as insignificant as everything else in this place, began to inch up my arm. Through the elbow, the shoulder, into my chest. My chest was tight with anger or something and felt stomped on and began to smolder. Something was smoldering in the policeman, too, and his voice changed, becoming at once scornful and serious.

"Listen, Mr. Erdman," the policeman said derisively. "Listen," he said, changing his tone. "What I'm about to say is very serious."

And surely enough, he was speaking in a very serious voice.

"That man who visited you is an acknowledged Communist agitator."

"What man?" I feigned ignorance.

"You know what man I mean," he said. "Josip Klančnik, known to his accomplices as Jelenc."

"If he's a Communist agitator," I said, "why haven't you arrested him?"

"Oh," Benedičič said. He said he found it very interesting that I knew the language of professional conspirators. That I knew their verbal feints and snares. But I was mistaken, he said, mistaken if I thought they'd set a police informer on my tail. That man really is Jelenc and they follow his every step. The trail brought them to me at the hotel. Why don't they arrest him? Because they still need him, because he'll lead them to others, just as he'd led them to me. He said he was speaking frankly with me, that even he wasn't averse to social change, but that I had to understand these things couldn't be achieved in a revolutionary, bloody way.

I told him that he, too, had probably confused me with somebody else, just as Klančnik or Jelenc had done before.

He said I was a slippery character, but that he saw right through slippery types—slippery, it was the word he used— and that I wasn't going to trick him. Not him. He'd dealt with too many of them. Slippery types. And their slippery slickness.

I said that was insane.

He said I had created a clever cover for myself with my connections in the city's better circles, "and believe me, we do know what connections," he said, "even in-ti-mate connections."

I said that was going too far, that they'd better leave me in peace, I said, that the whole lot of them should just leave me alone, for God's sake.

He said they were going to leave me in peace, I just needed to tell them what I was doing in their city without putting on a phony business front or feigning interest in anthropology or telepathy or what have you, that I just needed to tell them what I was doing here, that was all, nothing more. "Once we've cleared that up," he said, "you'll have your peace.

"But as long as that remains unclear," he emphasized, banging his pencil down on the desk, "you'll remain suspect. Rightly or wrongly, you'll be suspect."

Suspect? What does that mean, You'll be suspect? Why doesn't he just say suspicious? And that much I am, I'm definitely suspicious. Suspicious to myself, not just to him. For an instant I thought how I really didn't know what I was doing here, and how this entire corner of the world was moving in some direction, and that I was going to slide somewhere. I thought of how the world had swayed and moved beneath my feet when I got off, when I got off the train to find something here. I haven't found anything. I've found a corner of the world where everything is confused and everything is insane. So what am I supposed to explain to this person? What am I doing here? He doesn't believe I'm waiting for Jaroslav. He doesn't believe I'm an expert in special laboratory equipment. His thoughts and his calculations run a different course. So do mine. Should I tell him I've come here for that sphere in the church? Should I tell him that?

I got up and walked to the door. As I took hold of the door handle, his voice stopped me.

"And one more thing," he said to my back. I stood still.

"If you've come back," he said; I turned around and tried to find him through the ray of light, "if you've come back, which is also possible, then register with the police and there'll be no problem—peace in Bosnia."

"If I've come back?" I asked, and I felt a sudden electric current run through me. "How do you mean that?"

He was leaning back, sunken in that chair of his, watching me as though he knew more than I did, as though he knew me better than I did.

"Just as I said. Lots of them come back. It's nothing unusual.

"Some people can't adjust to emigration, or they're drawn back by who knows what. I don't care if your family was German and I don't care if that's why they left. Lots of Slovenes have German surnames in these parts, and a few Germans have Slovene names."

"I haven't come back," I said. "I'm here entirely by coincidence. I'm waiting . . ." He's insane, I thought. He doesn't understand a thing; this policeman is insane.

"I know, I know you're waiting," he interrupted. "You've already said that. But there are also some people who don't even realize they've come back. Or they've gotten stuck and can't move forward. Or even backward. They can't move anywhere. So take my advice: Find yourself a job, register a permanent address, and stop wandering around aimlessly. The whole town knows who you are by now. It's unacceptable, do you understand? I can't be responsible if something happens to you. Or if you do something to somebody. Understand?"

I nodded.

"Make a decision before your ship starts going down, because once that happens, you know what the outcome will be: *Das Schiff ging unter mit Mann und Maus.*"

And I, who know something about psychology, anthropology, telesthesia, phrenology, psychiatry, schizophrenia, telepathy—in short, about human beings—I, who know something about how a human being behaves with himself and in relation to others, how he reacts and how he feels, how he senses, I let myself get lectured to by some police department bureaucrat. He was talking to me about myself as though he were my keeper or personal physician or father, who saw and knew everything that was happening and would happen to me. And I just stood silently and nodded like an idiot. To think that I could be dressed down by some paper pusher whose job was to collect facts about people and who pretended to know human nature. I'm no Nazi or Communist, I'm not a spy or agitator, I'm no revolutionary or thief or pimp or con man or smuggler, that he can treat me this way. So I did what I ought to have done a lot sooner. I pushed down on the door handle and, without a word, walked out and slammed the door behind me, so that it groaned in its hinges. He called out after me, but I was already in the stairway and out the door and suddenly I really didn't know whether I'd come back or hadn't come back. Was it an accident that I'd gotten off the train at this station, or could I have just as accidentally gotten off at Trieste and had something similar happen to me there? Then I remembered that I was waiting for Jaroslav and that I should go to the post office to send a telegram. The clerk, who knows me by now, would type it and I'd wait for an answer.

# 3 1

AS I LEFT THE POST OFFICE I RAN INTO ENGINEER FRANJO
Samsa. I felt awkward, but I was still so tense from all the
police intelligence looming over me just a short while before
that I couldn't worry too much about this discomfort. He
tried to get me interested in another Russian party. They
were all going. Russian songs, plenty of vodka. Then some
jazz for entertainment. All proceeds would go to support
schools for Russian émigrés. I hesitated for an instant, thinking about the occasional flash of silken undergarments
worn specially for the dancing season. I thanked him, but
said no. He kept insisting and said his wife would also be
pleased if I could come. For an instant I thought his eyes
flashed with subtle meaning. Did he suspect? His Margerita
would be wearing a short skirt, kicking her legs seductively,
and when she sat down, the silk fabric would slip down her
thigh ever so slightly. I'd be delighted to stop by sometime,
but I really can't tonight. I have some new material about
telesthesia to study. He looked at me astonished, then nodded understandingly. Aha, telesthesia—your anthropological
research, right?

Rightrightright?

  And you and your Russian parties and your jazz enter-
tainments.

■  ■  ■

I didn't go to their famous party, of course I didn't. With my luck I would have run into that person with the pink fingers, who would have watched me for the rest of the evening with his ridiculous policeman's eyes, which he probably thinks are so piercing and penetrating. But I met other eyes, running into Fedyatin's gaze. In that disgusting dive down in the old town. I'd been there once before, soon after my arrival—or my return, more likely my return? I'll never know what drew me down there. But, as though I had weights around my ankles, I stopped outside its dimly lit windows. Inside it was dark with males. At a big table two fat men were stuffing their faces with food and standing drinks for the tables around them. They were timber merchants, hauling timber downstream to Belgrade or someplace. Not them, of course—they traveled around by train, stopping here and there, making deals and eating like pigs. They were gorging themselves to an extent I'd never witnessed before. On top of all the meat, they kept knocking back pitchers of beer, and then brandy, brandy-meat-beer-brandy-meat-beer: They were starting to go red in the face. For me these quantities would have been fatal. But these two, with their infinitely long digestive tracts—how long do you suppose they were in yards, in miles?—these two kept pouring and stuffing it in and all that machinery down in their guts just worked, digested, and absorbed. I took some time to observe this activity from the bar and wondered how long it would last and whose heart would give out first. Then I sensed someone steadily watching me. At first I couldn't tear my eyes off these two, but the eyes I felt on myself were unmoving and persistent. There he sat, the old man, in the corner where I'd seen him once before. It was that Russian muzhik, Fedyatin, the man of God, the Rasputinite. He'd chosen me to bore into with his godlike eyes. He wasn't alone. That stocky, burly fellow, the youngish one with the bullish, smooth-shaven neck, was sitting with him. I went and joined them. I don't know if I sat down at their table solely in order to find out at last what the story was behind this scraggly, squalid person who might occasionally have been divinely possessed, as Ondra the lover of his Moravian flowers and mud thought. Or if I did it just because there was room at their table. I don't know. Inevitably I sat down at their table and we became acquaintances of a sort. At least acquaintances, if not drinking buddies, because then we started drinking considerable quantities of stinking brandy amid the clouds of smoke in that stinking tavern. Actually, the stocky fellow and I drank, and Fedyatin only sipped slightly, because he doesn't really drink; he's in a perpetual stupor, or a trance, or divinely possessed, or whatever. The empty brandy glasses began lining up and the stocky fellow's name was Ivan Glavina, the stocky fellow hated the timber merchants and he hated all merchants, he hated landowners, real estate magnates, and industrialists, ladies in silk clothing, their tennis playing and automobiles, he hated Jews, hotels, popes, and Communists, highfalutin whoring, all of it bought and sold, usurious and corrupt, all of it prostituted and debased. I didn't argue with him, I understood him. Just days before, the man had lost his job for causing a ruckus in some quarry or some such thing. I could understand him. Fedyatin didn't say anything; if I remember correctly he just banged on the table for a while and muttered something to himself. I don't know why he did it, but he banged on the table with both fists, as if he were punctuating the stocky guy's profanities and shouts. Could he have been trying to argue with him? I don't know. The stocky guy shouted and cursed, Fedyatin banged with both fists on the table, and I drank the stinking brandy and thought about Marjetica, about her silk underwear, about Lenka and Jaroslav and Trieste. I could sense that, very close to the inn where we were sitting, the river flowed past. Darkly, silently, it flowed beneath the bridges to some place down there that I will never visit. Because the river flows, people come and go, and I'm sitting here in this tavern with a glass of stinking brandy in my hand.

When I woke in the hotel room, I was seized by a sudden fear. I had drunk so horribly much the night before that I must have been trying to kill myself. That very night, I must have intended to destroy myself utterly and completely. But suicide, which, by the way, is a punishable offense here, is not what I came to the place of my birth to commit. Something else, some fear that's seizing hold of me and squeezing me around the heart, forced me to drink with those two men. Down in the tavern I could sense there was something wrong in the air of this city and this world. Something is under way and something is building, and I honestly don't know what bad things are going to happen. That stocky fellow with his neck shaved smooth, Ivan Glavina. His neck is shaved just like that officer who struck a soldier in the street. It's not just Glavina's neck—his face is shaved so close, so totally, that the skin is raw in places. He's covered with red spots and abrasions and you can sense some dangerous blood beating, circulating, welling up under this fellow's skin, ready to burst right out of that face or drive this stocky fellow, this Glavina, to do something that could turn out very badly.

THE STOMACH IS EXTREMELY SENSITIVE TO ALCOHOL. ALCOHOL, which absorbs moisture, dries out the mucous membrane that covers the stomach's inner wall: The exposed tissue turns a reddish color, and with excessive use the stomach turns into one big wound, which has as a consequence chronic infirmity and related debilitation, and in acute cases quick onset of death. A drunk never has any appetite, because his stomach is sick, but he does have an unquenchable thirst for drink, which ruins him even more. "If drunks could see their own stomachs, their stomachs would turn in disgust—they're that ugly!" reads a manifesto of the Union of Sober Youth bearing the title "Drunkenness: Our People's Greatest Misfortune." Accompanying the manifesto are two photographs: a healthy stomach, which in cross section looks like a well-formed half-moon with evenly distributed folds and muscles, and a drunk's stomach, which is hideously distended by the drink it has to carry, all corroded, a mass of extrusions and lesions. The article's author, the heart and soul of the Slovene temperance movement, added a photograph of a healthy heart, the motor of the human body working tirelessly, incessantly from birth to death, and a picture of the heart of a drunk, subject to greater blood pressure, and consequently prone to have its valves wear out or some artery burst: heart attack.

In 1938, drastic warnings such as these, which ought to turn any reasonable person away from drinking, no longer have any effect. At its annual congress, the holy crusade was forced to acknowledge and reluctantly admit that its twenty-year campaign in this cause had produced too meager results. Its members had to concede that, despite their many lectures and direct involvement among the populace, person to person, soul to soul, as it were—despite the public health and hygienic advisories—alcoholism was unexpectedly on the rise, instead of suddenly dropping off as they'd anticipated when they established their extensive and active organization. The Temperance League had done everything in its power. The Alcohol-Free Production Cooperative had organized countless classes throughout the country to promote the nonspirituous use of grapes and other fruit. Representatives of the Union of Sober Youth had propagated their ideas with relentless fervor in various young people's organizations and circles. Yet after so many years of hard work, they had to acknowledge that the number of taverns was growing and that they were getting fuller and fuller, that instead of alcohol-free fruit and grape juice there was more and more moonshine being made, that even among members of the Junior Union of Sober Youth there had been instances of covert drunkenness, and that, after all this, the drinking of that forbidden bootleg, rubbing alcohol, was on the rise and causing serious brain damage and unpredictable violent reactions in people.

Thus, the congress of the Temperance League, which had been called together in the dangerous weeks before Lent and in the heart of the danger zone, a city that was surrounded by cellars full of wine and kettles for making moonshine, proved to be a tumultuous one. The disunity that, in view of the movement's waning influence, had been palpable among the membership now became articulated with full force in the form of vehement polemics, demands for resignations, and even the dissolution of individual committees. The greatest differences were over the presumed causes of this state of affairs, since, as the truism goes, it's impossible to treat the symptoms without going after the root cause. Thus, for instance, the proponents of alcohol-free production maintained that one-on-one ministries among drunkards and maybe even the poorly attended lectures should be dropped, since all those activities were yielding insignificant results. You had to attack the problem at its source, and that was the production of alcohol. All efforts should therefore be redirected toward alcohol-free production. One of the members of the Temperance League argued with all the fervor a member of that organization could muster that the cause of drunkenness lay in chaotic social conditions, hence the entire movement had to be redirected toward social activism. Before anything else, you had to help people, and alcohol-free production would then be a logical and natural consequence of orderly social conditions. But a member of the Union of Sober Youth disputed both arguments. You didn't have to help people, he shouted at the climax of his speech, you had to change them. You had to involve them in organizations that would change their consciousness. Get the young marching, exercising, setting up tents, organizing rallies, and cheering great ideas, and the danger of alcoholism would vanish of its own accord. Let the young be intoxicated with great ideas and they'll never be intoxicated by alcohol again, the representative of the Union of Sober Youth concluded his speech.

In this fashion the morning session of the congress ended in a total split, with the polemics and fights continuing through the noon break, even as some of the participants investigated the alcoholic conditions amid the lilac arbors of the Lent district and distributed leaflets with the aforementioned photographs of a healthy person's and a drunk person's stomachs, and as the Alcohol-Free Production Cooperative gave the other members a demonstration of ways of distilling fruit into respectable juices.

At the beginning of the afternoon session a history professor from the local secondary school directed his calm words into the tense atmosphere of the hall, which was rustling with the curses and catcalls of the temperance movement's various factions. He said that, foremost, he wanted to object to the statement by the representative of the Union of Sober Youth. Never had young people marched as much as they were marching these days, and they had never been involved in such an array of organizations on such a mass scale. But how did these marches and mass rallies of various mass youth organizations end? In mass drunkenness—he raised his voice slightly, and the hall began to drone. And not just drunkenness, but also brawls, he added. The Slovene youth were brawling with the German youth, the leftist youth were brawling with the rightist youth, city youth with rural, with lads of rival villages, using bats and knives. It is precisely membership in these organizations, the professor continued over raucous objections from the representatives of the Union of Sober Youth, that is the cause of the drunkenness and the brawls. Be the pretexts what they may—white stockings on the legs of German youths or the hawk's feather in the cap of a Slovene youth—when all is said and done, the professor continued calmly as the noise in the hall grew, there have never been so many ideas claiming to bring order to human affairs, the youth have never been so intoxicated with these ideas as they are today, intoxication with ideas. . . . The professor's words were lost amid shouts of angrily protesting sober youths. One of them could no longer restrain himself; his collar loosened, he ran up to the speaker's podium and called out: So in your opinion, we should all start drinking? Then he brushed back the hair falling over his forehead and raised one arm. The hall fell silent. He approached the professor, brought his face up to the other's mouth, and said: Exhale! The professor grew agitated and backed off in fright. The sober but decisive and aggressive youth turned to the audience and said distinctly amid the silence: He refuses to exhale. With a trembling hand, the professor adjusted the collar of his shirt, as though it were strangling him, and cast bewildered looks all around. It struck me as strange, the youth said, that he spoke so calmly, without any kind of enthusiasm. The youth gazed about the hall victoriously, and then he returned to the professor again. May I ask you something? he said and then immediately proceeded to ask, Where were you when we were distributing leaflets, and the members of Alcohol-Free Production were demonstrating ways to preserve and boil fruit? The professor didn't answer. Well, where were you? the youth repeated amid the silence, which by now was not just agonizing but dangerous as well. The professor shifted his weight from one foot to the other. I was going to say, he said, when you interrupted my speech, he said, I wanted to say that there's one other reason why our efforts have been unsuccessful. . . . People also drink because of the newspapers.

The newspapers make them drink! the youth cried out, and the hall exploded in laughter. That's right, it's the newspapers, the professor said amid the laughter echoing among the light fixtures high up under the ceiling. There's some incident every day and . . . uncertainty. . . . The youth stared fixedly at him, the entire hall stared at him, and the professor fell silent.

Well? the youth asked again. Are you going to exhale or aren't you? The professor loosened his collar again, then looked down at the floor, somewhere around the toes of his shoes, shoved his hand into his pocket, and left the hall. This turned out to be a long walk, because the door was on the opposite side of the hall from the rostrum and the eyes of all the congress participants followed him in total silence as he went. The professor looked at no one, and everyone could observe that his lips were pressed tightly together. But as the large door creaked closed behind him, the entire hall burst out in laughter. Repeating the young people's radical slogans, the sonorous voice of the representative of the Union of Sober Youth resonated amid laughter, applause, and the stomping of feet. A moment later the Hymn of Sober Youth boomed forth from their young throats. Then the falsettos of the female members of the Alcohol-Free Production Cooperative for the preserving and boiling of fruit joined in, followed by the powerful male baritones of the moderate, reform-minded Temperance League.

In this way the congress of the temperance movement unexpectedly maintained its unity, despite the dangers of a hostile separation resulting from their recent failures. Later, moderate members of the holy crusade did bring up the possibility that this time the professor might actually not have drunk anything over the noon break. But that changed nothing, since it was a well-known fact among all members of the holy crusade and temperance movement, and even among members of the various committees and the junior league, that this insignificant person had in the past many times pulled himself out of the alcoholic ooze, only to sink back in again. Adherents of the various factions didn't perceive the victorious performance of the Union of Sober Youth as a defeat for themselves. After all, such values as youth, unity, and temperance had carried the day.

■ □ ■ □ ■

## 3 3

LIKE A CRIMINAL RETURNING TO THE SCENE OF HIS CRIME, THIS morning I walked to the lower town to seek out the tavern where I'd spent last night guzzling brandy with those two strange characters, instead of going to the Russian party with jazz. In the morning light the tavern seemed even darker. The floor was black and the bartender who was washing the glasses greeted me with an abbreviated wave of the hand, as though I were an old acquaintance. The place was empty, but I could swear I could still see their faces—Fedyatin's and that of Ivan Glavina, scraped raw by a precision shave.

Then, in the Café Central, I absently listened to Marjetica. She said that her friends' attitude toward me was getting worse and worse. Last night Dr. Bukovski, the coroner, the bald guy, had come out with a fascinating theory that made me listen to her more closely. The police were interested in me because they suspected I was an international con man and cheat with some important assignment in this city. The stories I tell, if he gave it serious thought—that's what he said, if he gave it serious thought—are pretty unlikely, after all. Where was my license or documentation showing that I sell special laboratory equipment? Did I even have a single sales prospectus from Stastny and Company, Vienna? And if, ultimately, I really were who I claimed to be, if I really did what I claimed to do, then I should go start doing it. Up until now I haven't done anything except wander around, and people have reported seeing me in some pretty questionable company. But Bussolin had taken the high road, Marjetica said. You can't just condemn a man like that, he had said, and even if there is some truth to all this, then it's probably all political. And politics is always a matter of conviction.

I made no response to these ridiculous accusations. And if a response were necessary, what should I have said? How am I supposed to defend myself against these suspicions?

I asked her if maybe she didn't have some roof repairs to attend to. She gave an embarrassed smile. But I kept repeating that banal phrase, for which she alone was to blame. That time when she came to get me, hadn't she said she had some roof repairs to attend to? Had she said it or hadn't she? She nodded. But she couldn't today, it was out of the question. Why couldn't she? She refused to explain. Were they having another jazz party? Did she have to get ready? I became pushy, aggressive; I was still sick from the night before and strangely irritated. She looked at me in despair, as though there were something wrong with me or I couldn't talk straight. But I was speaking up quite loudly, so that people sitting at the neighboring tables began to turn around and stare at us. Maybe she also had some roof repairs to attend to with that flycatcher, Bussolin? You know that Boris and I are friends, she said. He's a truly decent person. And handsome, I said. Such a trim little mustache he's got. With a sudden, unambiguous motion, she put her cigarette out in the ashtray. She picked her gloves up off the table. I don't know why she behaved like that. I just wanted for the two of us to head over to that empty apartment, where we could be alone and where we could watch the snow melting on the windowpanes, where we could listen to the wind howl, howling down the wooden walkway over the courtyard in a way totally unlike the wind singing through the pines in the Pohorje, where it roars and frightens her. She left without saying good-bye, while I wanted nothing but to feel something of her warmth near me, her gentle movement and soft words. Nothing but to not be alone and to be with her, the only living thing I have in this town. And she ought to be with me, too. After all, she did say, that last time when we were in the apartment on Carinthia Street, when we were repairing the roof, she did say that last time that more and more she's afraid of something—what, exactly, she doesn't know—that I know how to calm her down, to excite and calm her at the same time, that she can hear the strange, drawn-out song of the Pohorje wind and sometimes its distant roar, just as she could when she lived in the country, in that house on the wooded hillside, and she would hide under the covers and press the pillow over her ears; she really ought to be with me. But she's listening to the stories being told at their jazz parties instead of being with me, the one who knows the right things to say. But that's not the issue; I don't care. What's important is that she needs me, that the best thing for her is to be in that apartment with me, that I need her, because I can't keep emptying glasses of that disgusting, noxious brandy—and I can feel it doing its damage—with those people down in the Lent district until I can see the face of that Ivan Glavina so bloated with blood, it could just burst out of his face.

When the waiter came I tossed some money onto the table and shoved the table back so that a cup fell to the floor and rolled under his feet.

I went to the hotel and slept till evening. I woke up with an anxious feeling in my chest and confused about where I was and what was happening.

■ □ ■ □ ■

# 3 4

THIS EVENING THERE WAS A DISTURBANCE OUT IN THE STREET.
I opened the hotel room window and saw two groups of
young people shouting insults at each other. It was about nine
o'clock. They hurled insults back and forth, then each group
retreated to its own corner. Preparations are under way for
some event tomorrow. The city has come to life. Uniforms,
hats, guardsmen, the hotel filled with noisy guests, politicians,
downstairs music, singing—rhythmic, enthusiastic, hymnal,
ultimately drawn out and drunken.

My Margerita has lost all sense of moderation, of the law, of
her status, of decency, of hotel staff, of everything. She's come
to see me again. Who knows where they might have been getting ready for tomorrow's festivities? She has left her company
and come to me. Her eyes were watery and she smelled of
wine. She laughed strangely and smoked one cigarette after the
other, then she went to bed with me and fell asleep beside me.
It's spinning, this world is spinning faster and faster and there's
nothing I can do about it. It's spinning, sinking me into a deep
sleep as it spins.

Wildly loud march music woke us early in the morning.
The drum major must have given the downbeat to his brass
right under the hotel window. It blared and boomed. It threw
us out of bed. I went over to the window. Lots of young people
in uniforms surrounded the band. Somebody with a red stripe
on his sleeve walked among them, adjusting their neckties.

The kids were shoving and collecting in units of some kind. There were also gentlemen in black suits assembling. Marjetica put on her clothes, somewhat absent and somewhat confused. Last night she'd been drunk, no doubt about it. Today it will be my turn. She doesn't look at me at all as she gets dressed. It doesn't bother me in the least that she's leaving. I want to be alone for an hour or two, to stop the spinning in my head and in the earth's axis. She put her coat on and stood in the middle of the room for a few moments. Then, all dressed in her boots and overcoat, she threw herself back onto the bed and buried her head in the pillow. I thought she was going to start sobbing. But she didn't. She was totally calm.

"I'm not going back," she said into the pillow after a space, so that I scarcely understood her. I didn't answer. I was watching the crowd gathering on the square outside the hotel. Even the girls were in uniforms. Must have been some Eagles or Hawks or Scouts.

I turned away from the window, from the clamor of the march and the gathering crowd of young people. She still lay there, motionless. But I knew that beneath that calm, her heart was beating furiously. I thought about that heart of hers, beating beneath her white skin. I thought about how she really was in rather a hopeless predicament, and I thought of going over to the bed and beginning to lift the overcoat off of her, then the skirt, until I dug down to her white skin and heartbeat and reached and crawled right into her hot insides, down to the source of her morning despair.

For a moment it was quiet again. Down on the street the march was over and they were getting ready for another one. The men were tuning their trumpets and clarinets and flutes and French horns, blowing the spit out, adjusting the straps, and any second they would begin the next one.

"You can't stay here," I said.

I could see she was breathing faster and that she'd shoved the pillow aside with her hand, as though trying to get more air. Then she turned over with a jolt, her whole body at once, and for some moments she lay on her back and stared at the ceiling. Down below they'd struck up the next march. She raised her hands to her head and pressed them to her temples and over her ears. She lifted her head and looked at me like some kind of wounded or sick animal, with her hands over her temples and ears. I couldn't tell if she was squeezing her head in her hands in order not to hear the brass band, or because some inner strain and fear and anxiety were threatening to blow it apart. I was a little afraid for her when I saw that look, and I took a step toward her. But at that instant she started, as though I were about to harm her. She drew back on the bed and a moment later got up. She left. She left without saying a word.

I turned on the faucet over the sink and for a long time just watched the stream of water as it dashed against the porcelain, sending drops of water flying to the walls and floor. I dashed cold water in my face and dried it with a coarse towel. I walked over to the window and threw it open. In a powerful wave the music washed over and through me, into the room. Young people, arranged in rows four abreast, were singing the words to the military march: King Peter's guards went marching, went marching. . . . Several officers and civilians were nodding in enjoyment, while someone else was cueing the crowd to applaud. The drum major was turned with his face toward me. He was brandishing that huge baton, and at one point I could feel he'd seen me. There I was, standing at the window in my undershirt in the cold morning air, and I had the sense he couldn't take his eyes off me. He kept glancing up, and finally he smiled and waved to me. Several people turned to look upward. I sat down on the floor next to the window. I lit a cigarette and listened to the march, the music, the drum major, the young people, the parade, everything as it moved off into the distance. Everything was moving down Alexander Street and it was quiet in the room, quieter and quieter.

PERHAPS THE DRUM MAJOR WOULDN'T HAVE PERFORMED IN quite as many marches, and perhaps so many young people wouldn't have followed after him in such a variety of uniforms, if he hadn't had a son. It's a well-known fact, which doesn't need repeating here, that a special relationship exists between father and son, between son and father. The drum major wanted his son to look up to him, and his son did look up to him when he marched at the head of the musicians with his baton, the leader of the band and of the parade. Could he have looked up to a clarinetist, anonymous in the crowd? This is why there's a very simple answer to the question of why the drum major was a drum major and nothing else. He will never suffer the fate of some other people in this town, such as the limping postal clerk, or Gretica and Katica, or the coroner, pursuing his anthropological interests in the morgue. And after all, there was always a need for drum majors; not just anyone could do it. He was a capable drum major, just as lots of drum majors of other kinds were capable, so there's no need to draw any unusual conclusions. Music was music. Ideologies and regimes didn't give a shit about music. Whenever his winds struck up a march, people just felt better, and the drum major felt best of all if his son—little, big, or all grown up—also happened to be standing on the sidewalk. This is why the drum major used to conduct the Radetzky March, and it's why he conducts the March of the South Slavs now, and why he'll keep conducting and marching on Sunday mornings. He'll march at the head of the "Horst Wessel Lied"—*die Fahne hoch*—and, just as he's getting on in years and growing less ramrod straight, he'll get out of that in time to lead young working people in march time to the tune of "East and West Awaken." While Erdman sits hunched in his room, listening to the march as it fades into the distance, the drum major will be marching. And behind him the young people will march. The year is '38, and young people aren't marching only here. This is the time when young battalions the world over are in love with a disciplined stride, a hearty song, taut muscles, and a clear voice. From east to west, young people are marching. They march for the Reds, they march for the browns, they march for German and then for Russian socialism. They march and sing victory songs for extending the national borders, for the defense of the nation's Lebensraum. Young people who will not survive march behind the drum major, who will. The city they march through today is nothing but the echo of that great Central European continuum drumming and echoing with marches that young people repeat in their sleep and hum as the parade marches by. Down by the Drava, in a slaughterhouse next to the mill, the livestock moos when a procession with flags at its head comes marching over the bridge from the other side of the river and passes the slaughterhouse. It moos and then oddly howls a greeting back at this morning song, a preslaughter greeting. Like the bulls in Spain that are falling to their knees just now, bloody and powerless.

Soon the parades in this town will whirl together in an insane, bloody dance. Very soon all the factions marching today to different tunes and bands will be grabbing each other by the throat. Germans and Slovenes, Communists, National Socialists, clericalists, nationalists, Yugo-nationalists, Serbs, Bulgarians, Cossacks, workers and peasants, professional athletes and waiters, schoolmates and colleagues, brothers and sisters, daughters and mothers, fathers and sons will all have a stranglehold on each other and will grunt the words to their marches with lips bloodied, eyes pulled out, skulls crushed, bellies pierced. Through slit throats they will rasp out the young, brilliant, heroic songs of Sunday mornings in 1938.

## 3 6

IN THE AFTERNOON, PEOPLE STARTED RETURNING FROM THE stadium, where a political rally had been held. The city was full of uniformed people, civilians, handsomely dressed women. Singing could already be heard from the taverns in the afternoon, and groups stood around on street corners calling out slogans or taunts to each other. I wandered among the boisterous, undisciplined crowds and remembered the silence that had taken over my room for a short time that morning. At Main Square I ran into Gretica, one of the two middle-aged blossoms. She was walking with a slicked-back gentleman. His hair, I mean—it was slicked back as though he'd just stepped out of a barbershop. This struck me when he lifted his hat and said hello to me, as though we were two old friends. These women tell everybody everything about everyone. I have no doubt they gossip about Marjetica and me, too. Anyway, how could that be kept secret, with the two of us passing through their vicinity in broad daylight? Gretica kept her slicked-back fellow waiting and babbled something at me. I don't remember any of it, except for her pointed invitation. This roly-poly little mannequin pronounced it with such emphasis that it was impossible to miss: Why don't I come visit them sometime, why don't I come knocking one door farther down . . . if I have occasion to come take care of any business involving the house. She winked at me slightly, but still too brazenly, and then she took her fellow under the arm and the two of them walked off down Gosposka Street. I knew I was going to finish this day drinking. Not just because it had been so unrestrained and full of loud people but also because of the morning, because of this wretched morning when I'd been unable to find or pronounce a single right word or gesture. I found Fedyatin and Glavina at Beranič's. They were with some others. Glavina was being loud. He had money. He was making himself out to be a bigger troublemaker than he probably was, in fact. He was telling everyone about his fight with the owner of the company and its employees.

But still a troublemaker, if lacking affiliations; an angry man unable to understand why anybody should be allowed to give orders to him, since he did his job well. For the miserable wages they gave him there. And even those he tended to drink away. He's no drunk, but since he's without family, the money tends to get in the way. He's unusually attached to Fedyatin. They'd probably run into each other in some stinking dive down in Lent, drinking schnapps, just as I'd found them now.

On Government Bridge, very close by me, a horse that was drawing a peasant wagon took fright, rising up on its hind legs. The peasant held on to the reins and lashed it persistently with a whip until it calmed down somewhat. You could see that the peasant, dressed in his Sunday best, was afraid of the horse. And that the horse was afraid of Fedyatin. I only later remembered that Fedyatin was walking nearest to the street and that the horse reared as we walked past it.

Glavina didn't care to go to the hotel restaurant, though it seemed to me that Fedyatin would have gone. When we parted, I caught sight of Dr. Bukovski through the glass door. He was holding his hat in his hands and talking with somebody. It was him; you couldn't mistake the bald spot. Once again a suspicion overcame me which I immediately resisted. Surely the bald fellow couldn't be here on account of me. Presumably we don't live in some kind of commune where each person is responsible for everyone else, where each person would look after one of the others and all of us look after

Marjetica. I remembered what the doctor's wife had said about Marjetica. In a voice oozing concern, she had in fact said that everyone had to keep an eye on her so that she didn't go bad or get lost. In any case, I refused to give in to this suspicion. Baldy was there on some business of his own, and that was that.

Slightly woozy, I dropped off to sleep immediately. I could hear singing from outside and the hoarse shouts of the last rally-goers, and the entire day with its marches and crowds played and replayed itself in my sleep.

A knocking at the door woke me. Dazed, I followed the concierge, who had gotten a telephone call for me. It was her. She wanted us to meet. Right away, tomorrow, the very next day. I stumbled back to my room and fell back asleep without a single thought.

■ □ ■ □ ■

## 3 7

FINALLY, THE THING I'VE BEEN EXPECTING ALL ALONG BUT refused to admit has happened. The suspicion had been there all along, hovering just over my stomach somewhere. The doctor wasn't in my hotel by accident, and it wasn't an accident that people came looking for me when I was with Margerita. It's obvious that they've known all along what was happening. Slowly and surely they've been collecting information. They've probably also set a few traps for me and staged a few chases. This has been a real investigation. Now they've taken it as far as they can go and they think they're about to bring it to a thoroughly appropriate conclusion. I've been waiting for this to happen, soberly and exceptionally focused. I don't know what got into me to buy flowers just then, of all times. I'd never bought her flowers, partly because they were drowning in them in that house. They had to appear on the table, in your hands, wedged under your arm at every possible opportunity, and that rather bothered me, just as everything had been making me jittery recently. Still, I bought the flowers. And, what was stupidest of all, I just tapped on the door. I didn't barge in noisily, I didn't seize the door handle decisively and turn it. If I had at least knocked loudly. But I just tapped, pitter-pat. I imagined her sitting alone in the total quiet of that room, and suddenly pricking her ears up at that silly tapping on the glass pane of the door. Which is almost certainly why the door didn't open immediately. Even Engineer Samsa, as he stood on the other side looking at the shadow I cast on the translucent glass, must have been taken aback by that tapping. He must have either caught his breath or straightened his tie before he firmly pulled the door open and, in the same breath, said, "Won't you come in?"

I knew we'd eventually be discovered. But I'd always thought it would happen in flagrante. That we'd be lying in bed when somebody would start banging wildly on the door. I always thought she would be present at that meeting, too. Engineer Samsa would leave the office one morning and start banging on the door to the vacant apartment on Carinthia Street, causing the walls in that empty space to reverberate and echo, while the two of us looked into each other's eyes and realized the inevitable had happened.

"Were you expecting someone else?" he asked in an abrupt but still controlled voice. He was red in the face. So he'd drunk two glasses of muscatel, but he was calm and collected. Well prepared. His voice was straining to conceal the agitation he had to be feeling inside that chest, where his heart was pounding irregularly. I behaved pathetically and stupidly. I tried to make something up on the spot. "I've come to help," I began to babble, but he cut me short. "Repair the roof," he said with a sneer. Yes, that's how far things had gotten. That woman had simply given away everything. They'd put her in a vise, and out of spite or some accursed sadism that came over her at the moment, she'd begun to recount some ridiculous details. I felt that I'd much rather leave. But when I saw that his eyes were fixed on the bouquet of flowers I was holding, I suddenly felt spellbound by this big, powerless person. "Well, come in, then," he repeated. I stepped into the empty room. His briefcase lay on the table. He'd come from work. He'd dropped some very important business to come deal with this personal matter.

If I had ever imagined a scene where a jealous husband and his wife's lover met at the site of the covert action itself, then I'd imagined it just this dramatically. Primitive male instincts are released in both men. Dangerous passions are inflamed in both. Both can feel her warm body in their gut, and they're going to have to fight for it now. But with good reason, these scenes are the butt of countless jokes and a favorite comic theme of caricaturists. We simply can't fight over females, because the question of how we're going to preserve our idiotic and illusory dignity always comes first in those enormously agonizing moments. In the eyes of civilized peoples, the most ridiculous possible image is that of a jealous man who's lost his senses and does who knows what in his helpless agony. And, indeed, both of us were very dignified and polite to each other, as though some misunderstanding had occurred between friends and the two of us were going to clear it up man to man. Only his red face, living proof that he'd had to drink two glasses of muscatel to bolster his courage, and the ludicrous flowers I was holding shifted the impeccable form of what we were doing into the sphere of the ridiculous.

We sat down, at opposite ends of the table, with our eyes fixed on the same blank wall, looking over a shoulder at each other. I had the feeling he was going to take his briefcase off the table and pull some papers out of it. He said exactly what's supposed to be said at a moment like that: You think you're a free man, traveling from one place to the next. And you also think you can indulge yourself in a little adventure here and there without any consequences. But you don't give a thought to the consequences, the threat to family life. You also don't give a thought to the fact that the person you're dealing with may be very sensitive. I couldn't tell if he meant Margerita or himself by that. But he kept going in that vein: For you this is just one more adventure along the way, while for us (again, I didn't know whom he meant) this is deadly serious business.

When he came to the end of his prepared speech, he buried his head in his hands, as though he were in extreme pain or thinking something over. Then he suddenly straightened up and asked jerkily: And what now? What is it you want from me? This took me by surprise. What did I want from him? I wasn't the one who had asked for this conversation. I wasn't the one who had spent all morning lurking in this apartment, waiting for my wife's lover. Do you want me to convert to Orthodoxy, get a divorce, and find a new wife? he asked in a high-pitched voice. No, I don't. What is it you want, then? He sat back down and buried his face in his hands again.

Then he changed tone, becoming warm and confiding, as though he were explaining his problems to an old friend.

There followed the tale of him and Margerita. What she meant to him and what he meant to her. How they'd gotten to know each other, and the fact that he was older. Why they didn't have any children—I asked him to spare me the details—and why she sometimes behaved so strangely that he felt, that he had to feel, responsible for her. And that he'd never leave her. He got nervous, because I was silent for the most part, and in the long silences he glanced around. I was sure he had a bottle someplace. Why hadn't he just put it on the table? Everything would have gone a lot more smoothly. I had to understand that I had no right to destroy a human being's happiness with my detachment and total independence. He had to ask me to stop stalking her. Here I objected. He corrected himself to say everything had to stop, this he had to ask me. And that I had to understand he didn't have anything at all against me personally, but he had to ask me not to visit them anymore. This took me by surprise. First of all, because I hadn't visited them in a while, and second, because that made it sound as though it really were possible that, after all this, I might still come visit them.

He had the feeling that I agreed to his demands. He was satisfied. As I left, we shook hands. He followed me out onto the walkway. He thought I'd go down the stairs, but, flowers in hand, I asked him to make way for me, because I was going in the opposite direction. Clumsily, he stepped aside, and I headed the other direction down the wooden walkway that juts over the courtyard and knocked on Gretica and Katica's door.

This is how Gretica and Katica unexpectedly got flowers.

■ □ ■ □ ■

## 38

I'VE MOVED. I COULDN'T STAND THAT HOTEL ANY LONGER. THE
room was too small. I seemed to feel it pressing down on my
shoulders, the ceiling pressing me down to the floor. At night
I'd wake up in a sweat to discover a microscopic space around
me. I couldn't move an inch in it. Wherever I tried to reach,
a wall got in the way, to the right and left, above and below
me. I felt so bad that something in my chest started to blow
me apart. Something was roaring inside and wanted out.
And wherever it charged, it ran into a wall. In the dark I was
looking with eyes wide open at the wall that was right in
front of me, so close I couldn't even move my head. The rage
inside my rib cage relented, and then I could feel my heart
had stopped. I was totally motionless. I knew I was going to
die if I didn't wake up immediately, that instant. But at the
same time I thought—and this I remember clearly—I thought,
How am I supposed to wake up if my eyes are already open
and I'm seeing with them—for instance, seeing the ceiling
right in front of my eyes? With the utmost effort I moved
one arm and then the walls suddenly parted. My whole body
dissolved and I got up, hitting my head against the bed frame
and my hip against the table until I felt my way over to the
sink and the light switch. When the light went on I felt
better. The light was weak and I could still feel some of that
anxiousness in my chest, but there was at least light and I
felt better.

This same thing happened to me again several times.

I don't believe these nightmares had anything to do with the bizarre events and people that had been bothering me lately. Most likely I'd been reading too much about occult physiology. Most likely I'd been reading too much about those things, with the result that I began to feel my whole body to be something extending into space and existing in a strange relationship to the mass of the objects around me, to their weight, density, and solidity—a mutual magnetism. Maybe I'd had more than enough of that hotel for other reasons. If only because of the staff, who had been looking at me suspiciously of late. They'd been exchanging meaningful glances at every visitor I received. I don't know what plot was being cooked up behind my back, but there's no doubt that Benedičič and that stranger Jelenc or Klančnik, the Communist agitator, had a hand in it. If they weren't one and the same thing after all, one and the same person in some split dual personality. And certainly one of the strangest occurrences that had been taking place one after the other in that hotel room lately took place one morning a few days ago, when I returned from a long walk I'd taken to Kamnica. I tried to unlock the door to my room, but I could see that the lock refused to turn. I kept trying to turn the key in the lock over and over, until suddenly the door yielded. It just gave way and left an opening gaping before me. Through the opening, way in the back—yes, it was way in the back, even though the room was minuscule—way back there I could see a stranger in a winter overcoat sitting on my bed. Actually, I didn't see his face. I couldn't make it out, because he was sitting with his face turned away, so that the light shone on his neck but his face remained in the dark. There was, however, one detail that I could make out clearly. It was a familiar, light, almost white silk necktie. It practically glowed from under the collar of the dark overcoat. He was absolutely silent and I expected him to say something again any moment. Then—and I have no idea why—I was overtaken by the kind of mute terror, the kind of becalmed terror that doesn't seize you suddenly, but that slowly permeates you from somewhere outside, that settles somewhere in your bowels and that you can't ward off with any effort. Try as I might to convince myself that there was really no reason for me to feel any fear or uneasiness, that terror just kept crawling up and down my body.

I turned and walked out with rapid footsteps. I left the door open. I went to the reception desk and, I have to admit, I lost my temper unnecessarily somewhat. I shouted at the desk clerk that I'd had enough and that I wasn't going to put up with endless strangers in my hotel room. That I paid my bills on time and expected to have peace and quiet in return. I hadn't come here to spend every waking minute answering questions. And that he'd better see to that. The clerk gave me a startled look, but I wasn't convinced it was all that sincere.

I know I was overdoing it, but there was absolutely nothing else I could have done at that instant. Why, in fact, didn't I throw the person out? Why did I have to shout at the desk clerk, begging for help in such a convoluted way? Most likely I'd had a real scare upstairs and the creeping mute terror was taking its toll. There was to be no help, of course.

"Sir," the clerk said, "I'm afraid I don't quite understand you."

"Come with me and you'll understand in a hurry," I said, grabbing him by the elbow in a sudden fit of rage. I held him in a steel grip until I extracted him from behind his desk. As he politely tried to slip free, I held tight to his elbow like a vise and dragged him up the main hotel stairway after me. I seemed to have given him a shove once we reached the hallway upstairs, causing him to stagger toward my door, and I seem to remember that at this point he got a little frightened. The door to my room was closed.

"Go on," I said. "Go in."

The clerk pushed the handle down. The door was locked. I pushed him aside and banged on the door and the handle simultaneously, producing a boom and causing a door somewhere farther down the hall to open an instant later. Probably some heads poking their curiosity out into the hall. I shoved the key into the lock, pushed the startled fellow inside, and followed him.

The room was empty. There we stood, me catching my breath and looking around the room impatiently, him looking at me, just at me the whole time, and gradually edging over to the open door. I raised a hand and pointed to the bed. He didn't follow my gesture at all, but kept moving closer to the door, and at that point everything in me just broke down. I no longer had the will to stop him. I tried to say something else and probably even opened my mouth. But just at that instant he had reached the open door, felt the free and empty space of the hallway behind him, and suddenly vanished. I caught my breath. I didn't know what had happened. In a minute I more or less regained my senses and went over to the bed where, just a few minutes before, a man wearing a bright silk necktie beneath an obscured face had been sitting. I inspected the bed from close up, but there were no traces on it. Untouched. Slowly, I removed the bedspread, but even under that there was nothing. The bedsheet was drawn taut, with all four corners tucked under the mattress, as though waiting for some drill sergeant's inspection. Am I losing my mind?

I'm not saying that the nocturnal shrinking of space, the walls pressing in, the motionlessness of my body, or my heart stopping—I'm not saying all that had anything to do with the day's events. I even think all that had completely different origins. But what happened with the stranger in my room was too much for me. That minute, I began to pack everything that was mine. And there was quite a bit of that. I'd amassed a ton of things in my lair in the course of less than a month. New and interesting things. Someday I'll describe them all so that I have some sort of record.

The hotel proprietress came to protest my rough handling of her employees. So it's only them that people are handling roughly, I thought, not me. Me everyone just leaves in peace, is that it, ma'am? That's what I thought. What I said was:

"Ma'am, there's no cause to get upset. I'm leaving."

Once I'd said that, she immediately changed her tone of voice. But it was already too late, I'd made my decision. There was no going back.

So I moved to the other bank of the Drava, to the room I'm in now, which really is a bit smaller than the other one, also a little uglier, I have to admit—also less tidy, and less clean. I have to admit all of that and even add that my belongings have taken up practically all the space here, so that I can barely maneuver past them. All this is true, and yet just as true is the fact that here in the Dvor—that's the name of this tavern with rooms to let—I feel much better. I can breathe freely and start over again, so it should be no surprise that this cramped, over-stuffed room is much more pleasant. And not just that, but also bigger, far more spacious and free, however strange that may sound.

NOW I FEEL AS THOUGH I'D JUST AS SOON LEAVE HERE, TOO. I wrote Jaroslav a letter from the other hotel. I was afraid they might have misplaced his reply, accidentally or even on purpose, so I asked at the desk there what had happened to the letter that had come for me. I sprang the question on them, to catch them off guard. They responded politely, but with extreme coolness. There are no letters for you, sir, they said. There has to be a letter, I said. What would we want with your letter, sir? they said. You could rip it up or hide it, I said. They were offended. Someone else came out and responded to my complaints very sharply. As though I were to blame for strangers sitting on my bed in their hotel. On the other hand, maybe my letter never did reach Jaroslav. But I can't admit this possibility to them. Maybe he's also moved to a different hotel. In which case, how are we supposed to meet when he comes here? And I'll bet that desk clerk will give him bad information. In the lavatory I looked at myself in the mirror and saw an unshaven, even shaggy face. Were my eyes really glinting that strangely, or was that somebody standing behind me?

Even in this hotel there are people asking about me. Are those Benedičič's people? Or the fellow with the silken necktie—Klančnik or Jelenc? I'm going to have to leave. What's happened to Jaroslav? Where is Lenka? What have they done with Marjetica? What is she afraid of? Why is she afraid of the forest booming? Questions drill away at me like some damned fat worms digging into my chest. I live wholly alone. And Fedyatin lives alone. Glavina, too, in his emergency shelter built out of wood, somewhere in Abyssinia. But fate has condemned the two of them to solitude. Over time they've managed to reconcile themselves. I'm alone because of misunderstandings that aren't clear to me at all.

Katica has told me that there was no rent collection last month. More recently they've gotten the news that the manager, a retired bureaucrat who lives next door, will be stopping by later to skin—or, rather, to collect from—them. Who knows whether in this time she's approached that door, or even the window that looks out onto the narrow street? If I could, if I had the money, I'd rent an apartment across the street and watch day and night for her to come. She might even stop for a while, at least when she was out for a walk.

I saw a young man with a grim face in the company of Glavina and Fedyatin. I didn't join them, because I had to keep moving. I wanted to visit that church. But I made a mental note of his face and his striped suit. His name is Markoni, and his father is the real estate magnate—or magnet—my acquaintance from the wine country, the vineyard owner and wine merchant.

I can't sleep and I can't stay awake. I have to calm down. I dreamed about the blue sphere again. It's close and I'm going to find it soon. I'm not much for visiting churches, but now I'm going to search all of them in town and in the vicinity. I'm going to find that sphere, just as I found that lawn and as I'm going to find the flower and bean patch in the suburbs. That lawn is buried under wet, crystalline snow. The surface slopes toward the river, sliding gently down. When I stood in the middle of the lawn I could feel its whole surface slowly sliding toward the river.

■ □ ■ □ ■

# 40

IN FEBRUARY OF 1919, SHORTLY AFTER THE OVERTHROW, A merchant by the name of Leopold Markoni, Ggb., pulled the shutters down over his storefront that displayed fine bottled wines and served as both an office and a wholesale showroom. Bent over as he turned the key in the padlock, he could see out of the corner of his eye several male figures approaching down the sidewalk.

He straightened up and headed back to the door, but then heard a gruff and insolent voice behind his back, which, in a Slovene mountain dialect, said, "How 'bout if we have some fun with the Kraut?"

The other two laughed, and Leopold Markoni thought it sounded like the laughter of the mildly drunk. He was about to step through the doorway into his store when the one behind him shouted, "Hey, merchant, don't move."

Markoni stopped and turned to look back. There were three of them in uniforms, with bayoneted rifles slung over their shoulders. One of Maister's peasant patrols that had scurried into the city from outlying villages and put on uniforms. The one who was talking big had been a hired hand on a farm. In his impudent, drunken face Markoni instantly recognized the face of an impudent, drunken hired hand. This is how a hired hand behaves when he's not working, when he drinks, when he has a knife or a gun in his hands. They stopped in front of him. The drunk one stood out in front, his cap with its tricolor cockade pushed up on his forehead, while the other stood in the background, in the dark. The drunk one giggled awkwardly, and it was obvious he wasn't yet sure how far he could go. Then he had an idea.

"You," he said. "You're not going to eat our food anymore."

Markoni was silent. For an instant he thought the man could be one of his vineyard workers wanting to avenge himself for God knows what, but in a flash he summoned all their faces, and none of them registered as similar. But the farmhand was there, and Markoni thought he could pick up the stench of barnyard manure on him. The farmhand leaned forward, and Markoni could feel the warm, alcoholic breath on his face. It was disgusting, but he knew he couldn't give this person any excuse. He knew this type—knew that the peasant was going to try to provoke him into some careless word or gesture.

"Well," the farmhand said. "So?"

"So nothing," Markoni said and bit his lip, because it was clear he didn't dare say anything, not even "nothing." The one in uniform thought hard.

"Nothin' don't mean nothin'," he said finally.

Markoni nodded. The aversion he felt within himself toward this man wearing a crumpled cap pretending to be military dress, the aversion to his alcoholic stench mixed with fear began to reach into his stomach like some empty, hollow void. The urge to shout at him, to hit him and show him who was who mixed with the cold sweat creeping down his forehead and the odd shuddering in his knees, for these degrading and arrogant insults refused to end. He could see the idiot in uniform turning to look at the other two, who had shoved their hands in their pockets and were waiting to see how this would end. He could see that the lout was growing dangerous, because this was dragging on and he still hadn't thought of any way to humiliate him. Then something obviously coursed through his oafish, drunken brain, something he must have experienced himself, since he couldn't have had much imagination—something clear and simple. He took a step backward, regained his footing, and shouted:

"Crawl!"

Leopold Markoni shuddered. He could see the other two shifting their weight from one leg to the other, and one of them said something to the raving man in the crumpled uniform. Definitely something that ran counter to the command he'd just given. Markoni thought he could hear the other speaking in Serbian, and suspected that he and this farmhand speaking a Slovene mountain dialect weren't understanding each other. And that just seemed to provoke the idiot even more.

"I said crawl," he roared.

Above the storefront, windows started opening. The idiot unshouldered his rifle and pressed the bayonet to Markoni's chest. Markoni could feel his knees starting to give way. He felt the tip of the bayonet pushing through his suit coat. He could see the peasant's dangerous eyes, which were glassy and most likely unaware of where they were and what was at stake. Markoni bent down and touched his hands to the ground. Then he dropped down to his knees and lay down on his stomach.

*"Crawlen Sie!"* the idiot looming over him shouted, and pressed the bayonet to his back.

*"Crawl!"*

Markoni began crawling in the direction he was pointed, across the wide sidewalk and down onto the pavement of the street, using his elbows for locomotion.

"Faster!"

He had no idea now what he was doing. He just felt the blade's sharp point at his back, just that articulated contact that could pierce straight through him any second with a metallic scrape against the pavement below. He crawled faster and faster.

"Turn around! Come back!"

He turned around and crawled back, arching up onto the sidewalk like a caterpillar. He came to a halt in front of the lowered green shutters. Then it was quiet for a time. He could hear the oaf breathing above him. The simpleminded volunteer was out of breath, as though he'd been crawling, too. He was excited and fearful. He knew he had done something he hadn't originally meant to do, because it exceeded not only his authority but the bounds of his imagination.

"All right," the farmhand said, catching his breath. He stood thinking for a while.

"You asked for this," he then added, almost apologetically. "Why'd you provoke me?"

Markoni could hear their footsteps receding into the distance. They were talking about something and trying to come to some kind of agreement.

Leopold Markoni stood up. He didn't brush off his wet suit. He didn't look up, because he knew the windows were open and countless eyes were silently watching him.

He staggered into his store like a lunatic. He sat down at the counter and began sobbing in despair at his pointless and horrible humiliation.

■ □ ■ □ ■

# 41

I DIDN'T DARE ASK HIS NAME. EVERYBODY CALLS HIM TON-
dichter—"tone poet"—or Maestro, and that's probably good
enough. The fellow didn't introduce himself to me. He just sat
down next to me, as though we were old friends. But then,
apparently we *are* almost friends, because apparently we met
out in the wine country that warm, sunny winter day when
the two landowning circles—Real Estate Magnate's and
Samsa's, German and Slovene—had such a nice time chatting
with each other. But there's less niceness between them than
you might judge at first sight. This day, so important for me
because it was when I learned about the latest racial theory,
was nothing like the sunny day when I'd first met the famous
local composer. Today clouds were pressing down onto the
earth, the sky was dark, there was slush on the streets again,
and the river was black under the bridge. The more I sit here
and the more the trains head for Trieste, the more inexorably
and steadily that river flows and flows along its ancient channel the other way, toward the Black Sea. We sat in the Grand
Café, with its view of the river and bridge. Maestro was telling
me about the choir he directs, a boys' choir, the local version of
the Vienna Boys' Choir, and he'll invite me to come hear the
unspoiled, clear beauty of their crystal-pure voices. He com-
poses, himself. His compositions have a patriotic cast. As he
says, they breathe the native soil, the Pohorje Mountains, and
the clear Styrian sky, which in his opinion ought to be green.

Because green is the true color of his native hills and pastures and of the green Styrian spring and the green rivers. I told him I thought the river running under the bridge was black. Only in winter, he said, otherwise it's green, and the sky should be green, too. This notion struck him as so artistic that he repeated it again a third time. I was more focused on the yellow color of the fine cognac that Maestro had ordered for me. I thought about how I simply couldn't afford to buy that kind of cognac anymore. My savings had dried up and it was only a matter of time before I wouldn't even be able to afford brandy down at the tavern with Glavina and Fedyatin. But I could see that Maestro wasn't bothered by my present state—by the shaggy whiskers I no longer felt like shaving, by my crumpled suit, or by my hair, which was as greasy as pumpkin oil. Sitting next to him—especially him, as clean and groomed and fragrant smelling as he was—I became aware of all these things about myself in an instant. Next to someone like that, you start thinking about your own slovenliness, and it struck me that this was my last chance to pull myself together (specifically, to work on returning my appearance to its original state, and my internal state . . .), to pack my bags immediately and take them down to the station, where there's a train leaving every day for Trieste. I'm going to do it tomorrow, I firmly decided as I was looking at his sweet-smelling face. And right now, today, I'm going to go to the post office and send Jaroslav a telegram. Maestro suddenly said that he sensed I had an artistic soul. I looked at him nonplussed, but I was even more surprised when he then edged right over next to me. He said the externals weren't important, and that what was important was what a person had deep inside himself, in his heart and soul. He said that he had sensed it—my artistic soul, that is—as early as the trip to the wine country, when I seemed somehow absent and refused to take part in their eternally unchanging discussions about money, which he finds repugnant, too. And your faces, he said, yours and Mrs. Samsa's, they just shone. So he knows, too, I thought. He knows something about Mrs. Samsa and me, too. But why, I thought, why would he then be sitting so close beside me if he knows about Mrs. Samsa and me? In that case he must also know I'm not a member of his boys' choir. I didn't say any of this to him and just drank the next cognac that he pushed in front of me with a rounded movement of his hand and an ingratiating smile.

■ □ ■ □ ■

# 4 2

THE INTEREST IN MAN CONTINUES TO GROW. THERE ARE END-less scholarly lectures about the human physiognomy and its influence on the individual's personality traits, intelligence, abilities, and qualities. About man and on behalf of man, on behalf of his future and a better life. But this is possible only if we know who is who and if we can tell that by the shape of his head. After all, someday we'll make it to the moon, but we still won't know the most basic facts about man. About his skull—it's especially important to know a lot about the human skull, because everything that makes man what he really is is hidden underneath that skull. It's 1938 and man wants to know who he is. He wants to know if it's possible to transmit thoughts over a distance, he wants to know if it's possible to see into the future, and he especially wants to know what's inside that skull, and he wants to know it at a single glance. The community of man has the chance to plan a rational future in which man can live a life that's worthy of a human being. It's 1938 and man is interested in man, and cares about him. Which is why he needs to know his qualities.

According to Weinert, the anthropologist, two fundamental criteria determine the quality of a race. Both of them have to do with the human head, or rather skull. The first is the index of the skull, and the second is its shape.

1. Cephalic index. Cephalic index refers to the correlation between the width of the head and its length. If we assign the

length of the head a value of 100, then its width should be three-fourths, or 75 percent, of the length, or possibly a bit more or less than three-fourths. A head with a ratio of 75 to 80 is mesaticephalic. If the width is less than 75 and the head in relation to that is narrower and longer, then you're dealing with a long-headed, narrow-headed, or dolichocephalic person. Widths registering 80 or 90 are brachycephalic.

2. Head shape. This is an indicator of the cultural worth of a race. Only long-headed people are intelligent and culturally inclined. Wide-headed people with an index of more than 80 are the most incapable and dangerous elements in human society.

Some anthropologists, most of them Slavic, have seriously disputed this theory. The most powerful counterargument is that among Germans today, 16 percent are dolichocephalic, 41 percent mesaticephalic, and 41 percent brachycephalic. Among the French, according to the same Slavic sources, the breakdown is 14–41–45, among the Chinese it's 25–52–33, among American Indians it's 17–43–40, among the Eskimos 86–9–5, and among blacks 56–38–6. Consequently, the greatest number of long-headed individuals is found among primitive peoples, not among the Nordic creators and Kulturträger, as Weinert and his school would have us think. Blacks score highest of all, the opponents of the theory of racial quality gibe, and accordingly ought to rule mankind. Moreover, they counter Weinert, Socrates had to have been a total cretin by the standards of racial theory, and Kant and Leibniz substandard broadheads with ratios of 85.5 and 90.3, respectively.

These investigations, which are so important for the future of mankind, remain incomplete. Before final conclusions can be reached, many practical experiments have to be conducted, and in the most difficult circumstances. Of course, qualified anthropologists will have to be present in order to determine firsthand the accuracy or inaccuracy of their theories of racial quality. In the years to come, anthropological experiments will be conducted in this and other areas.

■ □ ■ □ ■

# 4 3

AFTER THE NEXT COGNAC, WHICH THE WAITER BROUGHT IN A fine, fragile, spherical glass, I showed more interest in Maestro's creativity and his opinions. Maestro warmed his glass with the palm of his delicate hand, as though he were cradling a boy's ass in it, and he told me about his love for those creative spirits whom he would never equal, such as Wagner, for instance. Maestro would be happy if his own music gave a sense of the green Styrian hills and brooks, the clear-flowing rivers, and the clear green sky. His gestures struck me as unusually rounded, as though he were directing his boys' choir, and as though now and then while directing he even stroked one of the boys.

Boris Valentan—Bussolin—walked into the café. I saw that he noticed me, and I felt a little uneasy. Maestro was sitting just a little too close to me, and with his hand patting me on the shoulder he told me in confidential tones about his views on creativity. It was too artificial for me not to feel uncomfortable, despite the cognacs I'd drunk. Maybe that's why I raised my hand in greeting, which Bussolin interpreted as an invitation. He seemed to shrug his shoulders and turned toward the door, but then at the last second reconsidered. He came over to our table, ignored the hands that each of us extended to him, and sat down without a word. Maestro said that he'd just been talking to me about patriotic music, but Bussolin looked past us somewhere. He was clearly in a bad mood, and he was searching for the right words. Then he looked at me with his bright eyes, and in the firm, honest voice that I knew and disliked precisely for those qualities, he said:

"My dear Mr. Erdman, I've sat down at your table only because there's something I have to say to you."

He was speaking to me alone, as though Maestro weren't even there. Maestro edged away and measured him with a hurt look.

"It's your business," he said, "if you want to remove yourself from our circle. It's your business if you've chosen to abuse our trust. It's also your business if you've chosen to keep different company," he said, and his eyes flashed toward Maestro, who then edged even farther away. "And it's just as much your business if you choose to tramp around taverns with good-for-nothings and appear in public in the state you're in. All that doesn't matter, even if it does cast a particular light on us."

I had to catch my breath. What did he mean, remove myself? What different circles had I chosen? What sort of attack was this, what did it mean? Why was he telling me this?

"But it's not just your business and it does matter that you've begun broadcasting things among your new associates that you've heard from us, including intimate things, if I'm correctly informed."

I was amazed. What on earth had offended them all, among all their oriental carpets? What had happened between Marjetica and me was our business, and at most also Franjo Samsa's. As for what other circles were saying, there's nothing you can do about that. That's the way the world works, and that's how people are. As to what authority Bussolin was acting on, I was at a complete loss.

"You're not correctly informed," I blurted out pointlessly, for lack of anything smarter to say.

"It's not just the company you choose to keep, it's the fact that you abused our trust and now you're telling others about your experiences with us. To live with people who opened their homes to you and their hearts—yes, even their hearts, don't mock this—and then to betray them so shamelessly, simply put, is base. It's as low as a human being can go."

Bussolin was noble, Bussolin was an exceptionally good person—that's what she had said once—Bussolin spoke with feeling and commitment.

I didn't know what to say. Maestro butted in.

"I beg your pardon, Mr. Valentan, but Mr. Erdman has told me absolutely nothing about your circle. We were talking about music and one's homeland."

It turned out that Maestro spoke pretty good Slovene.

"I wasn't speaking to you," Bussolin said in the same firm and polite tone of voice. "What I said was addressed to Mr. Erdman."

"But this gentleman is sitting with me."

"Didn't you invite me over?" Bussolin turned and asked me. "Did you wave to me or didn't you?"

The two of them were worked up, but still polite. They exchanged their barbs with utmost dignity. Finally, Bussolin leaned back and examined Maestro carefully.

"You with your brachycephalic head are of absolutely no interest."

"What kind of head?" I asked.

"Brachycephalic," Bussolin said.

"This is an outrage," Maestro shouted, suddenly raising his voice as though someone else were speaking. "This is one more brazen attack on an innocent person," he exclaimed. "A person can't even sit in a café anymore without being attacked by brazen people."

## 4 4

"I HAVE NO INTENTION OF SPEAKING TO THAT, THAT RACIALLY impure person," Bussolin said in a quavering voice. "But I had to tell you things that concern you. You made Margerita unhappy, and then you betrayed her, and finally you betrayed all of us. You're a scoundrel and a traitor. You're a liar. You're a liar and a sneak. I don't believe one thing you say anymore. You belong down, down," and now not just his voice was shaking but also the hand he was using to point down toward Lent. "You belong down there in those filthy dives."

He threw some money on the table and strode decisively away. It was a nice speech he'd made, dignified and noble. He'd dressed me down with some choice words. After all, he could have struck me and thrown cognac at Maestro. He could also have spat at me if I was really as much of a lowlife as he'd shouted that I was, right here at this table, causing everyone to turn and stare. But Maestro was also shaking with rage.

"Now you see what these people are like. Chauvinistic people. Little people. Dirty people. Primitives."

And these are the people whose sky he wants to paint green.

This was how I came to drink one more cognac and became a traitor, a scoundrel, a liar, and a sneak.

But I did learn about racial theory. The theory of Mr. W., the famous anthropologist. Maestro then explained W.'s theory to me. He asked the waiter for a length of string and measured my head. He did some calculations. He nodded.

"Yes, I think that's right," he said finally. "I think you're mesaticephalic."

To demonstrate, he then measured his own head. His turned out to be an egghead, the kind of head that's the carrier of cultural qualities.

My mesaticephalic head couldn't quite understand all of this.

"But then," I exclaimed, "what if a person is a waterhead? What if he's a *Wasserkopf?*"

Maestro preferred not to answer this question. His head was nodding off. Even my mesaticephalic one was roaring from the cognac and from Bussolin's elegant speech. It had been an elegant, moving speech. Once I've had a chance to think it over properly, I'll feel sorry for myself. And I'll go on down there, where I belong.

■ □ ■ □ ■

## 4 5

BUT DOWN THERE, WHERE I BELONG, I COULDN'T RESIST MEN-
tally measuring Glavina's skull. It was the head of a broad-
head, there's no glossing over that fact. He was banging on the
table again. And Fedyatin was gleefully bouncing around, his
epileptic eyes shining. Glavina was banging on the table
because the woman he'd just been with hadn't washed. Oh,
she doesn't have to take a bubble bath like those whores you
visit, he shouted at me, as though I were at fault for his
woman not bathing. But the whore could at least wash herself, he raged. I was used to his shouting, because I knew this
gentle soul did it in order to give some release to the blood
circulating under his taut skin. This was obvious from his
raw, razor-burned cheeks.

"Why does she have to stink from the last guy," he then
added a little more quietly, emptying his glass of foul-smelling
brandy. "You know how the last guy stinks. The last guy
stinks inside a woman and coming out of her like a disinte-
grating fish. A rotten, saltwater fish." There was laughter at the
neighboring tables and Glavina pulled his head in between
his shoulders and looked around, causing the laughter to
stop in an instant. He cruised around the whole room with
this laughter-stopping look of his, until his eyes finally came
to rest on me.

"Why don't you get a shave?" he asked. I shrugged. He
drew the back of his hand across his face and muttered, "A

fellow has to keep himself shaved like in the service. Even if he doesn't have any money. Shaved and washed."

I nodded agreement. I could tell that people were growing more and more unhappy with me. With my beard, my clothes, my mesaticephalic head, my treachery. Thank God I at least have an artistic soul, as Maestro senses.

That evening Glavina really was unhappy with me. Normally the guy is pretty well disposed toward me, always happy to see me when I walk in, glad to talk to me about world politics, but sometimes he looks down his nose at me. Or maybe he's just got an excess of blood and strength and it's not me he's unhappy with, but himself. He wanted to find out if I was strong. He proposed an arm-wrestling contest and put his elbow down on the table. I wasn't up to this. This was going too far, this informality here where I belong. He was offended. He wanted to show me that he's strong, even if I am weak. He crouched down next to my chair and slapped his neck with one hand. Fedyatin clapped, and people at the other tables were standing up. I couldn't understand what he wanted, although it was obviously some kind of performance that everyone else knew well. He slapped himself on his fat, shaven neck again and some fellow showed me that I should straddle his neck. So I got up and sat down on his neck. He spread his arms out and there was a sudden silence in the room. I could hear him moving and panting underneath me. Slowly he began to stand up. His whole body was tense, and as he rose up slightly I began to sway, and I had to grab on to his short but thick hair. He rose faster and faster, and finally he jerked his body up the last bit of the way. I'm not exactly light, so what he was doing was no small feat. My head practically banged into the low ceiling, while down below there was thunderous approval. He had his arms still extended outward, while there I sat on his neck, practically colliding with the ceiling. He took a few steps around the room and I started swaying again like some huge, ridiculous puppet. Then he slowly let me back down and gave me a few satisfied pats on the back. His face was flushed totally red. You couldn't see the famous red spots anywhere on his raw neck anymore, because the blood was pumping everywhere, throughout his broad head and even in his eyes.

■ □ ■ □ ■

# 4 6

HIDDEN ON THE EAST SIDE OF MAIN SQUARE, RIGHT IN THE
corner, is a narrow street that not even all the local residents
know. If a stranger were to venture into this street at night,
convinced that any street leading off of Main Square had to
go somewhere—if he were to venture down the street at
night, he would notice that it isn't even lit. If the stranger
were drunk in the bargain, as Josef Erdman, an employee of
Stastny and Company—a firm producing special laboratory
equipment—has tended to be more and more of late, he
would walk straight into a wall. The problem is that this
street has no exit—it is, in fact, such an exitless dead end that a
building suddenly looms up in front of you, presenting itself
at precisely the moment when it's already too late. In this
sense, you quite literally run up against the Jewish question
in this street, because when you ask later what the name of
this odd street is, those in the know will tell you that it's Jewish Street and that it doesn't lead anywhere.

About ten paces down from Jewish Street is the Jewish synagogue, with windows looking out onto the Drava. The whole
block is known as the Jewish Quarter. For the most part, the
apartments in this neighborhood are in very poor condition;
the staircases are dank and their stucco is crumbling. The synagogue is also falling apart, slowly but surely. The Jewish
Quarter is very old. There have been no Jews living in it for a
long time. In 1497 they were expelled from the city, because

the residents owed them too much money. They resettled all over Europe, and many of them assumed the distinctive surname Marpurgo. But perhaps that was just an excuse. As is well known, the causes were profound and ancient. And so the Jewish Quarter has no Jews living in it, and even in the whole city you'd be hard-pressed to find a single Jew in 1938. At least, Dr. Bukovski couldn't find any. He will encounter Jews several years later. Yet, even if there are no Jews in the city, that doesn't mean there isn't a Jewish question. For in 1938 the Jewish question is the central question of all Central Europe, from the Baltic to the Adriatic Sea.

I LEFT THE LITTLE TOBACCONIST SHOP NEXT TO GOVERNMENT
Bridge and ran straight into Dr. Bukovski. He'd covered his
bald spot with a big black fur cap. I asked him whether he was
cold, and whether his head got a little chilly, not having any
hair and all. He walked past me wordlessly, but I shouted after
him to say hello to everybody for me—Marjetica, Bussolin, the
engineer, and everyone else. Then he turned abruptly around
and walked toward me.

"Do you," he said, "do you always talk to people on the
street? Do you shout after them?"

"Not always," I said, "and not everybody. Only my friends."

"Even when you're sober?"

Obviously he meant to imply I wasn't sober. I told him I
wasn't drunk. The only problem was that I didn't feel well. I
ought to catch a train, but I can't catch the train, and he'd
better not think I'm some international swindler or sneak. I
think my voice was shaking a little. Dr. Bukovski suddenly
started showing interest in my case. He stepped right up
close to me and looked into my eyes. I could see his pupils
moving back and forth, examining something in my eyes.

"Two weeks ago," he said, "you were a different person.
What's happened to you?"

Then he stepped back and thought for a while.

"Would you mind coming with me for a moment?"

"What do you want?"

"I'm going to show you something that will get you on that train."

We walked through the slush and I could feel the doctor glancing at me from under his fur cap. I tried not to trip or stagger. He was probably waiting for something like that, or why would he be scrutinizing me that way?

We didn't walk far. The hospital was quite close to the tobacconist's shop, the one with the seated Turk. It was almost across from my abode, the Dvor. Dr. Bukovski greeted people to the right and left, then he opened the door to a tiny building, an annex to the huge main corpus of the hospital. We stepped into a kind of office where some man in a leather apron stood up. Wordlessly, the doctor put on a white laboratory coat and fumbled through the coatrack for a while. He couldn't find anything suitable, so he finally offered me a blue work shirt which could have belonged to the man in the apron. He opened the door to the next room, and with a light, polite, slightly ironic bow he let me in.

The first thing I saw was a pair of bare feet jutting out from under a white sheet. It was a body covered with a white cloth. For a moment I was motionless, my eyes taking in the huge room, its walls painted halfway up in white oil-based paint which had faded to dirty gray. Around the room, lying on crude wooden racks, were several more corpses covered with sheets that had red-brown spots all over them. The wooden racks kept reminding me of the counter in a butcher shop. In fact, everything somehow resembled a butcher shop. The man in the leather apron standing behind us had a little black beard and eyes that were reminiscent of some black bird, a crow or a raven.

With a sudden yank, the doctor pulled the sheet off the nearest corpse. The naked male body had been dissected down the middle and then sewn back up again in broad stitches with thick black thread. The rib cage jutted upward, the head lay far to the back, and the belly was collapsed almost all the way to the surface of the wooden rack, with only skin left covering it.

"This one was picked up in Lent last night," the doctor said. "His liver was almost totally gone. Cirrhosis—hopeless, complete cirrhosis. That's what happens when a man surrenders to drink."

Then he walked from corpse to corpse, uncovering them and saying something, though suddenly I wasn't seeing or hearing anything. The fellow with the black beard and the apron helped support me. He was probably used to people collapsing in here. I leaned back against the wall and closed my eyes. My head really was spinning a little, perhaps in part because of the room's strange smell of disinfectants, of human beings, and of chemicals. When I opened my eyes, the doctor was covering the corpse in the corner.

Then he walked over toward me. Once again I could see his pupils from right up close, as I had earlier outside.

"Your pupils are unusually dilated," he said.

I could feel my unusually dilated pupils.

"Otherwise you look healthy," he said. "Except for your eyes. There's something wrong with the way you're seeing things."

He took hold of my arm and looked at his watch. He nodded and paced about the room. He left me standing beside the wall with that fellow, who was motionless.

Suddenly he exclaimed, "You once said you had an interest in anthropology. The morgue," he said, "is an excellent place for an anthropologist."

His voice seemed unnatural to me. The way he was walking around the room struck me as nervous. I wanted out of there, so that I wouldn't have to listen to his voice or see this room, and him pacing back and forth among the corpses in this room. He kept talking and exclaiming.

"Do you know," he exclaimed, "that in my whole life I've never seen a Jew? Living or dead? The whole world is obsessed with the Jewish question, and I still haven't ever seen a Jew."

When this person looked at my eyes, was he trying to tell me that my pupils were dilated because I was afraid, because huge waves of nausea were coursing through me, because I was trying not to look at anything? Was he perhaps trying to imply that those dilated eyes meant there was something wrong with my head, with my thoughts? Was he trying to tell me that I was basically healthy but just a little soft in the head? Why had he brought me here? Could it be because *he's* not quite healthy, because he can't control his thoughts, because his nervous pacing and arm waving, his exclamations, mean there's something wrong with him? This is the second time I've felt space slipping away in this city. The first time, it happened when I was standing on the lawn in the deep snow; that time, space started sliding down toward the river. No, I'm not sliding. I'm not even unbalanced or confused or crazy, even if I do have dilated pupils. But the floor under my feet is sliding, the doctor is sliding, that fellow with the little black beard and the leather apron is sliding, the whole world is sliding toward the edge of some insane abyss. The doctor talks and waves his arms. He talks about intelligence, intelligence. He pronounces intelligent sentences, he exclaims them louder and louder, he walks into his office and comes back with a piece of paper that he shoves under my nose, and now, when he's right up close, I can see his pupils, his eyes don't even have any whites to them, the eyeballs are covered with brown, finely chopped pupils that rapidly rotate and spin, spin inside the skull and back out again, while the whole world slides away down there.

DR. BUKOVSKI, THE CORONER, SPEAKING TO JOSEF ERDMAN IN the morgue one January morning in 1938: An Austrian regimental medic named Dr. A. Weisbach made some extraordinarily interesting observations in an extensive study titled *Körpermessungen verschiedener Menschenrassen,* which was published in Berlin long ago, in 1878. They should be of interest to every anthropologist. I've heard that you, sir, have a consuming interest in anthropology. Did you know, for instance, that Jews have a pulse rate of 77 beats per minute? You didn't know that? Doesn't that suggest anything to you? My dear sir— Jews have the fastest pulse rate of all! It's faster than any other group: the Slavs at 72 beats per minute, Hungarians at 70, and the poor Romanians at just 64.

It's a known fact, Bukovski continued, that Jews have aquiline noses. It's a known fact that the breadth of their shoulders is insignificant in comparison with other Europeans', but that's only the beginning. The thighs, my dear sir, the thighs! Jews' thighs are even shorter than Slavs' thighs: 487 to 491. And they're thinner: 287 to 297. The same thing holds for the size of their calves: The correlation between a Jew's calf and a Slav's calf is 196 to 212! But most significant of all is the overall length of the body: An Austrian Jew's is 1,632 millimeters long, a Slovak's is 1,660, a Czech's is 1,669, a Frenchman's is 1,667, an Italian's is 1,669, a Ruthenian's or a Pole's is 1,673, a Slovene's is 1,672, a Croat's is 1,692, a German's is 1,680, and a Norwegian's is 1,727.

A Jew's extremities are extremely short. If a Jew holds his arms outstretched, the distance from fingertip to fingertip is usually equal to the height of the body. At most 25 millimeters longer, but more often it's even shorter. Among non-Jews in Russia they've discovered a difference of as much as 203 millimeters—that's how much farther their outstretched arms reach compared to their height.

What can we conclude from these figures? On the basis of their anatomical characteristics alone, Jews are less suited to manual labor or military service than most other nationalities. Indeed, there is scientific evidence to support this, too. There's no hiding from science—it's the truth that nobody can escape. Look at the facts. At the time of one investigation there were 874,078 men enlisted in the Austrian army. And how many soldiers do you think each nationality contributed? Look at this table.

Clearly, the Germans, Hungarians, Czechs, Slovenes, and Croats contributed too many soldiers, and the Poles, Ruthenians, Serbs, Romanians, and—well, what have we here?— the Jews contributed too few. The Jewish shortfall is the greatest of all!

In that same year, Jews represented 5.5 percent of the personnel in military administrative units, while the Slovenes had only 2.7 percent. Similarly, there were more Jews in military training installations: 6.0 percent, as opposed to only 2.3 percent for Slovenes. Contrast that with units where real fighters are needed: the cavalry, for instance, where Jews register just 1.8 percent and Slovenes 2.3 percent, or heavy artillery, where the discrepancy is even worse: 2.0 percent for Jews and 3.4 percent for Slovenes.

And so, my dear sir, we've proven to ourselves with hard facts that we simply can't remain indifferent to this reality. A lack of physical ability, a lack of courage, fear of death, an absence of self-abnegation, extreme egotism, niggardliness, treachery, fanaticism, morbidity, intolerance, nonproductivity, cunning, and so on—I could keep naming the qualities that threaten Europe's peoples, even the smallest. Do you think the Jews are not a threat to the Slovenes? There's impatience in your voice, you speak as though you'd like to say someone else is threatening us. Didn't you say that? Who says that every thought has to be spoken out loud? Sometimes there's more meaning in what's left unsaid than in what's said. But it must be clear to you that that brood—you'll have to excuse me, but your resistance to my line of reasoning compels me to more forceful means of expression—that that vile and treacherous tribe has, has—please, please don't interrupt me—has spread across the entire world, and especially Europe, like some gigantic swarm of rats, undermining the foundations of a sound intellectual and economic life, and assaulting society, the individual, and human values with its guile and cunning.

Were you, for instance, aware of the fact that the Jews were not affected by the plague? On the other hand, they have a higher incidence of gastrointestinal disorders, hemorrhoids, and leprosy. No one has been able to determine the true cause, but that's probably just a cover for something left unsaid, not to say hushed up. And then . . . But I don't think it's really such a secret that Jews are very unclean people. That's been noted as early as Marcus Aurelius.

Jewry constantly, incessantly, and swiftly reproduces itself. Single males and females, even celibates, don't exist among Jews. The Talmud commands them to marry. You can say what you want, but they reproduce all out of proportion. Do I think it necessary to halt all that reproduction? Yes, I do. The proliferation of these traitors, these rodents, these dangerous rats has to be stopped immediately, this instant, because tomorrow it will be too late. But not just stopped—I am not shouting, who says I'm shouting?—not just stopped—and I'm only saying what I think—they have to be exterminated, do you hear, exterminated!

Do I need to catch my breath? I don't need to catch my breath. Let me just tell you this, and tell it to you personally: If you really are some sort of anthropologist, and if anthropology interests you in the slightest bit, then stop going on about those hairy women, those Amazons and wild tribes or whatever it is you keep rambling on about, and start dealing with issues of race, because anthropology is a social science, it's a question of the future, a question of the measures we're going to have to take in this area for the common good on the basis of strict scientific research.

No Jew has ever lain here. Yet this is a morgue, my dear fellow, this is where we study the human interior. The science of race is one thing, and a sick liver is another. Poisoning is one thing, and an ailing soul is another. Your pupils, sir, your pupils are extremely dilated. Don't you dare say, don't you ever again say that I'm crazy. Those are scientifically established facts. Your pupils—why are you leaning against the wall? Are you sick? Don't you dare think that the rest of the world is insane and you're the only sane one. I know cases like yours— your pupils, sir.

■ □ ■ □ ■

# 49

I SLEPT ALL AFTERNOON AND ALL NIGHT. I COUNTED ON MY fingers the number of hours I'd slept. I wanted to shave, but didn't have any shaving cream, and the razor was in such bad shape that I didn't dare. I'm not about to walk the streets with a gashed and battered face. Let Glavina say what he will. He shaves so forcefully every morning that he scrapes the skin off. They've told me I have to pay my bill. Just a moment, I said, please wait just a moment longer. How long a moment? they asked. Just a few more days, then I'll pay my bill and leave. I was composed and healthy and sober and I thought that the whole slipping world—at least the part of the world that contains this city—that it was less solid than me with my health and sobriety. Then I went walking around and stopped by the church on the upper bank of the river, St. Joseph's Church. I looked for Glavina and Fedyatin, couldn't find them, and walked around some more until I ran into that woman.

Liselotte dragged me along after her. You've really hit bottom, she said. Why don't you get a shave? You will get a shave, won't you? Of course you will. She kept twittering around me, and I just kept nodding my head. If she had told me right off what she told me later, I probably would never have gone with her and would have spared myself a lot of grief. But it was only after we'd walked all the way to their villa that she said: You know, Mr. Erdman, we think very highly of you.

"Really?" I said, matter-of-factly.

"Really, it's true. We're not like those people you associated with before, who left you high and dry," she said.

"That's what Maestro thinks," I said.

"Who?"

"Maestro."

"Oh, our genius," she exclaimed in delight. "Of course he does, and so do we all," she said. "We never leave anyone in the lurch. The abandoned and forgotten, all of them are welcome in our ranks."

I wanted to say that I didn't feel I was abandoned or forgotten or in need of being rescued, that I was going back to drink with Fedyatin and Glavina, and I don't have any idea why I didn't say it. She was so pleasant, even though she said the most ridiculous things and though I remembered that these people even bought souls, as rumor had it back among the oriental carpets, although they weren't particularly fond of Jews either, and ultimately the whole crazy world was talking utter nonsense, I thought, and there we were, right in front of the house, and in I went. No sooner were we in the entryway than she was twittering about how their genius, their Maestro, "who, by the way, as you've noticed, is too much inclined in some other direction, but all geniuses are a little different, aren't they"—she was already twittering there in her resonant voice that in Maestro's opinion I was a learned person, though I had let myself go lately, but those were all just little, cosmetic flaws, so to speak, and they valued the friendship of a man such as myself, and especially once you've shaved and pulled yourself together a bit, isn't that right?

What on earth do they value in me? I thought. What do they know about me, what qualities of mine could they possibly value, and what knowledge? But I would soon learn that they knew more than I could conceivably imagine. They even knew what things I'd said at Engineer Samsa's house. They knew I had very tolerant views on the nationalities question, a very pacifist attitude toward the social struggle and the differences between classes and races, that I was knowledgeable about the occult and anthropology, and that I was unduly modest and made myself out to be a person of no importance, a chance passerby, so to speak. Only about Margerita did they seem to know nothing, or perhaps they refrained from mentioning it out of the tact that was an inalienable part of them, a national trait. They even knew that I'd encountered financial difficulties, and they offered to help me out with a job if I planned to stay, and if not, then with a loan.

I listened to all this and nodded and thanked them, while Real Estate Magnate poured me some wine from his vineyards. Fine wines, excellent wines, he exports them to Germany, where the reputation of Lower Styrian wines is well established.

I was a little drunk, since Glavina and I had earlier put back a few glasses of brandy. Liselotte smiled at me and asked if I wanted some coffee. Maybe she thought I was too tipsy and that coffee would help. So I asked for coffee, though I didn't need it to sober up.

Here, Real Estate Magnate suddenly grew serious and said, In this spot you're standing on German cultural ground. With one foot (his foot was in a soft, high slipper) he banged on the floor: *Deutscher Kulturboden.* The cupboard behind me rattled. Liselotte brought in the coffee cups and I could distinctly feel her making some signs to Real Estate Magnate behind my back. REM laughed again. But we're not going to hide what we are, he said, and I didn't know if that was meant for me or for Liselotte. He got up and led me around the large living room. He was holding me by the arm and now I could see the pictures on the wall from close up. Some mustachioed men wearing bush helmets. Deutsch Südwestafrika, he graciously explained. The next picture: a salute to the German flag in Cameroon. Third picture: a sharp-looking group of young uniformed men marching down the street. They're marching smartly, but the row is disorganized and familial: Kaiser Wilhelm II and his sons. Young, handsome, decisive men: Prince Friedrich Wilhelm, Prince Oskar, Prince August Wilhelm, Prince Adalbert, and in the midst of them the old man with his manly gaze and stride. "A prolific old guy," I observed. REM looked at me as though he were trying to discover some derision in my remark, but I had meant it in all seriousness. The strength, the stride, the ambition, the will: It's all in that picture. REM smiled.

He stomped on the floor in his soft, slippered feet a few more times, humming something that was like a hymn or a march and keeping time with his hand as it hit against the back of an armchair.

■ □ ■ □ ■

# 50

LEOPOLD MARKONI SR.'S PROBLEMS WITH HIS SON LEOPOLD Markoni Jr. began at the moment when, by all of his father's calculations, the son should have changed from a boy to a man. He had forgiven the boy his failures at school, because he was perfectly aware that school was just school, and not the school of life, that the school of life was life itself—in other words, friendships, sports, the military, business, maybe a prostitute now and then, if she was clean and not too troublesome. For ages he had forgiven his son his overly childish, stubborn outbursts and his predilection for those revolting cookies that Liselotte and the cook endlessly mixed, rolled, and baked. He couldn't understand why his son, who one day would have to take over everything he had built, hung around the kitchen and why his bed was full of crushed cookie crumbs, left over from the previous night's gorging. He forgave him all this and much more, because he was convinced that some day, when the boy had matured, everything would change. But suddenly and with horror, Leopold Sr. began to see the difference between his one and only son and his son's contemporaries, who were becoming resolute men and firm heirs of their fathers. Leopold Markoni Jr. was different. He was unable to firmly answer questions that his father or one of their guests put to him. He was unable to look you in the eye. He was unable to give a firm handshake. He couldn't remember interest rates. He didn't play soccer. He didn't have a clear voice and a decisive gait. He didn't want to help in the store. He didn't like going out to the vineyards. He wasn't decisive, strong, and sharp. He wasn't like his father. He would lock himself inside his room and eat cookies in bed.

Leopold Markoni Sr. knew too well that a boy like that, had he been born among Spartans, would never even have survived childhood. The environment and times we live in, he often said at meetings of the cultural league, or Kulturbund, demand of us a Spartan spirit. Simply put, this wasn't a time for cookies.

Deep inside, REM bore a wound he never spoke of to anyone. Some nights, that wound ate away at his heart and roared within his breast, keeping him awake until morning. He knew that back in 1919 he had crawled over the pavement simply because the thought of truly decisive action made him feel an enormous void in his stomach, cold sweat on his forehead, and a shaking in his knees. He knew that back then he hadn't been able to overcome some accursed, mean-spirited coward in himself, and he was petrified by the thought that his son might, with all his being, have inherited that trait of his. It had surfaced only a few times in Leopold Sr.'s life and, sad to say, once in the presence of that stinking peasant in the crumpled uniform. It came out only occasionally and was hardly worth mentioning, but it showed in his son in an unusually pronounced way.

This is why he decided he had to do something. Like a Spartan parent, he decided to throw his son, such as he was, into the water, and to let him swim as best he could. He registered him for a camp where young Spartan men were trained in the spirit of Schlageter and Horst Wessel, where they were imbued with manliness, decisiveness, and the mission that awaited them. This was no ordinary camp. It was a comradely but tough, almost military, school of life. But the news that an old friend from the cultural union brought him was hopeless: The boy refused to make friends with his campmates, he kept to himself, was last to get up, couldn't make his bunk according to standard, was clumsy, slow, absentminded, and probably also a little lazy. The words that REM was hearing fell on him hard, like stones, even though they were spoken in a friendly voice and confidentially. The next blow came that same fall. Leopold Markoni Sr. was returning from a business trip. As he stepped off the train he saw a crowd of people, a brass band, and local luminaries. Indignantly, he was pushing his way through the crowd when he suddenly spied his son, Leopold Markoni Jr., amid a group of young men. He was standing beneath a banner on which was written in large letters OUR CITY'S HEART GOES OUT TO OUR BROTHER CZECHS AND SLOVAKS! REM's eyes clouded over. So that's how it is and how it'll be. He struggled to overcome that familiar void in his stomach and was not even conscious of walking toward the boy, whose grim face and features were reminiscent of Leopold Markoni Sr.'s own. He wasn't even conscious of striking that familiar face so that it gave a loud smack and twisted into a surprised and startled mask. He grabbed his son by the jacket and dragged him, flushed red, from the train station. But what was worst of all was that his son hadn't gone to the station because he'd wanted to, but because he'd had to, because some Slavophilic schoolmaster had ordered him to. That fact—that he had just bowed his head and gone, without even thinking whether he agreed or disagreed—that was the worst thing of all. Neither Markoni, father or son, slept that night. Each of them stared at the ceiling, seething with silent hatred.

That was the first blow.

■ □ ■ □ ■

# 5 1

LISELOTTE HAD GRACIOUSLY POURED US COFFEE WHEN I MADE the incautious observation that the Kaiser's family would look a lot more appealing if they weren't wearing their uniforms in the picture, at least not the sons.

"No uniforms?" REM asked, looking vexed.

"Right, just in civilian clothes. They'd look more relaxed," I said.

"Don't you like uniforms?" Leopold Markoni asked me, looking still more vexed. "Weren't you ever in the service?"

I didn't answer directly, but I did say that I was something of a pacifist by conviction.

At this, REM's face sobered completely. He caught his breath, as though he were preparing for a long, argumentative exchange.

"You know," he said, "I deal with practical things, and for that reason I depend on precise definitions. I'm not one to say things off the top of my head. I draw on encyclopedias for my knowledge—and ours, you'll have to admit, are among the most precise in the world. This encyclopedia," he said as he walked into the next room, "this encyclopedia, I'm positive, has an answer to your position," he said when he'd returned on light footsteps in his soft slippers.

"Liselotte," he called out, because she was in the kitchen fixing something for their guest. "Liselotte, where are my glasses?"

Liselotte came carrying a plate full of cookies.

"He's so proud of being organized," she said in a familiar, scolding way. "But he's so forgetful." She went into the room where his encyclopedias were and, apparently, also his glasses. She held them up to the light and carefully wiped them.

Ggb. was slowly leafing through a book.

"Aha, here it is," he finally said. And he read aloud.

"'Pacifism. A "peace movement."'' 'Peace movement' is in quotation marks, I should point out," he said. "'A "peace movement" with the utopian goal of eternal peace, which takes normal peaceful intentions—'"

I said that I wasn't a member of any movement, that I just . . . had my own ideas about soldiers, and uniforms.

"Hold on, hold on," Ggb. said. "'Which takes normal peaceful intentions, which are sufficient unto themselves, to unreasonable extremes.' This part is written in parentheses," he said. "In parentheses, it says: 'At its basis is the refusal to perform military service.' And here it goes on," he said, "here we've got you. 'Pacifist: An adherent of pacifism, by conviction an opponent of war, generally in favor of international ideas. Pacifists refuse to give their lives for the honor and freedom of their country. National Socialism firmly rejects anti-Germanic pacifism, which threatens the nation's safety and unity.'"

■ □ ■ □ ■

# 5 2

THAT FEDYATIN HAS SOMETHING PROPHETIC ABOUT HIM. SOME-
times I think he's outright hypnotized me. I try to clarify
things for myself. I try to convince myself that he can't have
any power over me if I don't adhere to his spiritual leanings,
if I don't succumb to some automatic, subconscious reaction,
if I don't permit a split, or anything that could lead to a hyp-
notic subversion of my consciousness.

But nothing helps when I see that the fellow is in some
kind of endless trance.

What should he be protecting himself from? Those problems are a part of him. But that terror he carries inside of him
is contagious. There's nothing he can do to me when he's in
that somnambulistic state that's uniquely his.

But maybe the entire point is that he doesn't force what's
in him on anybody else. He doesn't do any violence.

Quite simply, he's walking around with some horrible
visions inside, and all it takes is for you to know that, and
they slowly start seeping over into you. But I'm going to slice
that idiosyncrasy clean away.

I dreamed that they all had egg-shaped heads. The engineer, Margerita, Baldy, his wife, Bussolin, and all of his silken
and synthetic silk girlfriends who go there. At first I didn't
understand at all. Their heads just kept growing longer and
longer. Then I started making out words here and there—
they were talking about brachycephalics and dolichocephalics.

"I would seriously argue," Bussolin said as his head grew longer, "forty-one percent mesati- and fourteen percent brachy-," he said. Their heads kept growing longer, until after a while they were as big, as long, as their torsos. The doctor was holding Margerita by her little wrist. "The nerve center," he said. "The pulse beats seventy times per minute." The pulse. The eyes, mouths, and noses, too—everything was elongated. I determined that the underlying proportion was a third: one-third legs, one-third torso, one-third head. It was as though a baker had seized some dough and pulled it apart. As though an invisible force had latched on to their heads and was pulling them upward and down. The eggheads were saying, "Index three, index three." Then they turned and looked toward the corner and fell silent. Fedyatin stepped out of the darkness into a circle of light. All of them looked at him astonished, as though he had a different index than three, as though his pulse beat differently. And, in fact, Fedyatin then suddenly said, "Indeed, I don't have an index of three."

I ought to live only by day. My nocturnal life has become downright intolerable, at least the part that takes place while I'm asleep. I can still remember my dreams about Jaroslav and how he fell down all bloody amid the shattered glass, the laboratory equipment, how the little bits of glass, of test tubes and beakers, dug into him. What luck that I have Gretica and Katica. Lately they've been worried about me. They'd prepared for a visit from me. For a while they were as silent as before a storm. Then Katica insisted that I start taking better care of myself. That I find some work or at least finally give that Czech, that Jaroslav, a call. The one whose last name means Happy when it's translated. Stastny, I said. Oh what does it matter, Katica said, what matters is that I drink too much and hang out in taverns. Gretica said that I used to keep my trousers nicely pressed, but just look at how I was showing myself in public now. Now my trousers are like some policeman's, so baggy in the ass they hang down to the knees. Feeling offended, I said nothing. Then they rather sweetly started to give me advice. Katica was even on the verge of tears. But then Gretica forced me to take my trousers off. I sat back down in my underwear and watched while Katica pressed the trousers. Then she brushed off my jacket. I put the trousers back on and they were still damp and warm from being ironed. I did everything mechanically. Finally I borrowed some money and went looking for Glavina. I couldn't find him. He must have been hanging out somewhere with those jobless, unemployable characters, hatching some vindictive plot. Or maybe he was sitting somewhere with Markoni Jr., the heir of Ggb., the quiet young fellow with the striped suit and the grim face.

## 5 3

IT WAS AFTER THE CAMP AT THE PLITVICE LAKES, WHERE THE young men had made friends and trained under the slogan "Our people must live, even if we must die for it," when Leopold Markoni Sr. lifted his hand off his son. Just before that, however, he had raised it to him a second time. In actual fact, it wasn't until autumn that he found out what had happened. Leopold Markoni Jr. had returned from camp with a healthy tan, but quiet and distant in a way he'd never been before. After supper he'd leave the house, remaining stubbornly silent whenever they tried to extract information from him, about camp or about the friends he spent time with when he was away from home. He ate little, except for the homemade cookies that he kept taking to his room, as if to spite his father. That's how things went until autumn. Toward the end of September a friend of Leopold Markoni Sr.'s from the cultural league, who supervised the camping program, paid a visit. He'd come for an honest, man-to-man talk. Markoni was always in favor of that kind of talk. The friend had to tell him that they had released his son from camp two days early on account of numerous violations. Ggb. was silent.

"Your son," his friend said, "isn't suited to these things."

Ggb. wanted to know the reason for the dismissal.

"The boy isn't a straight arrow," the friend said. "He just doesn't have what it takes."

Leopold Markoni said that was no reason. That could be fixed, he could be trained.

"It's not just that," the friend from the cultural league said. "Poldi stole a knife from his tentmate. He hid it under his mattress."

Ggb. grabbed on more tightly to the edge of his armchair.

"And what's more," the friend continued mercilessly, "he's something of a coward."

Everything started going dark before Ggb.'s eyes.

"One night the camp guard caught Poldi in the kitchen. They thought some animal had sneaked in there. But they found Poldi, sitting at a table in the dark and eating. Not such a serious violation if you figure the boy might have been hungry, but his campmates thought that in more dangerous circumstances a fellow like that would be capable of even worse. Somebody who eats his campmates' food at night and on the sly is capable of sabotage, not to mention desertion."

Ggb. wanted to know what it was he'd been eating.

"Cookies," the friend said. "Cookies. Next morning after reveille they stood him in front of the patrol and the leader had some tough military words for him. And that's when the boy farted. I don't mean to say he was scared, but that's what it looked like. Or sounded like."

"What was that?" Ggb. asked, not having fully understood what his friend from the cultural league was telling him.

"He farted. Twelve times he farted. It was dead quiet all around and some of the boys counted."

"Then you mean he let some gas," Ggb. said angrily and all red in the face. "Not that he farted."

"I can understand all this must seem silly to you, and maybe it really doesn't mean anything, but at the time it caused—you can imagine what it was like. And the comments those Spartan boys made after the assembly was dismissed—it couldn't continue for all the helpless laughter—the comments were clear. If this happens to a guy when the leader yells at him, far worse is going to happen to him when he has to attack through barbed wire. Poldi didn't even try to repair the bad impression. Just the opposite: He started bucking the discipline. He stole the same knife a second time and then immediately confessed he'd stolen it, refused to fall in for assembly, avoided his chores, and finally we had to dismiss him."

"Dismiss him," Leopold Markoni Sr. said.

"Dismiss him," his friend from the cultural league said.

Markoni called his son and smacked him as he walked through the doorway. Ggb. knew there wasn't the necessary anger in that blow. If there was any, it had been meant for his friend from the cultural league. That slap had been more a matter of principle than anything else. But for Leopold Markoni Jr., that was his second public blow.

In the years to come, Leopold Markoni Jr. would finish business school. Whenever he needed money, he would put in some work for his father. In fact, that would happen rarely, because the young man would find other ways to make money. He would move out of the house and buy himself a striped suit and a silver cigarette case. His father wouldn't have anything to do with him and would avoid conversations about his son. Whenever he'd see him with Liselotte in the kitchen, he would go to his room or to the store. Now and then they would exchange a few words. Ggb. felt revulsion toward his son, and at night he would feel bitter at heart, thinking he ought to do something, but knowing there was nothing he could do. Leopold Markoni Sr. was not a bad man. Actually, he would make only one mistake. He would fail to do anything to help his son become an ordinary businessman. He had wanted his son to be brave, to know how to hate, and never to crawl on the ground in front of a drunken farmhand, even if the farmhand shot him or stabbed him with a bayonet. Could he help it if his most favorite photograph of all was the one with Kaiser Wilhelm II in a pressed and dazzling uniform walking with his sons?

■ □ ■ □ ■

## 5 4

MY NEIGHBOR, THE TOBACCONIST ON KING PETER SQUARE WHO
not only sells newspapers but also reads them, pointed his finger at a news item. I had to laugh.

Where are we now? Are we really on the verge of the out-
break of a bloody world war, as the great Tibetan pope pre-
dicts? All kinds of eccentrics and opportunists have been dis-
pensing that kind of ludicrous prophecy since the beginning
of time. It's supposed to start with a Russo-Japanese war.
Then both armies will get trapped in the sands of Turkestan
and they'll both be exhausted and reach a peace agreement,
but they'll establish their authority in their new territories at
an immense cost in human lives. The great lama announced
this in the temple of miracles, in the city of Peilingmian.
Finally an amusing day, not just at the tobacconist's but also
at G. and K.'s.

I paid another visit to Gretica and Katica. Katica sewed
my buttons back on for me. I lay on the couch in the kitchen
while Gretica put on coffee.

Gretica surprised me by saying that she isn't Wendish at
all, that she's German.

"How can that be," I said, "when you hardly know any
German?"

She said she'd been told that it didn't matter, that what
mattered was what you felt you were.

"Who told you that?" I asked her. She didn't want to say.

"Well, I sure don't understand; after all, the two of you are sisters, and Katica isn't German."

"She can be what she wants," Gretica said, "but I'm a real German." A craftsman she knows who's also a real German likes her because of that, she added.

"So he's the one who told you that?"

No, he didn't, and I should stop asking, because she wasn't going to say who had told her. What did Katica think of all this? Katica pointed a finger to the side of her head and made a twisting motion. Gretica got upset and said, "She's a fine one to talk, when that tax collector she cleans house for, that zio Rico from the coast, is always bad-mouthing Germans, as though they were some kind of Gypsies or Jews. All the well-bred people in this town are either Germans or Czechs, the rest are just plebs."

"What about Pristovšek," Katica said, "who brought you flowers and liqueur the other day? Are you going to say that about him, too?"

"Pristovšek is a gentleman," Gretica said. "You just let him be."

"But that's what I'm getting at," Katica said. "A Slovene can be a gentleman, too."

But Gretica wouldn't relent. From her eau de cologne bottling plant she even knew a few verses in German: *Die Slowenen und die Serben müssen alle, alle sterben.*

"So Serbs aren't gentlemen either?" I asked.

"The Serbs aren't and the Poles aren't. The Serbs take bribes and the Poles steal—and they're half Jews, anyway."

This was starting to interest me. "How about the Italians?" I asked. She thought for a while.

"The Italians are skirt chasers." Katica laughed.

"And the Croats?"

"The Croats are always causing some kind of commotion," Gretica said.

"But then they are Catholics," Katica said.

"Such Catholics—" Gretica waved her hand dismissively. She didn't elaborate. She would have nothing to do with the

French and that was that, because French kissing was unhygienic. "They shove their tongue inside your mouth—now what does that tell you?" Americans were rich, though a person could also come back from there poor and ruined by the mines. The Russians were Communists and didn't recognize marriage—they were all of them married to each other. The Hungarians ate garlic and stank of garlic. "Red pepper," I corrected her. "Well, then, red pepper," Gretica said, "it's all the same crap." "The Turks—" Katica giggled bashfully—"the Turks are circumcised." "She should know," Gretica said. "Recently there was a Turk here from Bosnia."

Katica was offended. "So what if he was," she said, "I bought a rug from him."

"Bought, right," Gretica said.

"Yes, bought," Katica said. Gretica just snorted. Katica couldn't leave it at Gretica saying nothing and just snorting; she had been stung. "So Pristovšek gave you that liqueur just because he's a nice guy, I suppose," she said.

Gretica's eyes turned to slits. "You're a fine one to talk, you are," she hissed through her teeth. I got up off the couch because the air in the room was getting too charged. I went over to Katica and put my arm around her shoulder, while I winked at Gretica.

Then we drank some of Pristovšek's liqueur and talked about various nationalities.

Next door the consumptive gave a few coughs.

I kept going back to visit them more and more often. Maybe partly because it gave me a chance to stop outside that door. I couldn't help it. My heart always started to beat faster whenever I climbed up that damp staircase, between those walls with black stains on them. I'd stand outside the door and listen to children squealing and the new tenants arguing inside. There had to be at least ten people living in there. If only because the toilet was constantly occupied, causing Katica and Gretica to complain fiercely. There were so many people breathing inside that jam-packed apartment, where before there were just the two of us inside, and it was so quiet that every word resonated between the walls. The snow melted on the windows and you could hear the water as it trickled into the gutters.

■ □ ■ □ ■

## 5 5

ALL THOSE YEARS, THE CONSUMPTIVE IN THE NEXT ROOM WILL continue coughing, outliving many of those who wrote him off in 1938 as fatality number 89. All those years, he'll hear the noise, the laughter, the loud conversations in the apartment next door, the intolerable fornicating, the scratchy gramophone, and the popping of wine corks. All those long years, he'll hear conversations about pressed trousers, and rustling and whispering and the squeaking of bedsprings. But when the last German leaves and the first of Tito's secret police arrive, he'll be fed up. One May evening he'll step out onto the walkway and start shouting down at Gretica, as she crouches on the courtyard floor and pours dirty water into the sewer. Every door opening onto the courtyard will fly open and the wooden walkway up above will be crowded with people noisily talking. Old lady Gruden will come and shove Gretica in the back so hard that the water will splash all over her silk skirt, and at the next shove she'll fall over her bucket into the dirty water.

"Kraut slut, Kraut slut," old lady Gruden will shout, while out of the apartments all around and from the walkway up above, from all sides, there will come such shrieking and shouting that Gretica's blood will run cold. Old lady Gruden will grab her by the hair, but Gretica will jab her in the belly with all her might. Then two men will run up and take Gretica by the arms. In a coughing fit that gets worse and worse, the

TB patient up on the walkway will shout, "Bring 'er here, up here with her, the Gestapo slut."

The men will drag her across the courtyard and up the stairway, with old lady Gruden pummeling at her blindly from behind. For all the perfume, for all the silk blouses, for all the hats, all the liqueurs and gramophones, for all the ration cards that they passed out right and left, humiliating them by forcing them to eat their whore-gotten butter, their meat, their sugar. The men will drag her up the stairs and onto the wooden walkway; Katica, whom they've locked inside the toilet, will be sobbing and banging on the door. The TB patient will run in to his apartment and, just as they've dragged Gretica to the top, will come back out bringing scissors. He'll grab her by the hair and, with a forcefulness you'd hardly expect from a sick and slumped man, he'll push her head out over the railing. With the other hand he'll chop into her hair, so that it falls in big clumps to the courtyard floor. Blood will drop onto it, too, dripping steadily out of Gretica's nose. Katica will keep banging on the toilet door long after the shouting and clapping have stopped, after everyone has retreated into their apartments and all that breaks the silence are Gretica's sobbing and the pounding on the wooden door.

## 5 6

WE REALLY ARE LIKE THE THREE KINGS, GLAVINA SAID AS WE were sitting around a liter of wine. Referring to him, Fedyatin, and me. It's true, we have been together a lot lately. We find a spot in some corner, I order wine, and they order brandy. Glavina drinks wine, too, sometimes, but Fedyatin only drinks brandy. We look through the smoke at the people who come and go—generally just men, or sometimes women of questionable character. Glavina knows a lot of people, he greets many of them, and sometimes some of them even come join us. Fedyatin and I are just quiet, for the most part. Whenever Fedyatin drinks a lot of brandy, he starts talking to himself in Russian and waving his arms. When he's in a mood like that, pronouncing in a monotone what I imagine could be magic spells—maybe back where he comes from he really moves people. Here nobody pays any attention. A few days ago we drank some rotgut. Dangerous stuff fortified with rubbing alcohol— we drank it in the shack where Glavina lives. In the part of town called Abyssinia. So there sit we three kings, though we resemble anything but royalty. Glavina waiting for some employment, me waiting for Jaroslav, and Fedyatin waiting for the Savior. Reason enough for us to be together. Otherwise, who am I to sit with? They've been avoiding me. Even Ggb.'s wife, Liselotte, avoided me in a wide arc recently. Somehow I don't really care. I admit, I'd like to see Margerita, just see her. I doubt she'd want to see me. But if she did, she'd probably be under careful guard, with Bussolin and his ladies-in-waiting, and the doctor's formidable wife: You know, sometimes she behaves very strangely.

I think about Margerita a lot. I remember things I didn't even notice before, when we were together.

And so we sit, and drink, and wait.

And drink, and wait, and sit.

And sit, and wait, and drink.

But at some point—and I can't say exactly whether it was in the middle of the day or in the evening—at some point, that same strange sensation that part of the world was sliding somewhere shot forcefully through me. At the moment, I was sober and I knew this wasn't from drinking. I knew that everything—this tavern and the three of us and everything on the table and all these people—everything was slowly and gently moving vaguely downward, toward the river. I was standing on a lawn covered with snow, and beneath my feet the world was gradually, surely moving downward. I was here and on the lawn and in the morgue, all at the same time, and all of it was slipping downhill. I stood up and grabbed on to a door frame. Then I was suddenly outside in the street, and here the world was shoved down tightly around my shoulders. On both sides the facades of the buildings were right up close. The street was running downhill, but I was taking rapid strides uphill, toward Main Square. I could feel I was getting nowhere, that the street was running downhill and that it was slipping out from under my feet so fast that I wasn't going to get anywhere. But then I made it. I stepped out onto that huge square and I could see the hand of the sign of the plague reaching high up into the sky and then slowly beginning to arch back downward toward the pavement. I grabbed on to an iron fence on the other side. I pushed some iron door open and entered a courtyard paved in cut stone. At the far end of the stone court-yard a wooden door stood ajar, and I stepped through it. Suddenly I was standing inside the huge nave of a church.

■ □ ■ □ ■

## 5 7

A FAINT LIGHT SEEPED IN THROUGH WINDOWS SITUATED UNDER the high vaults. The tall, dark figures in some paintings of saints reached from the floor all the way up to the windows under the vaulted ceiling. They were dark and veiled from the feeble and diffuse winter light. I leaned up against a cool pillar and doused my whole face with holy water out of a stone font. The familiar sensation refused to pass. The world's equilibrium had been disturbed, and someplace in the back of my head, in my chest, and in my shoulders—everywhere—I could feel the world stirring and moving, and that dim sensation suffused me with a chilly weakness. I took a step forward, down the middle of the moving church nave. It was sliding forward, now everything was sliding in the direction I was walking, and I grabbed on to a wooden pew, grabbed on to it tightly. When I lifted my eyes, I knew that this was that church, and the whole huge altar strewn with figures, golden carvings, silver clouds, columns, paintings with black backgrounds, and vivid figures floating in a black sky darted out of its mute, pliant repose at me. Way up above was that blue ball. There were figures inclining toward it from all sides, there were infants' heads fixed amid sunbeams, and some small, round windows. The old man with gray hair was shorter than the Son of God carrying the huge cross. The old man had gray hair and was bent over the blue sphere. Here it all was, and it was all so different. The old man with the blue sphere wasn't like the one I remembered. This was no gigan-tic, golden-haired he-man holding a sphere in his hands, making it look light and accessible to anyone who wanted to reach out for it. Just the opposite: It was heavy and unmov-able, and his arms were weak, his body hunched over, his hair gray. I also felt I wouldn't be able to reach for it or lift it, because my hands were holding on tight to the wooden pew. The nave was sliding, the entire church nave was sliding down toward the river, and suddenly I also felt it pitching slightly from side to side. All of the human figures started pitching with it and I could see the sphere shudder up above in the old man's hands. I could see he wasn't going to be able to hold on to it. It slipped out of his hands and dropped very incredibly slowly down onto the floor. It flew past all the pictures, past the black painting and the golden figures, it fell through the windswept skies, past the startled faces of the saints, and in slow motion landed on the floor, bouncing several times high in the air and then finally rolling away down the nave.

I could sense the nave sliding faster and faster, so I lay down on the floor and rolled up into a fetal position. It kept moving and swaying, only now it wasn't just beneath my feet, but it took my whole body with it. When I turned my head to look up, the sphere was back up there again and the old man was bending down over it. Now I could see that it had been dissected and sewn back up again in big, clumsy stitches with black thread from the morgue. Everything was so far up there, while down here below, everything slid inaudibly. Then I saw the smooth face of some man in a black suit who was bending down over me. At first I didn't know if it was Bukovski, or if those were Fedyatin's eyes in that face, but then I realized this was an unfamiliar face.

"Sir," an unfamiliar voice said. "Do you not feel well?"

The voice was coming from far away, and even his body stretched strangely all the way up to the vaults of the sliding church nave. Then I felt the nave come to rest, and the dizzi-ness began to dissipate. His body contracted, and now I felt suffused with a strange emotion, while at the same time something was squeezing around my heart, because I was lying here on the floor, because I was as helpless as a child, because the next time, I would find something, because I understood nothing and could do nothing.

"Sir," the priest said. "Shall I call a doctor?"

The nave came to rest, sliding only very slightly. So slightly that no one could feel it except me.

# 58

AND IT SHALL COME TO PASS IN THAT DAY, THAT THE LIGHT
*shall not be clear, nor dark. But it shall be one day which shall
be known to the Lord, not day, nor night: But it shall come to
pass, that at evening time it shall be light.*

I lay dressed on the bed in some anxious and senseless late-
evening half sleep. Footsteps clattered down the hall and a
woman's voice shouted something. Somewhere in the depths
of the hallway somebody knocked on a door, and I could hear
a male voice answering from inside the room. Then, right outside my door, another woman cried shrilly, "Fire, the whole
mountain's on fire." That cry of hers penetrated the bones and
veins in my body like a razor. It was so powerful that at first I
couldn't get up. For a moment I lay still on the bed and listened to the opening of doors, more and more numerous footsteps and shouts, a babel of voices all around. Then I suddenly
got up and looked at the clock. It was eight-thirty. I put on my
overcoat and stepped briskly out into the hallway. Somebody
in pajamas was running in front of me. He was totally confused, probably just roused out of sleep. At the top of the staircase he stopped and looked all around him. He turned around
and ran back, to fetch his clothes, I imagine.

Outside it was bright. The facade of the building next
door was drenched in a reddish light. People were coming out
of entryways, their overcoats hastily thrown on, some of them
with caps pulled onto their heads, and hurrying across King

Peter Square. Windows opened and isolated shouts vanished among the buildings. Someone walking alongside me was explaining: There's a terrible fire up on Kozjak, the whole mountain's caught fire. How, I thought, could a whole mountain have caught fire in the middle of this wet winter? A crowd of people were standing on a street corner, their agitated voices murmuring indistinguishable words, like some many-headed dragonlike creature. I pushed my way past them into an empty space. A totally illuminated space. Then I caught sight of the horrible fire.

The whole sky to the north was bloodred. An incandescent red glow of gigantic proportions was rolling in from the east. As though we had suddenly gone from night to day, only not a brilliantly sunny day, but one that glowed bloodily. The piercing light was incessantly shifting and moving in enormous waves. It pulsed and billowed and illuminated the landscape beneath it, the pathetically tiny people and their faces filled with terror. *And his brightness was as the light, and beams of light shot forth from his hands. His glory covered the heavens. Before him went the pestilence, and burning coals went forth at his feet.* There was complete quiet as that bloodred, heavenly horror coursed through an unspeakably enormous, empty space, eclipsing stars and covering the clear sky with its streams of light.

The scant clouds were flushed a glowing red, and from heaven to earth the spaces between them shuddered from the radiance of the huge beams rapidly shifting back and forth. I recall it being totally quiet. But others said later that in the background, behind those radiance-swollen clouds, behind the bloodred wall, they had heard a muffled rumbling. Others claimed the earth had shaken and that every movement of that light, stretched across the sky and throbbing like a gigantic organism, was accompanied by gusts of wind so strong that roofs all through town shook at their assault.

Yet the anxious crowd kept endlessly repeating and stubbornly insisting it was some big fire, and people tried to guess where such a terrible blaze could be. Only one person knew from the start that there was no fire, that heavenly forces were on the move, and that people would be petrified with fear in anticipation of what was to come over the world. As I passed from one murmuring group to the next on my way toward Government Bridge, I suddenly saw him. He stood in the middle of the bridge, with a large space around him. People stole fearful glances at the strange man who had cropped up out of some cellar, out of some smoke-filled tavern in the Lent district, and ventured out among the anxious populace. He stood with his face turned toward the fearful glow in the north, focused on something that only he could see amid the bloodred light. Suddenly, Fedyatin clearly spoke some words in Russian. His face was illuminated and transfigured by the wild light that had suddenly risen from beyond the Siberian steppes, and he could see *upon earth the distress of nations, the sea and the waves roaring. . . . And he saw the Son of man coming in a cloud with power and great glory.* From time to time as he spoke, he raised his voice, and I clearly recall him exclaiming: "*Khristos voskres. Voistinu voskres.*" These were signs sent by heaven, *and his brightness was as the light, beams of light shot forth from his hand, for therein lay his hidden power.* Age-old mountains crumbled to dust, the rough places made plain. *The chasm groaned and lifted its hands. . . . He did march through the land in indignation, and shall thresh the nations in anger.* Before him went a consuming fire, and behind him swept a flame that would destroy many countries. He could see the plains of his country all illuminated in this bloodred light, for he knew that it was written: *When these things begin to come to pass, then look up, and lift up your heads, for your redemption draweth nigh.*

By now the crowd was watching the overwhelming heavenly spectacle of the pliancy of matter in silence. The voices guessing at the fire's possible locations were quiet. Some faces were unable to hide their terror. I saw one woman, unable to bear the sign in the sky, flee into her house, sobbing. I saw people praying and others who were silent in their anguish.

Among them were interpreters and jokers. They went from group to group, making a big show of their fake omniscience or crowing their indifference. But the huge heavenly spectacle was also more powerful than they. It impressed itself on people's souls with its intensity, and as the red rays of light flashed across their faces, you could see the terror fetter and menace them. Shadows rapidly passed over the river quietly murmuring between its banks.

Then the light gradually began to fade and the stars came out in the sky again, but the night was darker than before. Silently, or exchanging a few muffled words, people began to part. Fedyatin remained standing all alone out in the middle of the bridge. I went up to him, but his eyes were glowing, as though some of the bloodred light had been trapped in them. He was still staring toward the north, but he silently lowered his arms in front of him. He didn't recognize me. He looked through me while I stood in front of him saying a few calm words.

I left him alone, and when I reached the end of the bridge and looked back, that figure was still standing there motionless, with empty space all around.

I went to my room and lay down on the bed. Outside it had suddenly gotten dead quiet. Not a voice, not a footstep down the sidewalk or the hallway. Nothing. Silence. I closed my eyes and saw the town and its people half-sunken in red. A sharp red light sliced my pupils in two and the images that had collected in them that day were also sliced in two. The people, the bridges, the mountain, the church tower, the lawn, and that sphere in the church—everything was half bloody. Even God the Father of St. Aloysius was swimming in red up to the waist.

That night, people tossed anxiously in their sleep, haunted by the powerful sign in the sky which glowed in their eyes and now in their heads. Even I can feel the anxiousness that's overtaken me. This is no anxiousness that reason can vanquish. It isn't the anxiousness of a wound suffered in love, which time can cure, nor the anxiousness of being awakened early by the music and noise of a brass band and a crowd. It isn't the kind of anxiousness that comes from anything human, thus transient and subject to forgetting. That horrible light stays in the eyes, making the whites bloody and red, whomever you look at. Thus it's an anxiousness that's impossible to dispel. Because it comes from beyond, from the unfathomable. It burrows into a person's cells and rests there. When it awakens, it flutters inside, causing a person to shudder and reel on the edge of the immense abyss he carries within.

■ □ ■ □ ■

# 5 9

BUKOVSKI WILL FINALLY HAVE HIS CHANCE TO SEE A JEW. A living one and a dead one. He'll see a lot of Jews.

In 1944, when Jewish Street is called Allerheiligengasse, but despite all the saints is just as dark and dead-ended as before, Dr. Bukovski will be arrested. One morning two Gestapo men will be waiting for him outside his villa in the Mozartstrasse and will take him in for interrogation. He'll have to answer, because he will have repeatedly given medical supplies to a stranger. During this time Dr. Bukovski will not have changed his scientific opinions, but the methods that will be used to solve the Jewish problem and, ultimately, the Slovene problem in this town—these methods never had and never will have Dr. Bukovski's support. And so, without a word, he'll give medical supplies to that stranger, even though he knows the supplies will go to the Partisans in the Pohorje Mountains. He'll be denounced by his attendant, who handles the business end of things in the morgue. The Gestapo will want to know the name of the stranger, nothing else. Dr. Bukovski won't know the name, because he doesn't know the person. They'll bludgeon and kick him for a week. Then they'll transfer him to Celje, to the prison known as the Old Bucket. There he'll be beaten at greater and shorter intervals for another month, until they send him to Buchenwald. In the autumn of '44 he'll walk through the iron gate topped by the inscription JEDEM DAS SEINE. For a short while he'll work in the quarry, but then, because of his professional background, they'll need him for anatomical chores in the so-called infirmary. There he'll have a chance to put into practice the anthropological knowledge he enjoyed expounding at the physicians' club, or to anyone who would listen. For in the so-called infirmary there, the skulls of Jews and Russians will be collected and sent in tin boxes to the anatomical institute in Strassburg, where they'll be used to scientifically document that particular type of subhuman personified by the Jewish-Bolshevik commissar. No one will know why, but after less than a month of anatomical and taxidermic work, Dr. Bukovski will be shot dead by a drunken SS officer. Probably not without a reason, because everything in this world has its cause and its effect, whether we necessarily understand the connection or not. Relatively well maintained thanks to the infirmary rations, his corpse will be thrown into a big pit. Like logs, Jews starved to death will be thrown over him, their thighs and calves still measuring, on average, about the same in length as they measured in the well-known study by Weisbach, with which he had once been familiar. But their width will measure scarcely more than the width of a Jewish bone. Dr. Weisbach hadn't calculated that width. What's clear is that the pulse of these Jews, whose bodies (1,632mm), thighs (487mm), and calves (196mm) will be falling on top of Dr. Bukovski, will not beat 77 times per minute, just as his will not beat 72 times. None of the pulses there will beat again, ever.

WHEN THE LIGHTS OF THE AURORA BOREALIS START TO FLARE
through the earth's atmosphere, a strange restlessness seizes the
magnetic needles of compasses. According to a scientific study,
the needle begins to shudder fitfully around its north-pointing
position of repose, and then jerkily points first west, then east,
over and over again. At the same time as these magnetic storms,
there are steady magnetic currents which appear in the earth's
crust and can interfere with or even disrupt signals being sent
by wire or cable.

The northern glow that excited and drove the peacefully
slumbering town slightly mad on the evening of January 25,
1938, was not just a thrilling show but an event of global proportions that reached very deep and continued to reverberate
at those depths for some time. An unusual celestial glow, huge
and intensely radiant, appeared all over Central Europe last
evening, the local newspaper reported next morning. People
thought there was a fire somewhere in the distance, and there
were fire alarms in many locales. This exceptionally powerful,
deep and dark red glow was seen not just here but also in Austria, Hungary, Bavaria, and Switzerland—all across the middle
of Europe. This phenomenon is very rare and had not been
seen since 1894. Some scientists ascribe the appearance of this
glow to increased sunspot activity. Last night after nine o'clock
our homeland was shaken by an unusual celestial phenomenon, another newsman reported. From nine until ten o'clock

the sky above Maribor and Styria flared up in a dark red, crimson color. Light rolled across the sky like incandescent clouds, between which rays of light fluttered in broad bands. Everywhere an agitated populace watched this unusual spectacle, which nearly evoked terror. Reports have come from Hungary of similar mass panic, and in Budapest they're saying a piece of the sun has broken loose, which, however, is probably not true. Last night between nine and ten o'clock Senj experienced an hour of acute panic, according to a third report. The sky ignited in a strident red color that illuminated the entire coast and reflected strangely off the sea. The light abated, but then strengthened again, while sharp, gleaming bands like lightning shot across the sky and a muffled drumming like thunder could be heard. Frightened, the populace streamed out of their homes toward the harbor, thinking something terrible had happened. Some fell to their knees and prayed, while others scurried back and forth in fright. All of them expected something even more terrible to happen any instant. The populace has not been able to calm down and is still confusedly trying to determine what it could have been and, more important, what it could mean. And so the reports went on. In one place people tried to save their property, in another they retreated into their houses, here they heard a loud thundering sound, there the sky flared up in total silence. In Jesenice they were convinced Golica and Stol and the whole mountain range must be on fire. In Zagreb they could see something drawing light across the sky. In Bosnia the light peacefully appeared and peacefully disappeared. In Hungary, because of the country's vast flatness, the event panicked the population as the incandescent sky strangely illuminated the entire puszta, from horizon to horizon. In Ljubljana there wasn't a single mention of the whole event, because a thick fog had covered the city, obscuring the sky.

Mr. Jakob Šešerek of St. George on Ščavnica was not nearly as agitated by the strange celestial phenomenon as his neighbors were. It did, however, excite him as an amateur astronomer, and he immediately undertook a complicated drawing, in which he preserved the northern glow for future generations. For him and other amateur scientists, the polar light had no significance so complicated it couldn't be explained. So, over the next few months, various explanations appeared, but common to all of them was the conclusion that the northern glow was almost certainly associated with sunspots. Similarly, they determined that the celestial phenomenon had been accompanied by exceptionally severe disturbances of the earth's magnetic field, as well as strong tellurian currents. At the time of the phenomenon the intensity of cosmic radiation diminished by 6 percent and shortwave radio reception was totally blocked. Thus scientists very quickly refuted the assumption that a piece of the sun had broken off, or that the northern glow above our region had been a fata morgana of normal polar light, or even that it was the result of mass hysteria and mutual hypnosis, a theory favored by adherents of what was then the most widespread science of man's irrational capabilities, occultism. Soon it became clear that something very peculiar had taken place on the sun at that time, that some powerful, elemental events had shaken it. The darker sunspots and the lighter solar flares that surround them, wrote one astronomer, are the visible sign of gigantic storms that originate far deeper within the core and then rush toward the sun's surface in the form of huge, funnel-shaped vortices. Just one of these vortices is large enough to swallow hundreds of earths. Sometimes there are instances when the jaws of one of these spouts is aimed directly at the earth. That's when compass needles on earth start to quiver and the aurora borealis's electric arcs ignite high in the atmosphere. But how very, very far away those storms rage—and how far away our earth is! A 93-million-mile-wide chasm of empty space yawns between them and it. How in the world does the news of those terrible crises on the sun's surface reach us across that broadly yawning void, and how do they cause such powerful reverberations on earth? Events on earth are just a modest accompaniment and faint echo of the powerful cosmic storms that convulse the sun. Like magnetic storms, the aurora borealis is just a distant echo of those gigantic natural events. Scientific studies also speak in detail—albeit broadly hypothetically—of electric currents, of coronas, of precisely calculated hues, they adduce numerous statistics in writing of the altitude of the northern glow, but none of them takes seriously the belief of ancient peoples that the northern lights are a dependable sign of wars, misfortunes, and all manner of human calamity on earth. They don't believe, as the Tungus of eastern Siberia believe, that they are the battle of spirits in the air. They don't believe, as the Baltic peoples do in their sagas, that the northern lights are the reflection of golden shields on which the Valkyries bear fallen warriors into the next world, Valhalla. They don't believe in Saint Paul's epistle to the Ephesians, where he distinctly writes of evil spirits coming from under heaven, of devils that wrestle like flames through the sky in the form of dragons and other monsters. They don't believe, as Luther did, that in those horrible signs and wonders in the sky, in those northern lights, perhaps God's wrath was showing itself too mightily. The scientists don't believe any of this. And yet, in awe, one of them asked: Where is the gigantic cosmic heart that beats on this cycle? And yet they concede sunspots influence people in some strange way that they have yet to investigate and explore properly.

And yet the slumbering town, which the glorious and fearsome celestial phenomenon had illuminated, was restlessly tossing in its sleep this night. The magnetic needles in human cells were shuddering dangerously within the restless, unsteady beating of that gigantic, cosmic heart, of whose whereabouts scientists have no inkling.

The night desk editor stayed awake a good part of the night, collected all the reports, chewed on his pencil, and finally wrote this headline, which appeared in bold type the following day: BLOODRED SKY OVER SLOVENIA.

# 6 1

THE SOUND OF TYPING ON A LATE-MODEL UNDERWOOD WOKE me. I could feel its clear, sharp blows scratching at my skin, trying to unlock my dream. It had something to do with Marjetica, some meandering morning erotic dream. She was here, in this wretched hotel room, or perhaps we were someplace else, amid her oriental rugs, under that lamp. Its fringe cast bands of light across her face as we lay there on the floor. She whispered something, but I couldn't make out a word of it. All this was happening in my room at the same time, with the red glow of the streetlights pouring in. The streetlights are red, I said. Odd color. She didn't reply. The room was full of that red light from the street, and then those mechanical sounds started to rap, more and more loudly and sharply invading my room. Then she spoke, and I can remember her words exactly: Well, now you've roused me but good, haven't you? I memorized that unusual word, because I'd never heard anyone use it that way before. The clear, sharp blows scratched at my skin and my intoxicating dream, finally causing me to wake up with the memory of that word. The restless compass needle spun wildly through my innards for a while longer, until everything gradually calmed down. The dream had been pulled apart and calmed at the same time. The feeble light of a winter morning, all around me my disheveled room, and yet peace. Peace to reflect, peace being chopped to bits by the blows of the typewriter one floor down, where there's some kind of office. In this peace, which resonated all the more clearly, the more distinctly as it was being disrupted by the keys of the Underwood, its slow, uneven blows. . . . In this peace I suddenly had a thought: This is my last chance to leave here. I've been in this town for a month and a half on account of some misunderstanding that I can't figure out. I came here because that's what Jaroslav and I had agreed to. I also came to see the town where I'd spent some of my childhood. To bring back some memento for my parents, to tell them what it's like now in this place where fat beans once grew in the garden, where I trampled some flowers, and where in some church I loudly demanded the ball that saint was holding. To bring back to them in their kitchen, which is almost certainly stuffy now, because they're always cold and they overheat the place; to bring back something they would like. But then I just got stuck out here. Didn't even send any postcards. I'd sent some telegrams to Jaroslav, who'd almost certainly left Trieste long ago. He's with Lenka now, in Vienna, or perhaps he's already back in Switzerland. And I'm still here.

Something truly must have happened that I can't get at with reason. I've traveled for so many years, then suddenly I get off here and stay. Could this have happened anywhere else? I've walked into some trap, gotten entangled with some people, woken up in some pit. And now this really was the last chance for me to break loose and crawl out, and when I take my seat in the train this evening, I'll remember Marjetica and everything that's happened, that tavern where I've spent so many nights—all of it will be just dreams. All those faces will flash past my eyes and get buried under the rumbling of the train as it races north toward Vienna. I got up and started quickly to straighten the room. I threw everything I could lay my hands on into my suitcase. I threw some dirty underwear straight into the wastebasket. I splashed cold water on my face. Only at that point did I get dressed and sit down on the bed.

For a long time I stared at my leather suitcase.

■ □ ■ □ ■

# 6 2

FOR THE PAST FEW DAYS, GIANTS HAVE BEEN MAKING A COMMO-
tion around town. Yesterday they charged into the tavern, too.
They were dressed in furs and they had big bells attached to
their waists. They cavorted around wildly, making me really
anxious when they started waving those hedgehog sticks of
theirs over our heads. They've come from the Drava and Ptuj
lowlands in the time just before Lent, harbingers of spring.
They rampage and run around endlessly, until they actually
start getting a little slaphappy under those masks of theirs.
Then they take off their huge, horned masks. Then they look
like some antediluvian creatures with huge bodies and tiny
heads. Stumpy, tanned faces. They have kerchiefs wrapped
around their heads. They sweat, and gulp down big glasses of
wine. Runners, they call them here, shadowy pagan phantoms
that have emerged from their lowlands and encroach on the
city. I thought about how those little heads under those terrify-
ing giant masks, especially with a hedgehog stick in hand,
must conceal really small and really dangerous, wicked
thoughts. Especially when they're a little slaphappy. But then,
my head is no better off. As one of the runners put his mask
back on, I noticed that his eyes were totally red. Another victim with the imprint of the northern lights in his eyes.

I paid for my glass of wine with money that I'd borrowed
from the two blossoms, G. and K., and followed the cavorting,
jangling giants out into the street. For a while I watched a knot

of people who had gathered around them, then I was simply swept away to the quiet northern end of town. I walked beneath their lighted windows, where that very minute over tea and pastries they were telling some new tale of the occult, or possibly discussing municipal, national, European, world politics. They were probably also talking about the hotel in Vienna that burned down. In the morning I'd been to the post office. Nothing. Only my friend, the postal clerk, who looks at me as though I were a different person. She shakes her head reluctantly. She doesn't smile and show her white teeth anymore. Suddenly I thought that perhaps something had happened in Trieste or Vienna. It's been ages since I'd read a newspaper, ages since I'd associated with people who report fresh news from the papers and radio to each other every evening. I went to the public library. I was surprised. In Vienna a hotel had burned down and in Austria incredible political machinations were under way. What if Jaroslav was in that hotel? Was he trampled by a mob? Did some stray bullet hit him? I also found something for Fedyatin. In his country various politicians, ambassadors, generals, and so on are being condemned to death and immediately shot or hanged.

I sat in a park for a long time without a single thought. A warm February wind was melting the snow, producing gurgling streams this evening, too.

I told Fedyatin about what I'd read. I could have sworn he chortled under his beard. Or maybe that's just how I perceived it through my warm, brandy-induced fog. I told Glavina that all hell had broken loose in Austria and that I wasn't going back there anymore, because hotels were burning down and mobs could trample you underfoot. Glavina said he didn't give a shit. Germans, Jews, Slovenes, he didn't give a shit for any of them. They eat like pigs, they drink, they drive around in their automobiles and go whoring with those sweet-smelling women in their silk underwear. And what am I supposed to do? Jerk off? he shouted, as even more blood rushed into his raw-skinned face. A thin, silent fellow was sitting beside him. This young man, Poldi Markoni, drank little, very little, and he behaved very distrustfully toward me. "Can't you find any whores at all?" finally came the question from this silent fellow, Poldi Markoni, with sunken cheeks and smooth eyebrows that were scarcely visible under the yellow lamps muffled in clouds of smoke. Glavina doesn't care for hookers who don't wash and who stink from the last guy. More and more blood rushed into Glavina's face. The blood seeped out through his abrasions, with little red droplets oozing out, just as little droplets of sweat might ooze out. He and the thin guy with no eyebrows have cooked something up, for sure they have. The thin guy didn't drink anything, while I drank a lot. I drank a lot, and I could tell they were cooking something up and I could see the drops of blood seeping out through Glavina's scraped, shaven skin and that they both had red eyes. They had that glow in their eyes and no matter who you looked at, they all had those eyes, like Angora rabbits'. All these people have that bloodred reflection in their eyes and I probably have eyes like that, too.

I walked across Government Bridge and stumbled into some rivulets of melted snow that were dribbling across the pavement. I gazed at the river and thought again about sliding into it, letting its muddy waters carry me on their gentle waves neatly down into the Black Sea, or wherever it flows. But there's a whole clammy zoo of fish down in there.

■ □ ■ □ ■

# 63

AT FIRST FEDYATIN AND I DRANK DOWN IN THE LENT DISTRICT.
Actually, only I drank, while Fedyatin cast querying looks
around the room, because there was a lot of noise that night.
The singing and the pounding on tables between puddles of
wine shining dimly and dribbling over the sides began early
that evening. Fedyatin's eyes shone feverishly, his pupils dancing back and forth, as though he took fright at every new
ghost that walked into the place. Each time, the men guf-
fawed loudly and those whores with them squealed so much
that it was a delight whenever some pirate or monk or death
with scythe, cloaked in white sheets, walked in. The most
laughter was provoked by a group of nuns that suddenly
materialized among the men, sat on their laps, and reached
for their glasses. The men roared with enthusiasm, slapping
the nuns on their rears, while the nuns responded by stroking
the men's necks and occasionally even reaching under a shirt
or two. They drank out of huge glasses, with drink spilling
out over their nuns' habits. Then the nuns gathered, whispered something to one another, and headed toward the door.
At the door they stopped and all of them lifted their skirts at
the same time, revealing knobby, hairy men's legs underneath.
This provoked such an uproar that you couldn't hear who was
shouting what. One little drunk who had been following one
of the nuns around the room with a liter of wine in hand,
pouring it out for her and patting her on the rear, suddenly

lost his composure. All the others were roaring with laughter at him, and he lost all self-control. He lunged at the nun with his fists, but the men in nuns' habits repulsed him so forcefully that he went skidding prone across the floor. The nuns vanished in an instant, but the little fellow went running to the door and shouted after them into the night. I watched Fedyatin's nervous eyes amid the chaos and all the images, which behind that high forehead of his were evoking who knows what, to give him such nervous eyes. I left him alone. In any case, Fedyatin doesn't care if he's alone or with people, on the street or in a tavern, outside an Orthodox church or at the railway station watching the trains. He sees everything, and he sees it in his own way.

The streets were crowded with masqueraders, drunk people, laughing faces. I tried to avoid these characters, because I had the feeling some of them could get aggressive behind those masks of theirs. Especially the executioner holstering an ax and carrying a whip in hand. He would snap and crack the whip at people's feet, causing them to jump back. He chased one woman into an entryway, and I think that earlier he had even given her legs a good lashing. She came back out with her hands covering her face. She was probably crying.

Through the windows of Tscheligi's Restaurant you could hear an accordion and drawn-out singing. I went inside. The place was so smoky and saturated with the warmth of human bodies that I was disgusted by the wine I managed to wrangle for myself at the bar. I think I spent the next hour or two roaming the city in the direction of Station Street, where a huge, stuffed Joseph Vissarionovich collided with me. In his hand he had a bottle with VOTKA printed on it. On Franciscan Street some women surrounded me and made all kinds of fun of the fact I was alone. And I really was damned alone in the midst of all this gobbledygook. Suddenly it occurred to me that the engineer's crowd was probably at the Grand Café. For a long time I stood on Main Square and looked up to where the shadows were shifting energetically back and forth, as though some other world were concealed there. I looked at my watch. It was around eleven.

I instantly made a decision. I'd go up there. I knew this was a totally insane idea and that I had absolutely nothing in common with those people anymore. I also knew it wouldn't be good if I went up there, that nothing good would come of it. But some things in life happen all by themselves, and then there's no stopping them.

There was a crowd at the entrance. A doorman in livery was holding back people who were pushing to get in. It's not at all clear to me why he let some of them inside but not others. Did he know them? When I jostled my way into his vicinity, he gave me such a look from head to toe that there really wasn't any more hope. I fumbled through my pockets, trying to find some money to give him for a bribe. There was very little in my pockets, woefully little. A gnawing reproach shot through me—why hadn't I taken that Judas money from REM? But before I could muster all my dinar notes, some group left the place, the door opened wide, and the doorman rudely shoved me away. Feminine laughter went jingling past me and there was a strong scent of perfume.

I stepped aside and listened to the doorman quarreling with the masqueraders. But everything was so predetermined that, hope or no hope, I had to get inside, and what was meant to happen that night happened.

A nun came running across Main Square. One of the group from the Lent district. She was holding her skirt up, the more easily to negotiate in long strides the ground swaying underfoot. A moment later I caught sight of some gendarmes who were racing across Government Bridge. Arms wide outstretched, they were running after the nun and calling out halt, stop, or something like that. The nun stopped for a second, and though she was obviously drunk, she confounded them by making catlike leaps to the right and left, and then she dashed straight toward us. She tripped on the edge of the sidewalk and went flying into the wall of the building. One of the gendarmes came racing after her, while the others stopped, as though to wait and see how the chase was going to finish. Then some in the group called out: Leave that one, let him be. The gendarme hesitated for a moment, then swiftly turned around and ran after the others, who were already racing toward Gosposka Street, where they vanished. The nun got up quickly and walked determinedly to the door. There's a fight outside the Central, she said in a deep voice. Our hawks are whipping the Kulturbund.

She shoved the doorman aside, who shouted something after her; then he too disappeared somewhere inside. The masqueraders made the most of the opportunity and they were suddenly all inside. They drew me along with them, although at this point I no longer had any idea where I was going or what I had to do up there.

■ □ ■ □ ■

# 6 4

I WENT UP TO THE CLOAKROOM, THOUGH I DIDN'T HAVE ANY-
thing to turn in. They were selling ribbons, confetti, and that
sort of thing there. I bought a pirate's eyepatch for myself and
put it on.

Among all the Cupids, cats, Arabs, chimney sweeps, Indians, Othellos, Spanish knights, and heroes from every con-
ceivable operetta and tragedy, mine was the only really original mask. The mask of a drunken, grimy, lonely Erdman with
a black eyepatch and confetti stuck in his hair. Some ostrich
kept sprinkling it onto me, a big fellow dressed in a ridiculous
costume with long ostrich feathers and material on the sides,
and a long neck that stretched from somewhere on his back
up over his head. He was drunk and standing behind me
when I leaned up against the bar, and with a silly smile on his
face he kept sprinkling that confetti on my head.

I drank a glass of wine and then another. Waiters and
women who kept rubbing up against me with their soft
breasts kept shoving me away. The ostrich shoved me away. It
seemed as though everyone was just shoving me away from
that bar. I had to grab on to it tightly, and suddenly I felt
warm and pleasant in the midst of that crazy, jostling sea of
humanity. I tried to spot them. They weren't in the main hall.
None of the dancers was wearing a mask that was reminiscent
of anyone in their group. Actually, my gaze shifting from face
to face, from one grotesque to the next, from one beauty to

the next, was in search of just her. I was trying to find only Marjetica, and I have no idea what moved me to search for her with all my being and find her at any cost.

Then, after a while, I spotted Baldy. He was wearing an unbuttoned white shirt with ribbons draped around it, and right in the middle of the bald spot on top of his head he was wearing a red nose. While dancing he must have run out of breath and pushed it off his face up onto the top of his head, so he had a big red honker up there. That nose was sticking out of his head like some big, fat, wrung-out male organ.

I wanted to go up to him and say something totally normal, Where are the others, where are the ladies, or something like that, as though there were no gulf between us. I'm positive that's exactly what I planned to do, but just at that moment the nun materialized before me again. Her masculine face was framed by her white wimple, scratched and with some dried blood on it from her tumble.

"Why do we hawks work out, if it's not to clobber Germans? We really whipped them," he was saying, possibly to me. "We gave it to the Krauts, we let 'em have it good. But I'm not spending the night in the Graf," he was saying to anyone who would listen. "I know when it's time to pick up and run. I've spent a night there before, and let me tell you, the bunks are hard and the food's no good. The cops aren't ever gonna get me in the Graf again."

When the nun with the heart of a hawk had vanished, arm in arm with the ostrich, and I had an unobstructed view of the dance floor again, all I managed to see was Baldy with the wrung-out, red penis on his head wending his way toward the bar.

So that's where they were. Without a thought, I picked up my glass and shoved my way toward the bar. Outside the door the crowd was even worse. People were craning their necks and looking inside. Somehow I managed to squeeze inside, at the cost of every last drop of my wine, which I spilled on some Arab's robes. Inside it was so dark I couldn't see anything at first. Then the place brightened, and a tall flame leaped toward the ceiling. Ooohh, the rubberneckers at the door exclaimed. An instant later a fire-eater had swallowed all that light, and the exclamations of wonder turned into energetic applause. He took a deep bow and his half-naked assistant handed him a long dagger. He showed it all around, and by now I could make out his face sufficiently to see that he was smiling and winking at the ladies. He was going to swallow that dagger, too.

They were all there. At first I caught sight of Baldy, who still had the honker on his head. Bussolin was dressed all in black as some elegant Zorro or whatever. The engineer sat there in his jacket with his tie loosened and a straw hat on his head. One of the ladies was obviously a rabbit, the second was sweating under an enormous wig, and the third was squealing and applauding. She wasn't there.

Because I'd irrevocably decided to go sit at their table, and since I couldn't do it with an empty glass, I swapped my empty glass for a full one at the first table I passed, while Turban was swallowing his dagger. There was no alternative. I couldn't sit down and let them pour my wine like they'd done for the hired hand out in the engineer's vineyards. Several chairs were unoccupied, and one of them had to be Marjeta's. They didn't even notice when I sat down, because Turban was starting some new stunt and their eyes were fixed on his charming smile. I watched their enchanted faces and thought about how they were going to change when they finally saw the guy with the eyepatch sitting at their table.

And change they did. Squirrelly was the first to notice me. I didn't know whose she was, but I was pretty sure this was the first time I'd seen her. I was sitting at the end of the long table, with them sitting on both sides, their faces turned toward the performer. Most of the men were sitting on the other side, which meant they had to turn away from the table in order to watch the performance. She probably thought she wasn't seeing straight. She looked at Turban and then at me again, and then her expression hardened. I could see her nervously twisting the squirrel's tail that lay across her legs. With one knee she nudged her neighbor, presumably Baldy's wife, who didn't respond at first, but then leaned over toward her. Squirrelly whispered something to her and pointed in my direction with the hand that held the squirrel's tail. The second lady refused to be shocked. I caught her fixed gaze, which bored into the air in front of her. The look on her face was a mixture of anger and an expressive how-dare-he! The performer had finished, and he and the half-naked woman were bowing and thanking the crowd for their applause and their cheers, until finally to everyone's delight he took the turban off his head, freeing the black hair which fell across his face, and he set it on the head of a woman sitting at the nearest table. The oily hair stuck to his sweaty forehead and he bowed in rapturous gratitude for the renewed applause. And at this point there was a new, still more surprising trick in store for those seated at the engineer's table.

The men slowly began turning their chairs back toward the table and, one after the other, discovered me there. Baldy's wife nodded, tight-lipped and meaningfully, while Squirrelly quickly and with urgent gestures explained to some ancient Greek or Roman lady about me. Gravely, the engineer poured himself some wine. Baldy adjusted the honker on his head, while Bussolin's face flushed red with anger and surprise.

Elsewhere there was a steady commotion of exclamations and laughter, but at this table there was dead silence for quite a space. I can recall every detail and every gesture. The whole evening is still vividly before my eyes, though I wasn't exactly sober. Indeed, if I'd been sober, I almost certainly wouldn't have done anything like this. I expected what was going to happen, but they didn't. My gaze wandered from face to face, trying to engage each person's eyes, to the extent they didn't nervously evade me.

Bussolin was the first to pull himself together. He stood up like a true avenging Zorro and prepared to say something. At that instant some cuddly little animal scampered up to the table, but when it saw all those taciturn people and Bussolin's face, all red and tense as it got ready to perform, it grimaced and scurried away.

But before Bussolin managed to compose his speech, the engineer tugged at his sleeve.

"No scenes, please," he ordered. "Sit down."

Bussolin sat down and with an agitated gesture poured himself a glass of wine. The hand holding his glass was shaking slightly.

"We have not closed our door to anyone who wants to come into our house," Franjo Samsa said proudly.

A moment later he corrected himself.

"What I mean is, we haven't denied anyone hospitality at our table." He cast a meaningful look at those present around the table and added with particular emphasis, "No matter how undesirable a guest it is."

They were still silent. Then Bukovski came to. He refused to have his mood spoiled. He pulled the honker back down over his nose and leaned toward me: "Boogah, boogah!" He really was funny and everybody laughed. Except for me, of course.

They all started chatting excitedly about Turban's feats. Only Bussolin remained silent and absorbed in thought.

Baldy was in such a good mood that it was only a matter of time before he became totally reconciled to my presence. Now and then I caught some remark or other of his made at my expense, but they all seemed pretty acceptable. He was trying to bring out the humorous side of it all. Like this, for instance: This blackguard has come to steal our prettiest girl. It didn't seem funny to me, or to Bussolin. But the engineer laughed, since what else could he do?

■ □ ■ □ ■

## 6 5

THEN TWO THINGS HAPPENED AT ONCE. THE ORCHESTRA IN the hall played a fanfare, the roar of human voices subsided, and you could hear a voice that was announcing "a very entertaining, if no longer very timely, performance." At the same moment, I saw Squirrelly's horrified look and the grim face of the avenging Zorro, which had completely stiffened. I knew she was coming. She stood behind Bussolin's back. She was wearing a Harlequin costume with a ruffled collar and some kind of cap that didn't match. She was all silken and beautiful. I knew how her hair smelled. I could feel my hands dampen as I broke out in a cold sweat. She also stood there as though she'd been fixed to the floor. The master of ceremonies came into our area and announced: See the Abyssinian Emperor and the Leader of Rome in an amusing performance! I heard the raucous shifting of chairs and could feel the people shoving their way past me—but the whole time, all I could see was her, just her. I don't know at what point I signaled to her to come sit in the empty chair next to me—whether it was when Samsa was still there, or later, when we were left alone. The bar cleared out in a minute, and in the entire place only we remained: she, Bussolin, and I. There was probably also some drunk asleep in a corner somewhere, but I had the feeling that in the whole world there were only the three of us. Bussolin stubbornly stayed where he was. He sat there like a stubborn child who's had something taken away from him, or been wrongfully punished. She was beside me, right next to me, looking at her glass. Silence. All three of us were silent. I noticed that the engineer hadn't gone into the main hall. He was standing in the doorway, not paying the least attention to us. But he was also in the room with all his being. From time to time a deafening laughter invaded the silence. You could hear parts of speeches and individual words: family of nations, Italian empire, *giovinezza, giovinezza,* Chamberlain, our tank battalions, our bow-and-arrow brigades, and the like. On the stage the Abyssinian Emperor and the Leader of Rome were playing the fools.

Then, in a silence between two waves of wild laughter, Marjetica said, "Pour me some wine."

I was about to get up and fetch her a glass, but she reached out an arm and held me back. She pointed to an empty glass in front of her that somebody had already drunk from.

I poured her some wine. She drank half of it and then pushed the glass toward me. Bussolin's face twitched—I saw that clearly. I finished the wine that was left in her glass.

Then things proceeded very quickly. Revelry broke out in the hall. You could hear laughter and shouts, the shoving of chairs. A number of people came laughing back into the bar. A burly, fat, close-shaven fellow in a black shirt, riding breeches, and boots came running in through the door—he didn't look a bit like Mussolini—and behind him a little guy in a beard and an unmistakable Haile Selassie wig. A gaudily gotten up, high-spirited crowd came racing in behind them. The fat man stopped next to my chair. I could hear him panting and I could see the drenched underarms of his shirt. With energetic shouts, the people were encouraging little Haile Selassie, who set off in pursuit of the fat Duce. The Leader of Rome over-turned several chairs and vanished through the door. With great dignity, and laughing, the little guy slowly walked after him. The play was drawing to a close. The bar was filling up again. Everyone coming back to the engineer's table, each and every one of them, turned to look at us curiously. Casually, and laughing, but in a way that said Now wasn't that funny, but here something serious is taking place.

And it really was. The band struck up a slow tune and several couples rose immediately. At our table everyone was waiting to see what would happen. Bussolin was engaged in a grim struggle with himself. The engineer was talking to Baldy, but he seemed a little worried to me. I may be mistaken, but I thought I heard a male voice—I don't know if it was Baldy's or the engineer's—saying *Sure, sure, but she's drunk far too much.* I stood and she automatically got up, too. I stepped aside and followed her, and I had the impression that everyone coming in our direction stepped aside for us. I wasn't looking at anyone anymore and I have no idea what happened back there after this. We stepped out onto the dance floor and danced—for a long time we danced. She leaned her head on my shoulder. I could feel her body willingly submit in my arms, I could feel her thighs, and, with each dance step, the empty space between them. For a short moment I saw Baldy spinning Squirrelly a little too fast, I caught the worried, confused look on his face, and that's all I remember. Just as I memorized every gesture anyone made around that electrified table, so I have absolutely no memory of what happened around us as we danced. I'm convinced it was the same for her. We didn't say a word. We moved slowly, listening to Russian love songs or some such, if we listened to anything at all. I can still hear the only words that she whispered in my ear while we danced. No—that she breathed in my ear. In her throaty voice she breathed: Why did you come, why did you come, you shouldn't have come, don't you know? I had one more lucid moment, right at the end, before we left. Damned slyly and observantly I looked around, searching for familiar faces. I made the most of that moment. I was suddenly calm, clear-headed, and sober. I did that wholly on purpose and premeditatedly. I made sure that none of them were there. They were probably all still sitting at the table and waiting for us to return. But we weren't going to return, my friends, we were leaving that instant. I pulled her along after me. She probably thought we were stepping outside for some air. She followed me. We went down the stairs and we were suddenly outside, with several bums leaning against the doorway. I'd completely forgotten that I probably didn't look much better than them myself. I kissed her on the hair, the cheeks, the lips, in front of everybody. Somebody said something rude, and somebody else tittered. I grabbed her hand and pulled her along, without knowing where I planned to take her; I took her toward the bridge. It was at that point that she came to. My coat, she said, it's in the cloakroom. I knew she was never going to come back if she went for that coat. I knew she'd stand outside the cloakroom, that she'd lean against the counter and think, and that she'd finally go back where she belonged. Leave it, I said. I took my jacket off and put it over her shoulders.

"I have to," she said. "I have to do it."

■ □ ■ □ ■

# 66

SHE STOOD THERE SHIVERING AND THAT "HAVE TO" SOUNDED like it meant something completely different. We were at the edge of the bridge. She bent out over the railing and stayed leaning against it for some time. I was freezing to death and I knew that I had to do something, otherwise the whole thing would be ruined. I had to reinforce that "have to" of hers with some wonderful word or gesture.

But then she suddenly turned around, looked at me smilingly, and then burst out in atypical, slightly nervous laughter.

"Look at you," she said. "I'm afraid."

I fingered the black eyepatch on my face and bared my teeth. I howled like a wolf and then all the way across the bridge I kept wailing like an idiot, so that what few passersby there were kept pausing and looking back at us. But at King Peter Square her mood shifted again. She stopped like a stubborn mule and refused to go on. I couldn't understand what was wrong with her, because she was also refusing to speak. I stroked her and whispered something encouraging in her ear. Her ears twitched, but she refused to go on.

Then she looked at me forlornly and said she wouldn't go there.

Wouldn't go where?

There, to my room. She wouldn't go to the Hotel Dvor. She'd feel like a real whore there, she said after a bit. That's what I am, isn't it? A whore?

"You're my sweetheart," I said.

"I'm afraid," she said.

She leaned against the entryway of that tall building and looked at me for a long time.

"What's come over you?" she said.

"I'm in love," I said in total seriousness. "Head over heels."

"Too late."

Yes, that's what she said: Too late. When was soon enough, in her opinion? And what does it look like when it's soon enough? And forever? So that you can become a friend of the family, a Bussolin?

I didn't say any of that. I was in despair. I really do love her and I wanted to have her and that's why I despaired. Because all the signs were that now she was going to say, Too late, that she would repeat this again, shrug off my jacket with a lovely gesture, and walk back across the bridge, back to her people.

Then I had an idea. A strange idea, a dangerous idea, but at that moment just an idea. I don't even know how I could have conceived an idea like that. Maybe because of the Abyssinian Emperor, or because I was desperately searching my memory for all the places in this town where I could take her.

"All right," I said. "We won't go to the hotel. We'll go someplace you've never been before, where no one knows you. We'll go to Abyssinia."

"Abyssinia?"

"That's right."

"To those shacks?"

This surprised her. It was something different. It was *mysterious*.

"I'm so silly," she said sadly. "I'm going to just up and go to Abyssinia.

"Let's go to Abyssinia," she said, and then as we walked she repeated the word. Abyssinia, Abyssinia. She walked under cover of its mysterious sound. "But Abyssinia's a long way off," she said after a few steps. "Don't you have a car?"

"No cars in Abyssinia," I said. "You can only go there on foot."

The trip to Abyssinia took a long time. Every twenty or thirty steps, we had to stop. Each time, she tugged on my sleeve, looked at me, and uttered something like this:

"Such a young, such a capable man, and he doesn't even have a car."

And then again:

"You don't even have a bicycle."

"Do you know what you are? You're an international fraud and a cheat. You've fooled all of us. But you've broken my heart."

Just before we got to Abyssinia, she started to hiccup. She was hiccuping uncontrollably, and I had to guess when she was going to hiccup next.

We walked past gardens and finally wound up amid those shacks, the barely habitable dwellings of all poor people. We were spattered with mud up to our knees as we walked through the puddles, because there were no lights there. Every now and then the moon shone forth from behind the clouds, revealing the land of Abyssinia to us.

■ □ ■ □ ■

# 67

IT WAS WELL PAST MIDNIGHT WHEN WE REACHED GLAVINA'S shanty, which smelled of sewage and urine. As I walked up to a window, she slid on something slippery—some garbage or whatever—and she clutched at me. Glavina's lodgings were a curious cross of wood and bricks, the remains of railway cars, and cardboard that he'd stuffed into the window frames. I pounded on the wall with my fist, and some lamp or other went on in the next building. My Harlequin was shivering there on the muddy pathway with my jacket over her shoulders and shifting from one foot to the other. I banged again and somebody yelled furiously from the window of the neighboring building, Quiet out there, for Chrissake, or something like that. Inside I could hear a bed squeak and then Glavina poked his nose out the door.

"It's me," I whispered.

"Who've you got out there?" he said out loud, because he didn't understand why anyone would have to whisper here.

"You can see," I said nervously. "We need a place for the night."

He went back inside and I could hear him grumbling. I think he made his bed and hid his dishes. Then he came out, wrapped in a blanket, and stepped through the puddles on tiptoe. He went up to Marjetica and inspected her.

"You and your masquerades," he grumbled, and vanished into the darkness.

When we were inside, I could hear him banging on a neighbor's door. He'd left us a lamp and a bottle on the table.

"It's chilly in Abyssinia," Marjetica said. "I'll catch a cold."

I think she was starting to feel sorry for herself. But there really was a draft coming through the gaps where Glavina had done a poor job of shoving in the cardboard.

"Don't worry," I said. "We'll warm this Abyssinia right up." I poured out a glass and sipped the liquid in it. It was rotgut. "The Abyssinian Emperor offers you the very finest from his cellars," I said as I grotesquely mimicked Selassie.

She drank a little of it through chattering teeth and said that she knew this drink, that it gave you a headache, and that it made people behave rudely.

She was losing her sense of humor. She feared that she might have made a mistake. I put my arms around her and felt her resisting me. I took the glass out of her hands. We lay down fully dressed and covered ourselves with the only blanket left on the bed. I stroked her hair. I kissed her hair, her eyes, mouth, neck, breasts. My hands were shaking. I was sick with desire and the closeness of her. But I love this woman, I thought. Something must be happening to me to send these damned jitters up and down my body.

Maybe it was the cold. Maybe it was because she was so different. She couldn't. She unfastened the ruffled collar and threw it on the floor. My cap, she said, where did I lose my cap? I unfastened her silk blouse and stroked her breasts. We struggled to get that clown costume off her. I started kissing her, all of her, awakening her body to warmth and to life.

There was a sound as if someone had coughed, as if there were a room on the other side of the wall and someone in it had coughed. She rose up on both elbows and listened.

"There's nobody there," I said.

"Yes, there is," she said.

We lay back and stared into the dark. Here was the body of the woman I loved and I couldn't get close to her. Her cool, silken skin, the cold tips of her breasts, her hand which I'd touched. All that was here and all of it devoid of love.

I got up, poured out a glass, and offered it to her.

"I can't drink," she said. I emptied the glass of rotgut, which gives you a headache and makes you behave rudely. She grabbed my wrist and kissed my hand over and over. She stroked my face and reached under my shirt and then I could feel her pulse beating. I could feel that her lips were suddenly warm, that her body could move, that she was rapidly freeing herself of those silken garments, that now she could. Now my sweetheart could.

Could she make her heart and pulse beat faster, lose her head completely, and whisper something in my ear and moan and finally not know where she was?

She could. If she loved me, then she could.

She sighed for a while longer, half asleep. I edged her head onto my chest and stroked her hair. It was just like in that empty apartment, where the wind assaulted the wooden walkway. She began to breathe evenly. I listened to her breathing and didn't move. Then the weird masks I'd seen that evening paraded before my eyes. I don't know if I was asleep or if this happened while I was awake, but somebody bent over us and sprinkled confetti over our bodies. Somebody was grinning at us grotesquely with eyes that were nothing but brown, chopped-up little pupils, spinning pupils, and somebody said: Boogah, boogah, sure, sure, but she's drunk far too much. I shuddered and opened my eyes. She turned in her sleep and moaned oddly. Then, in her sleep, she said very quietly, "I'm afraid."

I covered her with my jacket, so that it would be like it was when the wind sang its strange, drawn-out songs through the crowns of the pines in the Pohorje and she buried her head under her pillow, so as not to hear anything until she fell asleep. Now she slept.

■ □ ■ □ ■

# 6 8

LATE IN THE AFTERNOON OF THE SATURDAY BEFORE THE START of Lent, Ivan Glavina and Leopold Markoni Jr. visited an acquaintance of Glavina's in an apartment one entered straight off of Barracks Square. Glavina's acquaintance was a peddler who sold his knickknacks at local village fairs, but most often in the market on nearby Vodnik Square. On this day he'd closed his stand and had put away all the masks, confetti, ribbons, brass horns, and whistles—things that no one would care about anymore when Ash Wednesday came. For a while the two of them sat there, teasing the old peddler and calling him a Jewish leech. Out on Barracks Square you could hear the early-bird revelers singing and women squealing, and now and then some elongated mask from the neighborhood would appear at the door. The residents of the Lent district celebrated their Carnival in the streets, roaming from tavern to tavern and drumming on the front doors of houses as though they had nowhere to stay.

"And here we just sit," Markoni said. "But we can't just keep sitting." He suggested that they dress up. Glavina wasn't especially keen on this idea; it was just too stupid for everyone to go crazy all at the same time and behave like silly, crazy people. Markoni suggested they dress up and walk around town for a while—say, up in the vicinity of his father's store. This struck Glavina as a more interesting idea—to go give the old wine merchant a little scare: Ggb., REM, walking through his vineyards as though those vineyards were his domain and those peasant workers his children. They turned their over-coats inside out and put on identical masks with red cheek-bones, a puckered forehead, and a drooping mustache.

"Wearing a mask like this," Markoni said, grabbing the ped-dler by the collar of his jacket, "you can be a completely differ-ent person." The peddler shook himself free.

But Glavina said, "That's bullshit. If you ain't got the balls without a mask, then you ain't got 'em with one."

"Oh," Markoni said, "I'd have them without the mask, too."

"Bullshit," Glavina said. "Like hell you would."

Markoni Jr. admired Glavina. He was raucous, he spoke loftily of women and gentlefolk, standing at a bar he could lift you up on his shoulders whenever he felt like it, he was strong and insolent. He had all the traits that Markoni wished he had, but that always turned against him whenever he tried to realize them. Glavina also had something in him that Markoni knew very well: hatred. Glavina knew how to hate superbly, better than all his teachers and mentors. The hatred that had satu-rated young Markoni in the form of sermons about German cultural space, about the commandments of German blood, and about loyalty had been demarcated on all sides by disci-pline, by fathers, teachers, and camp commanders. But Glav-ina knew how to hate everyone equally, and for no reason. In a very short time Markoni and Glavina had become terribly close. They had something in common, even though Markoni wore a pressed, striped suit and a green trench coat, and car-ried a silver cigarette case, and even though all Glavina had was rotgut in dirty bottles down there in Abyssinia. The hatred that had been cultivated in Markoni at camping retreats spon-sored by the Junior League of the Kulturbund was in Glavina's blood. A natural-born talent, so to speak.

They climbed up a narrow alleyway and came out onto Carinthia Street, and then in the City Restaurant they lifted their masks just enough for each of them to toss down a glass of wine. They reached the Markoni store just as a salesclerk was getting ready to pull down the iron shutters.

REM was standing at the counter, talking with his manager. A short while before, he had suggested they close early that day.

"People have gone out of their minds, wearing those masks," he said. "And we'll probably get a stone or two thrown at the storefront."

At that instant, two identical faces appeared outside the glass door. The manager nodded toward them. REM glanced in that direction and indignantly turned his back to the door. He could feel the two masks were still there, staring at his back. He could read this in the eyes of the manager, who was looking toward the door and waiting for the two masks to leave. The manager angrily waved his hand. This didn't frighten the masks; quite the opposite—the two long faces with red cheekbones and droopy mustaches started to bang against the pane of glass. This was too much for REM's sense of decorum. He walked over to the door to call his clerk or even to whisk these two impudent fellows out the door—or, rather, away from it. But now the door was opening and one of the two masks began snarling at him, causing him to flinch. Then the snarling mask started to pull the mustachioed, red-cheeked disguise off its head, to reveal the grinning, snarling, dark face of Leopold Markoni Jr. REM angrily shook his head.

"What kind of silliness is this?" he said. "Don't you have anything better to do?" He was in a very bad mood, disappointed at his grown son's childish behavior.

"Turn your coat right side out, Poldi," he said. "And cut that out. It's beneath a serious person's dignity."

At this, the other one, his son's colleague, came right up close to him, took his mask off, and exhaled heavily, producing a strong odor of cheap wine and bad personal hygiene.

REM involuntarily took a step back. A sharp pain coursed through his chest, and he could feel the blood drain from his head, his temples go cold, and cold drops break out on his forehead. This wide head with the short forehead on a fat neck, this alcoholic stench, this crumpled lining of an overcoat turned inside out, covered with sweat stains and who knew what else, even with holes and burn marks in places—in an instant all of this overwhelmingly reminded Leopold Markoni Sr. of something that he preferred not to remember.

Just this kind of boorish head, this raw face, just this kind of farmhand stinking of manure, who dared to put on a crumpled uniform, just that kind of person, that very person responsible for his humiliation so long ago was standing here in front of him. REM went so pale that his manager worried for him. REM leaned against the counter with one arm and tried with all his mighty will to subdue the terrible agitation that had so overcome him he had been powerless for a moment. Then he collected himself and realized he was somewhere else, in his store, and that this was nothing more than a bad joke. Out of the corner of his eye he caught the surprised look on his clerk's face as he came in the door. And then he turned to his son, who was blood of his blood and had befriended this kind of person.

"Who is this person?" he asked in a hoarse voice.

"Who who?" Leopold Markoni Jr. answered. "He's my friend, that's who."

This person, who was mercilessly like the farmhand with a cockade on his smashed cap, this drunken, impudent person standing here in the middle of his store, as though he were in some tavern or his pigsty, this person was the friend of his son.

"Turn your coat right side out," he said, "and stop this at once, Poldi."

Poldi didn't know what it was he was supposed to stop, but he did know Glavina was watching him. He also felt himself seized by a growing agitation. He heard his father's authoritarian voice and he knew that Glavina was watching him. He nervously looked for his cigarettes under his coat turned inside out. Then he felt the contours of his cigarette case in the pocket of his jacket. He pulled it out and opened it to light a cigarette, in order not to be the Poldi that someone could order to stop doing something. Glavina could see that this had turned out not to be the prank it was originally meant to be, so he headed toward the door.

"Wait," Markoni said. "I'm going, too."

But that's when his father grabbed him by the shoulder and, taking two steps, shoved him behind the counter.

"Whoa, sir," Glavina said, "what's this now?"

As if that voice behind his back had released an invisible force in him, he suddenly raised his hand and slapped it across the face of Leopold Markoni Jr. The blow that landed on Poldi's face, his third public blow, across his temple and eye, was so violent he staggered from it, and the silver cigarette case which he still held open in his hands went flying across the floor, the cigarettes spilling out of it. Glavina remained standing in the doorway for a moment longer. Poldi's whole body was shaking, and he glowered at his father. Glavina went out and stood for a while on the street, as though he weren't sure what to do next. Then he took off his overcoat, turned it right side out, and set off down the sidewalk and past the display window with his mask in hand.

"Pick them up," REM said, and Poldi bent over behind the counter to begin picking up his scattered cigarettes.

# 6 9

I WOKE UP BECAUSE SOMETHING KEPT BANGING AGAINST THE wall. My eyes were practically sealed shut and I could barely open them. I didn't know where I was, but that irregular yet cyclically rhythmic banging succeeded in rousing me. When I could open my eyes to the world again, a sharp realization shot through my chest and brain: Abyssinia. I knew now where we were and what had happened. Marjetica was sitting on the edge of the bed, at my feet. She was leaning against the footboard, wearing her panties but with the clown costume and ruffled collar on her lap. She was covering her ears with her hands. The banging against the wall started again and I could hear a woman shouting, one woman calling out a man's name. The name was Jože. Jože with a very long *e* at the end, and then over and over again with longer *eee*'s, punctuated with convulsive sighs. As though she were up in the mountains somewhere calling his name. So there really was another room on the other side of the wall. So there was a squeaky bed on the other side, too, and a couple doing the same thing that we'd done last night, my sweetheart and I. If everything hadn't been the way it was, I would have called it a beautiful Abyssinian love song. The footboard on the other side must also have been leaning up against the wall, and in the same spot as our bed. This is what I assumed, and it couldn't have been any different, since during this whole business the fellow on the other side wasn't banging on the wall with his hand or fist. Then the banging got faster and faster, without any pauses, and then Jože gasped, and his name changed into a strange, melancholy sigh. Judging by the way she'd been calling out before, I thought she might scream, but she gave such a nice, melancholy sigh down there in Abyssinia that I've had that deep, melancholy sigh in my ears ever since. But my sweetheart had plugged her ears. When she finally dropped her hands onto her lap and clutched at the ruffled collar of her Harlequin costume, she looked at me with red, teary eyes. Some makeup had smeared on her face and her eyes were deep down inside their dark sockets. She was shaking with pure, black despair. I expected her to say, What have we done, what have I done, or something like that. But she just whispered calmly:

"Did we sound like that, too?"

I could feel my head start to ache.

"Does your head ache?" I asked.

She nodded. "Badly."

I reached out to touch her, but she slipped away. On the other side, a loud male voice was talking now. But the walls were so thick—made from the wood of railway cars—that you couldn't make out individual words. Still, she kept whispering.

"How am I supposed to get home?" she asked coldly. "In this getup?"

I didn't answer. I stood up, pulled on my trousers and felt the pockets. I lit a cigarette. I offered her one, too. She turned it down.

"I asked you how I'm supposed to get home," she repeated, in almost a professional tone.

I shrugged.

I'm in love with this woman. I keep repeating over and over that I'm in love with her. I expected her to be unhappy, to be sad, that I'd feel sorry for her, or whatever. In any case I expected something other than this questioning, which bordered on hostility. I struggled with this feeling, I tried to be mindful of her really pitiable situation, but at that moment I really didn't have any idea how to get her home in that Harlequin costume in broad daylight. And my feeling of total helplessness made me angry. She kept on with the questions.

"Don't ask stupid questions," I said loudly and sharply. I don't know myself why I said that or how I could say that.

I poured myself some rotgut and drank it down. She watched me with a look of revulsion. I sat and pretended to be pondering a way to rescue her from this dilemma. But I wasn't pondering at all. What should I have been pondering, when I wasn't getting a single good idea?

"There's no use," she said. "Go get Boris."

What Boris? Ever since I'd been associating with them, I'd forgotten that Flycatcher had a real name.

"Do you mean Bussolin?" I said peevishly.

An anger was rising up inside me. She told me to go get Boris. I'd always called him Bussolin when we were alone. And then, the very thought of me going to Bussolin's house and ringing the doorbell and asking Flycatcher for help put me in such a state that I could have done something really bad. I could have slapped her.

She could see things weren't good. But she wanted a solution to her problem now. When I think about it, I recognize she did all this out of profound and total despair. In fact, her calm tone of voice was sheer despair, all the worse for being concealed. That kind of quiet despair is worse than yelling and crying. It was a dark, silent despair.

This I realized only later. But first she got me ready to take a message to Bussolin. I was horribly powerless. Which excuses me for what I demanded from her. Demanded in utter powerlessness. She had to say: Bussolin the Flycatcher. She had to say: Go get Bussolin, that sticky flycatcher, and tell him I slept with you in the hovels of Abyssinia. I knew that I could do absolutely nothing to help her. I offered to find her some clothes. I offered to go find some friend (but what friend?) to pick her up, but she resolutely shook her head. I even thought of Maestro and his car, but that was a solution she could never accept. Never. Her eyes were teary as she gazed at the floor and had to say: Go get that con man and tell him that I made love with you in the hovels of Abyssinia as I never will with him. She repeated this after me, word for word. What was wrong with me? What was wrong with me, why was I doing this? It had to happen this way. Eventually this had to come to an end.

■  □  ■  □  ■

# 7 0

SLOWLY I PUT MY SHIRT ON AND WENT OUTSIDE. IT WAS SUNDAY
morning, a soggy late-February morning, and there weren't
many people outside the shacks. I called out to an old man
who was smoking on his doorstep and coughing. I asked him
whether he knew Glavina. The old man nodded. Did he know
where he might have spent the night, if he had a friend he
stayed over with now and then? The old man knew. I asked
him to go there and call him. He refused. He pointed the
shack out to me and told me to go there myself. I was afraid to
leave her alone. I felt through my pockets for some change to
give the old man. I found some, but the old man turned it
down. Go yourself, he said. I went and woke Glavina. I begged
him to go get that fellow, to tell him that Margerita had sent
him, and that he should come with his car to pick her up.
Glavina was upset.

"And now this?" he said. "Why don't you throw her out,
the slut?" he said.

He could see that I was dead serious, that I could have hit
him just then.

"Aw, all right," he said. "No need to jump down my throat.
I'll go." When I went back, she was already dressed. She was
sitting on the tousled bed in her Harlequin getup. She was still
holding the collar in her hands. She sat there in the middle of
the ill-lit room. Stuffed with cardboard and paper, the windows barely let any light through. The wooden floor was

unscrubbed, there was wine on the table, and a torn-off chunk of bread lay on top of a cupboard. She was beautiful as never before. Her face was dark, she had big, dark spots around her eyes. I tried to meet her eyes, but she kept looking away. In the corner next to the washbasin I discovered a comb. She took it without a word. She combed her hair and fixed it with her hands. She was beautiful. I'm in love with her.

We didn't exchange another word. I drank the rest of the rotgut, and she sat motionless, awaiting Bussolin's arrival and staring straight ahead.

I can't say how much time passed, how long I chain-smoked, waiting for some word or glance to link us again. What I can say for sure is that it stayed silent for a long time. Because when we finally heard the noise of the car approaching, it was mingled with a multitude of mostly children's voices. Which meant that it was getting close to noon and that the Abyssinians were finally up.

I OPENED THE DOOR AND SAW BUSSOLIN GETTING OUT OF HIS car. Glavina was sitting in front, grinning. Bussolin's behavior was irreproachable, though he'd clearly spent a sleepless night. He walked solemnly right past me, as though I were thin air. He pulled it off very elegantly. He wasn't patronizing a single moment. He didn't cast disdainful looks at the slovenly room. He didn't turn up his nose. He didn't do any of that. He stood about two paces inside the room and waited for his eyes to adjust to the darkness. The light from the open door fell on the middle of the room, but the bed was up against the wall, in the darkness.

Bussolin assessed the situation in an instant. There was nothing more he needed to do. This matter was resolved now for all time. He was calm and all-forgiving. He didn't say We've been looking for you all night. He didn't say What on earth is wrong with you. He didn't say I've been worried. He didn't say Franjo's a nervous wreck. He didn't say anything at all to her. He was so in control of the situation, so noble and so completely the good Samaritan, so utterly flawless, that I wanted to do something—anything—that would provoke him into an outburst or a sharp word. I didn't do anything. I wanted him at least to say to me You pig, you'll destroy this woman. But he was so thoroughly in control of himself, he didn't even say that, though he surely thought it and wanted to say it. His feelings got the upper hand only for a second. She was still sitting there, staring ahead.

"Marjetica," he said gently. "Marjetica, let's go."

And Marjetica went. In his noble and dignified composure he forgot to drape his coat around her shoulders. As a result, the Abyssinians who had gathered around the car outside squealed in delight when the melancholy masquerader appeared in the doorway.

Glavina came grinning into the shack.

"I'm going to Germany," he said, "and I'm driving back here with wheels like those."

He jabbed me in the shoulder and pulled yet another bottle of rotgut out of the cupboard, which we drank.

I could hear her moaning in her sleep. I took my jacket and drew it up over her head, so she wouldn't be afraid. I looked at Glavina's shaven face. I'm going crazy, I thought. Out of the pores in his skin, out of the little holes all over his face, I could see blood slowly seeping.

SUDDENLY IT STRUCK ME THAT I DIDN'T QUITE KNOW WHERE I was. Some building near the park was amazingly like some other house, I'm not sure where, in Vienna or in Linz. Then I walked through the center of town, and I don't know what was wrong with me that people were avoiding me. Maestro was standing outside a coffee shop on the corner of Slovene Street. When he saw me, he ran straight inside the coffee shop. I could see him through the window, hiding behind some big plant—the kind that thrives even indoors, in warm places—and he was peeking out at the street. Later I looked through another window, this one belonging to the orphanage of the Benedictine sisters. The cooks glared at me through the window and were incessantly saying something. I didn't hear a thing; I only saw them opening their mouths. Maybe they thought I was a beggar standing outside, mutely begging for bread. They giggled, too, but soundlessly. They wouldn't let me into the public library. Sober up, sir, a young woman said to me, and get a bath. Then you can come back. But I wasn't drunk at all. I grabbed myself by the fly and said: Fuck you. She got really upset. She threatened to call the police. A stocky man with a trimmed mustache came out. What is it you want? he said in a deep bass.

I don't know how I wound up in Abyssinia. Glavina and his skinny friend with the grim face were there in his makeshift shelter drinking rotgut and smoking. I wanted to see that place one more time. I wanted to see it with daylight eyes. It had looked different through nighttime eyes. I wanted to see its ordinary life. To smell that stench. To see Glavina, dressed and wearing his winter stockings, lying on our bed. Rummaging through the cupboard and crumbling bread with his fingers. To listen to the drip of the February snow as it melts off the roof. The wind as it howls through the poorly stuffed cracks in the windows. In the room next door they're yelling and arguing about some coffee that's run over because somebody crumbled too much bread in it. His grim friend Markoni is wearing a striped suit. His friend has slender fingers that he uses to stub out a butt in a metal pot and then pull a silver cigarette case out of his pocket. I smoked some cigarettes from his silver case. Glavina was cracking jokes at her and my expense, at our expense. The other was just silent, for the most part. I didn't speak particularly much either. I finished my glass of wine and as I left I saw that bit of garbage outside that she'd slid on. She'd almost fallen—she'd barely caught herself and then clutched at me.

I went to Lent and looked for Fedyatin. He wasn't there. For a minute I thought he might have left town. But he can't leave. He's come here and he doesn't have the foggiest idea where he is. All he knows is that his Volga River is awfully, awfully far away. He'll never get back there. He's old now, and this is where they'll bury him. Within a few years no one will even know that there ever was a Fedyatin. He's been forgotten in his village by now. I walked around the whole day and I didn't get the slightest bit tired. I knocked on Gretica and Katica's door. Some man in a white shirt came to the door. Maybe it was Pristovšek, delivering their liqueur, or the eau de cologne specialist. I went to the church and stood vacantly in front of the altar and looked at the blue ball that holy man was holding. I could feel myself shuddering. But not from fatigue; from my childhood memory of that ball, of that sphere. From something that was such a flash in my consciousness, I couldn't link it to anything. I'm sitting in a warm lap, stretching my arms out, and I want that ball. Nothing more, nothing else. How is it possible for just that to stay in my memory? Then that ball started to approach me.

All night long I had the bloodred sky before my eyes. I thought I could hear hundreds of legs tramping through the street, like on that night when all the windows flared red. I could hear the roaring of the pines in the Pohorje. The tops of the pines were red. They roared like the ocean. Then silence. Some people walked through the forest, among the trees, talking. Dr. Bukovski was standing behind a pillar in the church. He was holding a scalpel. Very slowly the sphere was slipping out of the old man's hands. I woke up with cold sweat on my forehead. I reached for the floor. The bottle had tipped over. There was just enough left in it for one swallow. I don't know how long I was in the room. I went downstairs just long enough to get a new bottle on credit. I practically had to beg for it. I pissed into the washbasin and rinsed the piss down with a gurgling stream from the faucet. I tried to hit the faucet's stream with my own, so that the two would merge and drain into the sewer system together. I couldn't hit it. I fell asleep on the floor. There was a red light in the window. Outside there was a fire. I wanted to open the window and piss on all of it. I just had to hold on tight, so as not to fall out. I dreamed of the ball in the old man's hands. It got closer to me and grew bigger and bigger. Then it became a blue apple. It was the same apple that Glavina had on his table in Abyssinia. The apple was round and resembled a ball, although its skin was slightly wrinkled. Glavina swiped at it with his hand. The apple dropped to the floor. Both of them laughed; even that quiet fellow Markoni in the striped suit, with the grim face and the silver cigarette case, laughed a little. You wouldn't dare hit it, Glavina said, like hell you would. But his hand dropped. Then he said a strange thing. Squash them, he said. His hand fell on the apple. Squash all of them, he said and hit the apple, so that it splattered all over the table.

I could feel I was falling after that blue ball. Falling through the window or past some pillars in the church nave. The nave wasn't sliding anymore. Now everything was falling into some abyss, including the sphere, stitched up with black thread from the morgue.

Did I sleep on the floor by the open window? Was I very cold? I can hear some voice. Maybe it's the doctor and he's giving a lecture. Do you not feel well? someone asks me. He goes away and I'm left alone. Something terrible has happened. Something terrible has happened and I can't remember what happened. Somebody looks at me and says something. He looks like somebody. Are you not feeling well? he asks. There's some word I have to say, but I can't remember it.

WITH THE FIRST BLOW, MARKONI WOUNDED BORIS VALENTAN only slightly, even though he had hit him in the face with the blade of the ax. Marjeta Samsa didn't see what happened, since the two men were standing close together and Markoni had pulled the ax out from under his trench coat. But when Boris Valentan turned around and raised an arm to protect himself from further blows, she saw the bloody wound on his right cheek and began to scream. Glavina was approaching Valentan from the side with an iron bar in hand. At that point Markoni struck with his ax a second time and hit his victim above the left eyebrow. Valentan staggered. When Marjeta Samsa saw that Valentan was falling, she fled down the cart trail that ran downhill. For a moment Glavina stood still amid the trees, but when he saw that Markoni was going to be able to take care of Valentan by himself, he took off after the woman. Markoni had gotten tangled in the skis that had fallen off Valentan's shoulders when he was first hit. This had allowed Valentan, seriously injured, to pull a hunter's knife out of his rucksack. Marjeta Samsa slipped and sank into the snow alongside the path. She looked back and saw Glavina approaching with iron bar in hand. For a moment she lost her voice. With desperate gestures she tried to find some object around her that she could use to defend herself. In the meantime Markoni had again attacked Valentan, who was shouting at Marjeta Samsa to run. Markoni hit Valentan again, but this injury wasn't fatal either. On the contrary, Valentan, who was strong, began defending himself desperately and tenaciously. Though severely injured, he managed to wound Markoni in the side twice with his knife. Marjeta Samsa had managed to pull herself out of the snow, but at that instant Glavina caught up to her. With his left arm he took her by the shoulder, and when she began to scream again, he hit her several times with the iron bar he held in his right hand, causing her to fall to the ground. Markoni called for him to come help, since Valentan was offering stubborn resistance. Glavina left Marjeta Samsa lying in the snow and dashed back uphill along the cart trail. From behind, he struck Valentan on the head with the bar, and when his victim fell to his knees, Markoni buried the sharp edge of his ax in his forehead. According to Glavina's testimony, Markoni then went over to where Mrs. Samsa lay in the snow by the path and finished her off with his ax. Markoni claims that Mrs. Samsa was dead when he reached her. Both of these assertions are false.

The murderers then dragged their victims some twenty to thirty meters down along the path, and from there about fifteen meters to the north into the woods. Here Markoni and Glavina continued to cudgel the victims, who still showed signs of life. The bloody tracks in the snow and drops of blood spattered onto the trees are proof that the decisive and absolutely fatal blows were not inflicted on the victims until here. This is particularly true in the case of Mrs. Samsa, whose head was shoved deep into the snow and who, in addition to the wounds on her head, had numerous injuries and lacerations on the fingers of both hands.

The killers then proceeded to rob their victims. They emptied out their pockets and the contents of their rucksacks. From Valentan they stole a camera, binoculars, shaving equipment, two shirts, long underwear, and a fountain pen. They tore a gold chain off Marjeta Samsa's neck and took a bottle of perfume, soap, and a fashion magazine from her backpack, among other things. The authorities discovered her silk underwear strewn around under a pine tree. This had probably fallen out of the rucksack earlier, but had been overlooked by the perpetrators. The murderers consolidated all items in a single rucksack and threw away the other, containing two towels, a woman's ski cap, and an apple.

■ □ ■ □ ■

# 74

ON THE SATURDAY BEFORE LENT, THE CITY HAD CELEBRATED IN abandon. One week later it was dumbstruck with horror. There had been more than a few violent crimes in the town and the surrounding area recently, but in its bestiality, as one person put it, the story that came out of that beech grove up in the Pohorje pines surpassed all comprehension. The killers were soon discovered, given that one of them came to the hospital that night to have knife wounds in his side attended to. At first he maintained that he'd been stopped in the woods by two strangers, one of whom sank a knife in his side without any reason. The doctor found his story suspicious and reported him to the police. The next morning the perpetrator confessed his crime and incriminated the other murderer. Journalists and curiosity seekers tried with all their might to determine the true causes of this crime. Although at first all evidence pointed to the probability of its being an armed robbery, it soon turned out that the perpetrators had not had any intention of robbing their victims, that they had done that after the murder and without any clear awareness of what they were doing, since there were many items they were unable to recall. After numerous suppositions, public opinion finally accepted the conclusion that the cause of the crime had been a trifling and insignificant offense in a tavern at the foot of the Pohorje.

■ □ ■ □ ■

# 7 5

IN THE TAVERN WHERE BORIS VALENTAN AND MARJETA SAMSA
were having dinner, Glavina started to harass them with loud
comments. After a while he even sat down at their table and
claimed that the three of them knew each other very well.
Valentan gently tried to persuade him to go away. Glavina then
started going after Marjeta Samsa and claimed that the young
lady and he were close acquaintances and that she would almost
definitely never have forgotten him. He poured himself some
wine from their bottle and reached for Marjeta Samsa's glass
several times. Valentan could no longer stand this and he asked
the innkeeper to make the annoying Glavina leave them alone.
After this intervention Glavina did leave their table, though he
continued to harass the two customers from the bar. He smiled
incessantly and nodded his huge head. Markoni remained
silent the whole time. Then the two men left.

They stopped at the foot of the Pohorje. There Markoni
took the murder weapons out of a bag: an ax and an iron bar,
the handle from a tire jack. He kept the ax for himself and
handed the bar to Glavina. The two men hid the weapons
under their overcoats and started to walk along a path uphill
to find a suitable place for their attack. Because there were no
tourists and Glavina and Markoni had begun to suspect that
the other two had reconsidered and would not climb the
mountain, they went back down. But at the foot of the
mountain, around 6:00 P.M., Valentan and Mrs. Samsa came

walking toward them, each of them carrying skis and a ruck-sack. This happened near the winegrower's house, where the trail forks. As soon as Glavina and Markoni had determined that the skiers had taken the northern trail toward St. Bolfenk, they followed and caught up with them. Mrs. Samsa probably suspected something or felt that she and Valentan had overly offended Glavina in the tavern, when they had forced him away from their table. Consequently, as Markoni and Glavina themselves testified, she asked them in a very pleasant tone of voice where they were going. Glavina just smiled, while Markoni replied they were going to visit an acquaintance in St. Areh. The couple let the men go ahead, but it's obvious they didn't want to run into the two men again, so they waited about three-quarters of an hour before resuming their trek. In the meantime Markoni and Glavina came to the beech grove above Cold Spring near the Chapel of St. Anthony, which is located a good ten minutes from St. Bolfenk. This is the place they chose for their attack. The terrain there is exceptionally favorable to an attacker. The footpath there is narrow and passes through a gully, the sides of which are steep and from two to three meters high. A victim attacked here cannot escape either to the right or the left. The men sat down on a stack of logs alongside the path and waited.

As soon as the victims approached—it was about 8:00 P.M. —Markoni got up and asked Valentan for a cigarette. Mrs. Samsa was walking some five meters behind Valentan, and Glavina was standing to the side under some trees. Valentan replied he didn't have any. At this moment Markoni pulled the ax out from under his trench coat.

# 7 6

THE INITIAL HORROR AND SHOCK QUICKLY GAVE WAY TO
curiosity. The most curious individuals, who are never lacking
for events like this, went to inspect the terrible scene of
human carnage and to verify in situ the two perpetrators' par-
tially conflicting accounts, which the newspapers were con-
tinually reporting. The most persistent individuals, who are
also never lacking and who know more than the others, kept
scouring behind the scenes for the crime's real motivation.
They refused to accept that a murder could be so pointless
and were unable to reconcile themselves to the thought that
what had happened was an abstract evil. An evil that had
brought a whole series of people, previously strangers to one
another, into closer or more distant contact, and finally to this
crossroads, where what happened had to happen. That evil
was a crack in a world which, through the aid of science and
good social intentions, anticipated changing everything that is
into perfection. That evil was a necessary crack in that perfection. And in 1938 this crack had begun to widen. This is why
they also refused to accept the possibility that the beech grove
incident—a crime that had left two absolutely innocent, honest, and good people lying in the snowdrifts amid the roaring
of the Pohorje pines—was just one component of that
abstract evil that was coming and already here. That the crack
was widening and that the world was trembling and slipping
from it.

This is why they kept sifting through the background of the crime and eventually came up with some results. In the course of the investigation the fact bubbled up that one of the killers, the older one, kept mentioning a third person, possibly a third participant, who had introduced him to both victims. And before long all the persistent investigators, together with the local newspaper, were asking: What will the mysterious third man say?

But Erdman has nothing to say anymore. The huddled city that looked him in the eye one dark night, on the first of January, has consumed him. Or maybe he's been swallowed up by his own abyss, which simply chose the place to draw him in. He lies in his room and searches for some word that he can't find and pronounce. Past his eyes dance images he can't describe. Let's spare ourselves his further testimony, which in the pages remaining could only recall the tortured and incoherent scenes of his disintegration. There he lies, and his consciousness, which almost certainly entered this story already cracked and damaged, now shatters like thin, fragile porcelain.

WHEN BOTH VICTIMS' CORPSES WERE DISSECTED IN THE MORGUE at the city hospital, it was determined, and also recorded in the postmortem, that Valentan had died from cerebral ischemia and a partial hemorrhage in the cerebral cortex. He suffered two absolutely lethal injuries: A blow to his forehead with the edge of an ax, inflicted with tremendous force, penetrated skin, bones, and brain, with the latter protruding from a wound that was 9 centimeters long and 3.5 centimeters wide. The skull had been shattered, with cracks radiating through the skull in all directions. The second lethal injury came from a blow with a blunt instrument, which cut through his right earlobe and shattered the bone at his right temple. A third lethal injury was delivered by a blow with the sharp edge of an ax beneath his right lower lip, which produced a gaping wound 9 centimeters long, exposing bone and teeth. Aside from these three severe injuries, he incurred several lesser injuries from a sharp object: above the left eyebrow, on the right cheek, beneath the right jaw, beneath the left lower lip, and on the left ear, as well as lacerations at the base of the nose, on the right cheek, and on both hands. Mrs. Samsa died of cerebral ischemia and hemorrhaging from the carotid artery. She incurred several forceful blows with a sharp and blunt object on the scalp, breaking the skull and causing cracks to radiate out in all directions. The bone at the left temple was crushed, and at the right temple it was broken.

She suffered several severe injuries to the face, inflicted by the sharp edge of an ax. On the left side of the neck the skin, veins, and muscles had been slashed through and the main artery severed. She also incurred numerous injuries to both hands: The right fourth finger was broken, there were two slashes on the skin of the right middle finger, the skin on the left hand was cut through to the bone, the left middle finger was broken, the left little finger showed several wounds, the back of the left hand was swollen and the skin scraped. Hairs were found in the wound on the right index finger, and there were bloody bruises on the left forearm and the right knee joint.

POLICE CHIEF SAMO BENEDIČIČ WASN'T SURPRISED WHEN THE
investigation produced the news that Josef Erdman was also
considered a suspect. This Austrian citizen, who had been
roaming the city like a lunatic, had seemed suspicious to him
from the very start. However, his suspicions had run along
other lines. Based on his experience working in a border
town, his first thought had been of politics and smuggling.
For a while he'd had him tailed, but Erdman's endless roamings through the town and vicinity soon became exhausting
and also uninteresting. Then Benedičič had assigned an
agent provocateur to him, but even those personal conversations had produced no real results. Chief Samo Benedičič
put much stock in personal conversations. He believed in
police intelligence, which examines all circumstances and
checks all the details, but he believed even more in his intuition. His infallible intuition had told him after one conversation with Erdman that something was wrong with the
man. Deep within, he sensed and knew that he wouldn't be
surprised if something happened in connection with him. All
right, he wasn't a smuggler, he wasn't a German spy, and he
wasn't a Communist agitator. But he was connected to a
murder. Thus Benedičič's intuition had served him. Of course,
he would have preferred to have some surprising bit of political business crop up out of that crowd that gathered at Engineer Samsa's house, or better still, that bizarre trinity who sat

the days away in the taverns of the Lent district. All the conditions were right for this: a laid-off worker and now shiftless idler who could be bought by anyone, an émigré religious fanatic who could be used as a cover, and an Austrian citizen born in this city, a traveling businessman who didn't choose his company, whether it was Slovene or German, upper class or the lowest social dregs. Or who, quite the contrary perhaps, chose his company very deliberately. In the work that Chief Samo Benedičič does, all options in all directions have to be kept open at all times. This is why he refused to accept easily the apparent motives for the murder. This is why he wasn't surprised when the investigators reported that Ivan Glavina was also talking about Erdman. Not even crimes can be put together in a really unusual and surprising way. Police Chief Samo Benedičič was pleased by this news, not because of the news but for the sake of his intuition. He immediately phoned the police magistrate to arrange for an arrest.

Josef Erdman was apprehended in his hotel room. He lay on the floor, with several empty bottles all around him. A suitcase stood by the door, packed and ready for departure. An expert investigator observed a thin, barely noticeable layer of dust on it, suggesting that no one had touched the suitcase in several days. As they put handcuffs on him, Erdman stared at the gendarmes with vacant eyes red from lack of sleep, or from drink. He compressed his lips so tightly that the skin at the edges was bloodless and white.

In jail he lay motionless on his bunk. He ate nothing. The guard who watched him through a peephole noticed that he got up only rarely, and then to drink prodigious amounts of water, as though he were trying to quench a fire within himself. At the first two interrogations he said nothing. When they confronted him with Glavina, he looked through him as though he were glass, and Benedičič thought this must be an involuntary defense mechanism. He was familiar with those kinds of cases, too. After he visited Erdman in his cell, he was convinced the prisoner didn't recognize him either. In the meantime an investigation into Erdman's origins had been initiated in cooperation with the Austrian police. It turned out that his parents lived in Linz, where they'd moved several years before the overthrow. But the firm of Stastny and Company had not been located in Vienna for many years, and nowhere else either. No wonder the telegrams he had sent to addresses in Vienna and Trieste had all been returned with the stamp ADDRESSEE UNKNOWN. The addressee didn't exist. When they confronted Erdman with these facts, he just shrugged. Yet this was also a sign that he had begun to cooperate in the investigative process. A surprise came on the next day, when in response to the question whether he felt himself guilty of inciting to murder, as the suspect Glavina claimed, he suddenly began to speak. He said he felt guilty, totally guilty, and that if it hadn't been for him, this horrible thing would never have happened. The police magistrate asked him to explain that. Erdman answered that from the moment he'd gotten off the train to look for that ball. . . . Ball? the magistrate asked. Sphere, Erdman said, the world. From that moment, he'd known that he would drag someone into the realm of evil. The realm of evil? Yes, the cosmos is split between good and evil, between spirit and matter, between soul and body, between the old age and the new. It's split and the sphere is sewn together with black thread from the morgue. With an astral body—that's an article of faith, but a person can see and sense things. Satan's early-morning agitator had confronted him, falsely prophesying the resurrection. In truth, the supreme principle was the principle of evil. The world lies in morning darkness, offering itself to the angel of evil. The magistrate tried to stop him. Where had he met Ivan Glavina? he asked. The fallen angel bends over a dead man in the morgue and takes his pulse, his heartbeat. The magistrate exchanged glances with the stenographer. He tried again, but now his voice was very gentle and lenient. Was it true that he had introduced Ivan Glavina to the victim, to both victims? Erdman answered immediately. The evil in him had slowly drawn the victim out to the place of execution. When the sign comes from heaven and the magnetic needle wavers, that is when the moment will approach. Evil creeps through the belly of this town, and it wants out. The bloody glow was the sign of its coming birth.

They called for a psychiatrist, who spent several days sitting with Erdman in his cell, involving him in conversations, and watching him, and he listened to him patiently and carefully in his office. This is referred to as the anamnesis of the illness. The first thing he established was the patient's extremely fragmented memory. Erdman could remember insignificant things from his childhood—a ball and some fat beans, some flower beds, he spoke about some Jaroslav and his sister Lenka, who clearly didn't exist in this world, if the information the police had gathered was to be believed, or who at least didn't exist in the place they were supposed to according to Erdman's words. He was unable to explain why he had gotten off the train on New Year's Eve. Then he decided he was here on account of laboratory equipment. He spoke in detail about his work and the trip south. The psychiatrist didn't bother him with questions that interested the police. For the anamnesis he also needed the opinions of people who had known Erdman during his short stay in the city. But he was already prepared for those answers from previous practice. One after the other, they told him they recalled him as a reasonable but rather standoffish and solitary person. He was given to alcohol and he associated with strange people. None of them would have thought there was anything wrong with his sanity. And yet, come to think of it, they would say, those odd stories of his about some stranger who came to visit him in his hotel room, and all those other stories, and his interminable roamings around town did make a person wonder. The psychiatrist hesitated a long time before making his diagnosis. It was probably a case of latent schizophrenia, which strengthened under the influence of alcohol and various mental stressors. The confused and picturesque figures in which Erdman spoke were ascribed to this and to a subconscious sense of guilt. He was the one who had introduced to her subsequent murderer the woman to whom he'd obviously developed an exceptionally strong emotional attachment. This realization produced a violent emotional shock which caused his latent schizophrenia to shift into an acute phase.

We don't know what to say about these scientific findings, for we've already heard a great deal here about a wide range of areas of human research. Many sciences and many scientists deal with the human soul, as well as the human skull and all the rest. But from the moment when everything collapses and crumbles for human beings, as it did so suddenly, if not unexpectedly, for Josef Erdman, it seems they should not be left in the hands of scientists. Because with their good intentions the scientists see to it that the degradation runs its course.

With all his sense of ethical responsibility, the psychiatrist considered what psychological antidote to prescribe to Erdman. At first he considered insulin shock, using the Sakel method. The shock induced by injections of insulin puts the individual in a coma that can last up to eight days, but he awakes from that a different person. Ultimately he chose the latest method of treatment. Just recently, one year ago, after extensive experiments on pigs in a Roman slaughterhouse, the Italian psychiatrists Cerletti and Bini had invented electroshock. Erdman's antidote would be delivered in the form of electroshock. For a time, his consciousness would be left hanging like a chandelier in an empty room, the psychiatrist told the police magistrate, half joking. Actually, it would float, because a chandelier hangs, but his consciousness wouldn't be attached to anything anymore. At that point, the doctor said, let's hope he'll be able to help move the investigation forward.

HE WAS GIVEN SEVERAL ELECTROSHOCK TREATMENTS, AND HE
no longer had to answer questions. Glavina retracted his state-
ments about incitement to murder, since he could see that he
wouldn't be able to implicate an idiot. Police Chief Samo
Benedičič thought that his intuition had been good, but that
he hadn't supported it with adequate reflection. He hadn't
thought of this possibility at all. The newspapers stopped
writing about a mysterious third culprit. For a while they continued to report the shifting testimonies of both perpetrators,
but the headlines got smaller and smaller. The whole business
shifted to the bottom of the eighth page and then finally vanished from the papers altogether. It revived again several
months later, when the court sentenced each of the murderers
to twenty years' imprisonment.

It is curious how quickly the human mind can forget about
two criminals who have been cast out, as well as their victims.
Along came new big events which flooded the town with their
omnipresence, instantly displacing the horror that had seized it
in those days after Carnival. The Nazis occupied Austria and
came within a few kilometers of the city. Ggb.'s friends from
the cultural league got ready to fulfill the commandments of
German blood, as they had written. In Moscow eighteen top
government functionaries were condemned to death. Everywhere decoys of parades marched, and young people prepared
to reorder the world once and for all. The snow on the Pohorje

melted. Daisies blossomed in the glades and among the trees that lined the paths. Gretica and Katica visited Erdman in the asylum. He walked back and forth, shrugging his shoulders and shoving his pale face at them. His pupils were rather dilated. He talked with them about his illness and recited his diagnosis in Latin. Katica asked the orderly for his suit, so she could press his trousers and brush the jacket. It wouldn't be necessary. Others were already taking care of these things, because Josef Erdman had regained his health sufficiently to allow him to go home. In any case, the cost of transportation would be less than if they had to support him here in the local asylum indefinitely and at government expense.

■ □ ■ □ ■

# 80

SEVERAL DAYS BEFORE EASTER, ERDMAN LEFT FOR THE TRAIN
station in the company of an orderly. His shoulders were
hunched and they trembled. The orderly observed him war-
ily, thinking of the trouble he would have with him until they
reached the border. They walked across Yugoslav Square and
from far off saw a group of people assembled in front of the
newly built Orthodox church. Another crazy man was standing there, arms outstretched, staring at the church door,
shouting, *"Khristos voskres! Voistinu voskres!"* Erdman didn't hear
him, and he didn't even turn to look at the growing crowd in
front of the church. The church where Fedyatin was raising
such a racket would explode in a powerful detonation within
a few years. It would be blown up so that not one stone
remained on top of another. Or even alongside another, for in
their pedantry the sappers cleared the square to the last frag-
ment. The crazy man kept shouting at the church door.

There was truly no shortage of madmen, murderers, and
demons in 1938.

The orderly turned Josef Erdman over to representatives of
the German psychiatric service in Spielfeld, together with his
identification, test findings, and a report on the state of his illness. He was kept in an Austrian hospital several days for observation. When they were satisfied he didn't pose a threat to his
environment, he was delivered to his parents in Linz. At first his
parents were shocked, but with time they grew accustomed to

their son with his twitching shoulders and pale face. Two years later, Erdman's father died. The day before his death he spoke about the fat beans that grew in some garden. That same year, the patient was detained and taken without any explanation to Germany, where a special commission for the purity of the race observed him. The scientists working in the famous euthanasia program studied his mental state thoroughly. Theirs was no small responsibility. There could be no mistakes. It was no small task to pierce a living human heart. This is why they had to consider it carefully and examine all the circumstances. They also measured his skull, which by contemporary phrenological standards was almost adequate to merit his release. But they had before them a diagnosis written by a psychiatrist in Marburg on the Drau. They concluded that the report wasn't accurate and in some respects even contradicted itself. They settled on a compromise. They didn't accept him into the euthanasia program, but even so, in case some latent hereditary disease did exist, they had him painlessly sterilized in the local so-called infirmary.

MANY YEARS LATER IN LINZ, ERDMAN SITS IN HIS KITCHEN, which is overheated and stuffy from the laundry hung out to dry above the kitchen range. Once again he tells a long and bizarre tale which his mother knows and gladly listens to. Actually, she doesn't hear it, because she's already quite old and deaf. But she knows her son's tale by heart, she knows what he's describing, and she knows that she had held him in her lap then. Erdman tells of a church located far away in some city to the south. In that church there is a tall and powerful male figure that stands high up beneath the ceiling. His mother gently nods and occasionally dozes off from the kitchen's damp warmth. That figure is the figure of God the Father. In his hands he holds a blue sphere, which every child thinks is a ball and reaches out for in his innocent, childish greed. If you're in the church and you listen carefully, you can hear the beating of the gigantic cosmic heart coming from the sphere. Now it beats calmly and regularly. Inside there's also a magnetic needle, Erdman says, and that needle quivers only very slightly now. But when the windows up above flash bright again in the bloodred northern glow, the heart will beat faster, and the needle will shudder at first, and then wildly spin from side to side.

■ □ ■ □ ■

# TRANSLATOR'S NOTES TO THE NOVEL

## Chapter 1

**3**   *Khristos voskrese. . . . Voistinu voskrese.*
"Christ is risen. . . . He is risen indeed." *Voskrese*
(Church Slavic) and *voskres* (Russian), a variant found
in chapters 58 and 80, are used interchangeably.

## Chapter 3

**10**   *Der Streit um den Knaben Jo.*
The title translates as *The Dispute about the Boy Jo.*

**14**   K. & K.
*Kaiserlich und königlich,* or "imperial royal," referring
to the old Austro-Hungarian Empire.

## Chapter 5

**19**   they've got these scheduled differently somehow
"These" refers to holidays, such as New Year's, Christmas,
Easter, and so on. Before 1917, Russia used the Julian
calendar, and all dates were out of sync with those in
the West. After 1917, Orthodox holidays (but not New
Year's) continued to occur on different days than the
equivalent holidays in the West. The protagonist is

vaguely aware of this, but in his disorganized thinking he includes New Year's as one of the holidays that falls on a different day in Russia.

## Chapter 19

**61**  center of the Sokol, or hawks', movement

Sokol, a gymnastic society originating in Prague in 1862, emphasized mass calisthenics to promote communal spirit. It was banned during the Nazi occupation of Czechoslovakia because of its association with Czech nationalism.

## Chapter 35

**114**  "Horst Wessel Lied"—*die Fahne hoch*

The first words of the "Horst Wessel Lied," a Nazi anthem, are *Die Fahne hoch*, or "Raise high the flag."

## Chapter 40

**130**  Ggb.

The abbreviation for *Grossgrundbesitzer*, German for "esquire."

## Chapter 48

**153**  *Körpermessungen verschiedener Menschenrassen.*

The title translates as *Physical Measurements of Various Human Races.*

## Chapter 49

## Chapter 50

## Chapter 59

## Chapter 65

■ □ ■ □ ■

# WRITINGS FROM AN UNBOUND EUROPE

*Tsing*
*Words Are Something Else*
DAVID ALBAHARI

*City of Ash*
EUGENIJUS ALIŠANKA

*Skinswaps*
ANDREJ BLATNIK

*My Family's Role in the World Revolution and Other Prose*
BORA ĆOSIĆ

*Peltse and Pentameron*
VOLODYMYR DIBROVA

*The Victory*
HENRYK GRYNBERG

*The Tango Player*
CHRISTOPH HEIN

*A Bohemian Youth*
JOSEF HIRŠAL

*Charon's Ferry*
GYULA ILLYÉS

*Mocking Desire*
*Northern Lights*
DRAGO JANČAR

*Balkan Blues: Writing Out of Yugoslavia*
JOANNA LABON, ED.

*The Loss*
VLADIMIR MAKANIN